"Turn around slowly," he said, keeping his voice hard. "Hold your hands up high, in plain view."

The figure turned, raising both hands to shoulder height. It was a young girl, with dark eyes, narrow face, and a faint mocking smile on her lips.

A twig snapped behind Kelso and a terrible thought touched his mind. Then the back of his head exploded and he fell, thinking: This isn't really happening.

Pain hummed in his ears like an electrical generating plant and the ground opened up to receive him, allowing him to fall forever.

Other Avon Books by
Malcolm McClintick

DEATH OF AN OLD FLAME

Coming Soon

THE KEY

MARY'S GRAVE

MALCOLM McCLINTICK

AVON BOOKS ◆ NEW YORK

All of the characters in this book are fictitious, and any resemblance to actual persons, living or dead, is purely coincidental.

AVON BOOKS
A division of
The Hearst Corporation
105 Madison Avenue
New York, New York 10016

"A Crime Club Book"
Copyright © 1987 by Malcolm McClintick
Published by arrangement with Doubleday, a division of Bantam Doubleday Dell Publishing Group, Inc.
Library of Congress Catalog Card Number: 86-19958
ISBN: 0-380-70818-3

First Avon Books Printing: Feburary 1990

AVON TRADEMARK REG. U.S. PAT. OFF. AND IN OTHER COUNTRIES, MARCA REGISTRADA, HECHO EN U.S.A.

Printed in the U.S.A.

RA 10 9 8 7 6 5 4 3 2 1

To Jeanette, who believed it was possible

Chapter One

Screams

When the call came into the duty room Kelso was refilling his pipe after it had gone out for the fourth or fifth time. It was 9:23 P.M., Tuesday, October 28. The others in the room were Karl Smith, a tall blond detective with ice-cold blue eyes, and Detective-Sergeant Meyer, small and dark, hunched over his desk like a bird of prey.

It was Smith's phone; he answered it without looking up from the *Penthouse* he was reading, pausing here and there to study a particular page closely. The overhead fluorescent lights lit up everything in a garish glare like the emergency room of a hospital. Even the smell, now that the cleaning lady had come and gone, was vaguely antiseptic over the aroma of tobacco smoke and the coffee that had sat on its warmer too long.

"Detective Section. Smith." The blond man cradled the receiver against his shoulder so he could devote both hands to his magazine. Kelso saw him raise his thin white eyebrows and nod. Smith always kept a perfectly blank expression on his face when he spoke on the phone, so it was impossible to tell whether it was a true emergency or merely one of his girl friends calling to yell at him. Smith's girls yelled at him often, for reasons Kelso found obscure but which probably centered around the callous manner in which he treated them. Smith was an unapologetic chauvinist.

He muttered something into the receiver, then replaced it in its cradle. Turning another page and peering at it for a moment, he sighed, leaned back from his desk, swiveled in his chair, and fixed his cold blue eyes on Kelso.

1

"Screams in the night," he said, with no particular emotion, as if announcing the time or a weather forecast.

Kelso knew that Smith enjoyed being subtly dramatic and couldn't be hurried, unless it was a true emergency, and even in that case Smith was likely to waste a few seconds. Kelso pinched up more loose tobacco from his pouch and began tamping it in, not so tightly this time, waiting for Smith to get on with it.

"What the hell are you talking about?" Meyer asked. The detective-sergeant's feeling for Smith was emphatic dislike. It was difficult to know if the feeling was mutual, since Smith rarely exhibited outward emotions, but Kelso suspected that Smith in fact liked no one at all. Probably he didn't dislike anyone, either; his approach to people was detached, clinical, as a botanist might approach a collection of bugs.

"Screams," Smith said calmly. "That was the dispatcher. There's a church at Wilhelm Drive and Amsterdam Avenue. St. Luke's. Or maybe she said St. Mark's. At any rate, there's a large parking lot next to it. Some sort of evening meeting just let out and some woman called up to say she heard screams."

"Coming from the church?" Meyer sounded skeptical.

"No. Apparently a path leads from the parking lot down into some woods. She thinks the screams came from there."

"Down in the woods," Kelso murmured, testing the tobacco in his pipe bowl with a thumb. Firm, but not too firm. This time it should be about right. He knew the church Smith was talking about but had never been there. It was an Episcopal church, if he remembered correctly, up on a hill. He'd passed it numerous times because it was on the way to the house Susan Overstreet shared with her Aunt Eleanor, but he'd never really observed it closely.

"So what are we supposed to do about it?" Meyer asked. "Isn't that the province of the uniformed guys? Loud noises? Screams in the night?"

"Don't forget the directive," Smith said.

"Screw the directive," Meyer snapped.

But Smith was correct. Last week Lieutenant Leill, head

of the Detective Section, had issued a directive instructing them to respond to any of several classes of calls after 6 P.M. The classes included possible assaults. To this end, a rotating roster of night-duty personnel had been posted; tonight the four names on the roster were Kelso, Smith, Meyer, and Broom.

"It's a possible assault," Kelso said mildly, striking a match and holding its flame just over the tobacco. He drew carefully, slowly, tasting the first sweet smoke. The tobacco was fresh and moist, maybe too moist; suddenly it flared briefly and went out, leaving him sucking at nothing with a dry rasping sound. "We're supposed to respond to possible assaults, according to Leill's directive. A couple of us will have to go." Sighing, he glared at the pipe and set it down in a large ceramic ashtray.

The fourth name on the duty roster for that evening was Detective Stanley Broom, but he was in the men's room and had been for the last twenty minutes. His stomach seemed upset tonight, something he'd eaten, and he'd been in there more than he'd been at his desk.

"I'll go," Smith said. "Meyer, you want to go with me?"

Meyer glared and said nothing. He would rather have attended a PTA meeting than accompany Smith anywhere, something Smith well knew. But Meyer wouldn't say so, he'd just sit there glaring, lighting a fresh cigarette and puffing hard. Kelso would have to break the deadlock.

"I'll go," he said, and Smith nodded with his dispassionate gaze.

"Leill is an idiot," Meyer said. "Only four men on call. What if Broom and I have to go somewhere and another call comes in and nobody's here to respond? What happens then?"

"The dispatcher gets somebody out of their nice comfortable house," Smith said. He stood up, cast a last look at the *Penthouse,* and slipped it into a desk drawer. From another drawer he took his service revolver, checked it, slipped it into his shoulder holster, shrugged into his light-blue suit jacket, and blinked. "Okay, I'm ready."

Kelso put on his jacket and walked out of the duty room

with Smith. They produced a study in contrasts. Smith was tall, thin, pale, blond, blue-eyed, almost sinister-looking in the way his eyes rode up under his drooping lids. His hair was cut short, his cheekbones were high, he looked like a well-dressed ghoul. Kelso was under five-ten, fifteen pounds overweight (mostly around his waist, from eating too much and exercising too little), with thick brown hair that was receding steadily with his thirty-six years, dark eyes, a rather large nose, and casual dress—corduroy slacks, crepe-soled shoes, blue Oxford button-down shirt, tan Windbreaker. He wore his .38 caliber Detective Special in a hip holster.

As they went out the door into the cold, lifeless hallway, Smith turned and said, "Hey, Meyer. Stay away from my magazine, okay?"

"I'm not interested in your filth," Meyer retorted.

Smith smiled and closed the door.

The upstairs hallway was practically deserted at this time of evening. Downstairs on the main level, uniformed cops milled around, sipping coffee from thermos mugs or paper cups from the detestable machine at the far end of the hall. Some of them nodded and Kelso nodded back. Outside it was Tuesday, October 28, cold and breezy, with light frost possible by morning.

"Let's take my car," Smith said. "I hate that bug of yours."

"I got it worked on," Kelso replied. "It only needed new points, after all that trouble I had with it. Now it runs like new."

"I don't care. I hate small cars. Let's take mine." It was one of the huge old LTDs. "This country can afford to spend millions on space shuttles and athletes' salaries, but they're too cheap to manufacture a decent-sized car. It doesn't make any sense."

"We'll take your car," Kelso said.

Smith had few pet peeves; anything relating to comfort or convenience was one of them. Smith wanted everything to be just right. Kelso liked his VW for exactly the same reasons Smith enjoyed a big car: it was comfortable, it was convenient, and he enjoyed driving it, but he'd never convince Smith. The wind made Kelso's face and hands cold. In three days it would be Halloween, and the trick-or-treaters would freeze their behinds. It was the way it was.

They drove out of the downtown area, out of the lights and into the relative gloom of a residential section with streetlamps far apart and dim. The instrument panel made more of a glow on Smith's pale features than anything from the street. Leaning back in the passenger seat with his hands in his jacket pockets, Kelso watched large dark houses slide past. The sidewalks were deserted.

"Do you read *Penthouse?*" Smith asked suddenly.

"What?" Kelso had heard him clearly, but the question had caught him off-guard and he wanted time to think about it. Sometimes Smith talked about weird things. "Do I read what?"

"Pent . . . house," Smith said, overpronouncing the word as if for a child.

"Oh." Kelso considered this. There was something a little odd about the man. It wasn't what he did—many people liked erotic magazines—it was his attitudes. "I've seen it, but I don't really read it."

"Do you think they're immoral?"

"Immoral?"

"Yeah. You know, the girls who pose for those pictures."

"I don't know," Kelso said. 'I've never thought much about it. I suppose it depends on your definition of morality. If you were a priest, you'd probably think it was—"

"To hell with that. I want to know what *you* think, not some priest."

"Oh." Houses loomed on either side of the wide avenue. The neighborhood was becoming expensive, more elite. Here was the church, ahead on the left, just across the next intersection. Smith stopped for the red light at Wilhelm Drive; there was no traffic. "I have a lot of trouble with morality," Kelso said. "I think it's immoral to hurt people, but I'm not sure whether women who pose for magazine pictures hurt anyone. Maybe it's a question of—"

"Never mind," Smith interrupted impatiently. "You're too philosophical. Things aren't simple to you. I wanted a black and white answer, not a lecture."

"If it bothers you," Kelso said mildly, "why do you look at that magazine?"

"It's fun," Smith said. The light changed. "Here's that church." He turned left into a driveway that slanted steeply upward and pulled into a large black-topped lot. For a moment the LTD's headlights shot powerful beams into thick woods, then Smith cut the lights and engine and they sat in darkness. No other cars were visible in the lot. To their right, a large church sat silhouetted blackly against the sky, its front illuminated by a single floodlight somewhere on the lawn.

"Where are the uniformed guys?" Smith asked, sounding annoyed. "We can't be the only ones responding."

"We waited around before we left," Kelso reminded him. "Maybe they've already checked it out." He peered through the windshield but could see nothing. It occurred to him that if someone had reported a scream, a patrol car should have been here rapidly; the absence of one should mean a false alarm.

Smith picked up the radio microphone and spoke into it.

"Unit Seven," he muttered.

The radio crackled and a young girl's voice said, "Go ahead, Seven.'

"This is Seven. We're at a church at Amsterdam and Wilhelm, responding to the call about a scream. But nobody else is here. Over."

"You're the only unit responding," the voice said. "Are you requesting a backup?"

"Jesus Christ."

"Unit Seven?"

"No. No backup. Why isn't there a patrol car here?"

"We thought it was probably a false alarm," the girl said.

"Shirley, is that you? This is Smith."

"Hi, Karl. Who's with you?"

"Kelso is. You know anything about this?"

"Not a thing. But you'd better watch out for ghosts."

"What?"

"Just a joke. You want a backup, Karl?"

"No. Unit Seven out." Smith replaced the mike. "It's a wonder the whole department doesn't collapse." His face was a pale oval in the LTD's dark interior. "Screams," he said. "Ghosts. I wonder if this whole thing is somebody's idea of a joke. Maybe Broom didn't go to the men's room that last time. Maybe he went out in the hall or into another office and phoned up about a scream, just to get back at us for putting salt in his thermos last week."

"That was your idea, not mine."

"Whatever. Well, you want to check it out?"

"I guess so."

They got out of the car. It was cold, probably not over forty-five degrees. It would be in the low thirties by morning. Kelso wished he'd brought his pipe; it would be good to have something to stick in his mouth, something to bite down on. Next to him in the quiet darkness of the parking lot, Smith was a tall shadow. Somewhere a dog barked briefly, four or five high shrill yelps, then quit. Down in Amsterdam Avenue a car rumbled past, turned the corner into Wilhelm, and accelerated away. Even in the darkness Smith's blue suit stood out pale and ghostly. It was a clear night, with stars but no moon.

"Shouldn't there be a light in this stupid lot?" Smith asked, walking to his left, away from the church.

"You'd think so," Kelso said. "Maybe it burned out."

"Maybe. Or maybe it was shot out or put out with a rock. Maybe somebody doesn't like cops, have you ever thought about that? Maybe somebody's waiting for us on that path the dispatcher mentioned."

"Don't get paranoid."

"I'm not paranoid. I'm just considering all the possibilties. I can't see where the hell I'm going." Smith returned to the car and opened the trunk. "I've got some flashlights in here somewhere." He handed one to Kelso. "There. Now at least we can see."

The metal was cold against Kelso's hand. He thumbed the switch and aimed the yellowish beam; it seemed weak against the darkness, but he saw the edge of the asphalt lot and the beginning of weeds and the woods that surrounded them.

"Is that the path?" Smith's light bobbed here and there.

"I guess it is," Kelso admitted, pointing his light where Smith's had stopped. A narrow opening in the high growth was just visible.

"Supposedly the scream came from down there."

"I guess we should go see." Kelso walked forward and stepped onto the path. It was dirt and led downhill between bushes and large trees. Unseen limbs stabbed at him from either side and his shoes came down on rocks so that he had to be careful to avoid twisting his ankles. He heard footsteps following behind, and Smith's light bounced past him occasionally, a yellow oval that darted across branches and weeds and went away again. Kelso kept his light aimed a few feet ahead, following the path, which kept turning and twisting sharply left and right. Sometimes a tree limb hung so low that he had to stoop. Things caught at his trousers, pulling like burrs or thorns, and things slapped at his bare hands, making them sting.

"Do you believe in ghosts?" asked Smith, behind him. "No."

Then the path made a final sharp turn to the right and they were in a large clearing, about thirty feet across, overhung by a canopy of dense tree branches and surrounded by thick dark trunks. The dirt floor was strewn with rocks ranging in diameter from an inch up to a foot. Kelso's light caught a large chunk of gray stone, like part of a statue.

"Look at this," he said, walking over to peer closely at it. "Something's engraved on it."

"I'd say it was part of a gravestone. What the hell *is* this place?"

"I can hardly make out the words. It must be pretty old." Kelso knelt down by the stone and moved his flashlight from one side to the other, making the carved words darken into relief. " 'Here lies Mary Carter,' " he read. " 'Born November 1, 1897. Died July 10, 1916.' Hmm. She died young."

"Nineteen," Smith muttered. "Do you think this is really her grave?"

"I don't know. This looks like the middle section of a larger monument; it's been broken off." He cast his light around the area. "Maybe all this rubble is what's left of the rest. Maybe lightning struck it."

"Maybe. But what's it doing out here in the middle of the woods?" Then his flashlight came to rest on something at the edge of the clearing, fifteen feet away. "What's *that?*"

Kelso stared. It looked like the base of a monument, probably part of the one with the engraving. It sat on the ground by itself, about three feet high, and a small pale object lay on top, more or less in the center. He stood up and walked over to look. Then he swallowed.

The object was a human hand, palm up, fingers slightly curled. In his flashlight beam the skin had a greenish cast, the fingers appeared thick, and his nose wrinkled at a faint foul odor. About an inch of wrist remained. Smith came up behind him and stopped.

For a while they stood holding their lights on the thing, looking at it, not speaking, surrounded by woods and cold and darkness.

Chapter Two

Mary's Grave

After what seemed a very long time, Smith cleared his throat—it sounded incredibly loud—and spoke. "Kelso, do you think it's real?"

"It looks real," Kelso said. Looking at it, he was reminded of the fake rubber or plastic things you could buy in the store, especially at Halloween, to frighten people with. Ghoul masks and witch noses, green decaying hands with long pointed nails dripping blood. At first he hoped that's what this was, just something purchased in a variety store and left here by some teenager to scare other teenagers. Maybe high school couples would sneak down here at night from some function at the church, to stand around and whisper and giggle and maybe do a little making out, maybe tell a few stories about the creatures living in the woods.

Kelso could picture one of them thinking what a good joke it would be to buy one of those realistic-looking hands and leave it atop the slab for others to find. Maybe they'd even hide behind some of the trees and wait for unsuspecting victims, so they could run out laughing after the screams had died away.

It all fit together. The scream someone had heard, that would be a girl encountering the fake hand. The woman who'd called in the report hadn't stayed around long enough to hear the laughter and howls that must have followed the scream.

All except for one thing: the hand wasn't fake, it wasn't made of plastic or rubber. Even in the darkness and the beam from his flashlight he could tell it was real. Just at

10

the thin narrow wrist it had been neatly severed from its arm, and now it lay there, obscene and nightmarish, on the stone.

"Yes," Kelso said, trying to make his voice sound natural, "it's real."

Smith moved closer. "Looks like it's bled dry. Drained. There's no blood on the stone, though. It wasn't done here."

"We'd better call it in," Kelso said. "The area will have to be searched, the sooner the better."

Smith looked up at him questioningly. "Why searched?"

"For the rest of the body."

"Oh." Smith nodded slowly. "Of course," he said very calmly, "There may not be any rest of the body, you know."

"Why?"

"Whoever lost this doesn't have to be dead."

Kelso nodded morosely. Smith was quite correct. He hadn't been thinking. The hand was evidence of—call it an assault—but not a homicide. For a moment he wondered if the victim might not be better off dead, then he cleared his mind of such thoughts. "I'll go up to the car and radio headquarters. Or you can. Take your choice."

"What do you mean?" Smith asked.

"One of us would stay here with the, uh, evidence. In case somebody comes around."

"Oh, yeah." Smith hesitated. He stood up and reached into a pants pocket. "Toss for it?"

"Okay."

Smith flipped a coin in his free hand, caught it, folded his fingers over it, and aimed his flashlight at his fist. "You call it," he said. "Winner decides?"

"Tails." It didn't matter to Kelso. Standing down here alone with this thing was as bad as having to trudge back up the path to the parking lot.

Smith opened his hand. The light gleamed on a quarter, revealing George Washington's head. "You lose, Kelso. Okay, I'll go call it in. You stay here with the . . ."

"Okay." Kelso nodded.

Smith walked across the clearing, found the path, stopped to look back.

"You don't mind, do you?"

"No. Not at all."

"It was fair and square, Kelso. You lost the toss."

"I know." Kelso sighed. "Just go on and call it in."

"I'm going." Smith hesitated. "You've got your gun, right?"

"Yes."

"I'll probably stay up there till the backup gets here, okay?"

"Yes. Okay."

"Well." Smith started up the path. Stopped. Looked back once more. "See you in a few minutes, then." He turned away, went up the path. Kelso saw him disappear into darkness; there was only the faint glow of his flashlight bobbing, then there was nothing.

He went to the middle of the clearing and peered again at the piece of monument with the engraving. Mary Carter. This must have been a family's backyard plot, or maybe the girl had been buried out here for some special reason. Probably she wasn't even buried here anymore, he couldn't see any signs of the actual grave. Unless it was beneath the stone with the hand on it.

Moving his light in an arc around the edge of the clearing, he tried to get some idea of where he was relative to the church parking lot and the street. Once, he thought he heard a noise, as of someone walking out there in the darkness, but then he heard a car engine; when the car's noise faded it was quiet again. The ground seemed to slope upward on the side of the clearing opposite the path and appeared generally level to his right, but he couldn't go exploring while he was supposed to be guarding the so-called evidence. He turned off the flashlight and stood in darkness.

The evidence. Evidence of what, he wondered. Possibilities suggested themselves, possibilities he tried not to dwell on. There were three, to start with.

One: someone had cut the hand from a dead body and left it here, for whatever reason.

Two: someone had cut the hand from someone who was still alive.

Three: the hand's owner had been alive at the time of the amputation but now was dead.

Probably Smith was right, probably nothing had actually taken place here, and the hand had been brought from somewhere else. Out there in the darkness, in the woods, or a field. Up in that church? Or even far away, on the other side of the city.

Kelso wondered about the owner of the hand. Fingerprints would, of course, be taken. If the prints weren't on file anywhere, identification would be difficult, maybe impossible. Either way, the hand's owner might never be found. It could be a tough case. He wondered if they were dealing with someone who was insane. Then he wondered, not for the first time in his career, if there had ever been a sane murderer.

It felt colder. He peered at the supposedly luminous dial of his watch, but had to turn his flashlight on it to read the time—10:05. He turned the flashlight off again and shoved it into a hip pocket. His nose and ears and toes were cold. His hands, too; he thrust them into the pockets of his Windbreaker. He stood motionless by a large tree at the opposite side of the clearing from the hand, facing the path so he would be able to see the lights of the cops who would respond to Smith's radio call. It shouldn't be too much longer. He shifted his weight from one shoe to the other and bent his knees slightly to avoid stiffness. Involuntarily, he imagined himself strapped to a table, something like a chopping block, with a madman brandishing a cleaver over him, wild-eyed and grinning. At the last instant would he pass out from fear? Or would he remain conscious long enough to feel the edge of the blade and then—

In the black quietness of the woods a sound met his ears: the snap of a twig. Stiffening, he strained to hear. The noise hadn't come from the direction of the path, he was certain; rather, it had come from his left. Holding his breath for a moment, he listened, fists clenched in his jacket pockets, eyes staring in an effort to penetrate the surrounding darkness.

The sound came again, louder. Now he could hear footsteps approaching, very distinctly, as if someone didn't at all care whether or not they could be heard. A madman with a cleaver, he thought. He opened his mouth and breathed cold air deeply.

Now the footsteps were loud and close. His eyes had adapted somewhat to the darkness, which here in the city was never absolute, though down in this woods there was scarcely any light. Dimly he could make out the dirt floor of the clearing, the somewhat lighter monument section in the center, and the stone on the far side. At this distance the severed hand was a small formless blur. Around him the woods and underbrush formed a black wall, blacker than the sky overhead.

Then a shape detached itself from the wall, like a piece of it coming loose, and a stone was kicked. Someone had entered the clearing and was standing maybe twenty feet away. Kelso suddenly wondered how visible he was. Wait, he thought. Wait and see what happens, maybe they haven't seen you yet. But surely his tan Windbreaker was highly visible.

The black form moved with a crunching of dirt, leaves, and pebbles. By watching it indirectly, from the corners of his eyes, he could follow its motion toward the large stone on the far side of the clearing, and now he realized that the intruder could very likely be the person who had severed the hand and was returning now to get it. Vaguely, he realized something else: that it wasn't logical, the criminal wouldn't have placed the hand on the stone and then come back for it. But cutting off someone's hand wasn't logical anyway, and besides that it didn't matter. What mattered was the immediate possibility that somebody was about to take the hand.

Carefully, Kelso took his hands out of his jacket pockets. With his left he found his flashlight and aimed it out ahead of him, thumb ready on the switch. With his right he drew his revolver. Taking a deep breath, he counted silently to three, then thumbed on the light and said sharply, "Hold it right there. Police. Don't move."

He squinted. The faint beam of light, which seemed to be weakening steadily from undoubtedly weak batteries, revealed someone who stood just at the stone monument section, facing away from him. Facing the hand. He got an impression of faded jeans, a dark coat, dark hair. He aimed the faltering light at the person's head.

"Turn around slowly," he said, keeping his voice hard. "Hold your hands up high, in plain view."

The figure turned, raising both hands to shoulder height. For a moment Kelso was afraid it might be the person who'd lost the hand, but the figure had two hands. Then he stared as his light illuminated a face.

It was a young girl, with dark eyes, narrow face, a faint mocking smile on her lips. A twig snapped behind him and a terrible thought touched his mind, then the back of his head exploded and he fell, thinking: this isn't really happening. . . .

Pain hummed in his ears like an electrical generating plant and the ground opened up to receive him, allowing him to fall forever.

Chapter Three

Interlude

In the harsh gray light from the stars the girl watched, faint amusement playing at a corner of her mouth, like a child at a magic show. The bald man ignored her, however, and knelt down to pat the pockets of the one he'd hit.

Using a penlight, he went through pockets and found a leather folder, inside of which were a gold cop's badge and an official I.D. card bearing a photograph. The penlight showed a solemn face, dark eyes, receding hairline, large nose. Beneath it, a number and a name: George A. Kelso, Sergeant, Detective Section.

The flashlight and the gun lay on the ground near the man's form.

The bald man returned the folder to its pocket and sat for a moment on his haunches. Across the clearing the stupid girl made a faint sound like a giggle. He scowled at her and stood up. At his feet the detective lay still, eyes closed, chest rising and falling with his breath.

"Go on home, Rosemary," he said to the stupid girl. "Go home now. Go on, scat."

Smirking in that idiotic way of hers, she moved away from the monument base—Mary's grave—and entered the woods. He could hear her shoes rattling and crunching leaves and sticks as she progressed up the hill toward the house. He knew that she would go around to the street then, and home.

Looking down again, the bald man considered taking away the hand, but then fear built up in him and he began wondering what to do about the detective. Should he leave him here? Alive? He thought he heard a noise, and peered this way and that in the clearing.

Someone was coming down from the church. He'd have to hurry.

"Good-bye, Mary," he said softly, and retreated into the woods, quickly and silently, like an animal.

Chapter Four

Ghost Stories

The lights were hurting his eyes. Someone was saying his name over and over, and his head throbbed. He was very cold.

"Kelso? Kelso?"

He raised a hand to his eyes, blinking, lying on his back. Faces peered down at him, out of focus. What had happened? He remembered and sat up, the pain stabbing at the back of his head and down his neck, producing nausea. Don't vomit, he instructed himself, or you'll be embarrassed. Someone knelt in front of him and he recognized Meyer, peering at him with an irritated scowl.

"Kelso? What the hell are you doing? What happened to you?"

"I don't know." He reached back to touch his head.

"No, don't mess with it. You're okay, there's no bleeding. Somebody must've sapped you from behind. Leave you alone for one minute and you get into trouble, don't you?"

"The hand," Kelso managed to say. "Is it still there?"

Smith's voice came to him. "It's still there, Kelso. What happened, anyway?"

He stood up carefully. Hands took his arms, steadying him.

"You want an ambulance, Kelso?" That was Meyer again.

"No, I'm all right. Just a little dazed." He shook his head. The pain stabbed again, but not as violently. "I was waiting down here for the backup. A figure came out of the woods, somebody—"

18

"You saw them?"

"I saw somebody. She went over to the stone, the base of the monument, and I was afraid she was after the hand. I ordered her to turn around—"

"A woman?" Smith asked. "It was a woman?"

"Yes, it was a woman. A girl. I identified myself, told her to turn and raise her hands. She did, and she just sort of smiled at me. Then I heard something behind me, and just when I thought I'd better get out of the way something hit my head."

"I don't get it," Smith said. "Some broad comes into the clearing and somebody bashes you, but she doesn't take the hand. What was she doing here?"

Kelso shrugged, slowly feeling better. The nausea was gone. He shivered.

"I don't know," he said. "I need some coffee or something."

"We've got a whole team on the way," Meyer said. "We're going to run heavy extensions down from the church and set up lights. We're going to go over this place with a fine-toothed comb, and also a team will search these woods. We'd better get you up to a warm room and get some liquid in you. Here, Smith, help me get him back up to the parking lot."

"I can walk," Kelso muttered. He swayed a little, then gritted his teeth and started for the path. It struck him that Meyer, usually surly and sarcastic and difficult, had actually shown human concern. Then Meyer's voice came to him from the clearing. "You blew it, Kelso. If you hadn't let somebody get behind you, we might've had a suspect. I guess you know you blew it."

Kelso smiled grimly through his headache. Yes, that was more like the Meyer they all knew and loved.

Smith led the way back up the path to the asphalt parking lot. Over his shoulder he said, "Did you remember to pick up your thirty-eight and your flashlight from where you dropped them?"

"Yes." Kelso patted his holster. "I don't know why I even drew it, it was only a girl."

"What's the matter, Kelso? You think a girl can't kill

you as dead as a guy? Listen, did you make the whole thing up, about the girl?''

"I didn't make it up, Smith. A girl came into the clearing. I'd say she was around twenty, dark hair, dark eyes, wearing blue jeans and a dark coat. I'm not making it up.''

"Okay, okay. Well, too bad you lost the coin toss. Otherwise it would've been me down there instead of you. Watch it, the path turns really sharply here. I'm getting to be an expert on this damned path. All I've done tonight is walk up and down it. By the way, you didn't happen to notice whether this broad had both hands, did you?''

"She had both," Kelso muttered, feeling tired and cold. He must have dropped his flashlight when he fell; now it hardly produced any light at all. He wasn't making any effort to figure anything out or to make sense of anything. All he wanted was to get indoors, get warm, drink something hot, eat something. Then he'd try to fit some pieces together. He struggled up the path, trying to follow Smith.

The girl's face stayed in his mind. She'd had a strange effect on him, and the more he thought about it the more familiar she seemed. Maybe he'd seen her before. Have to check out the mug books. But surely it wouldn't be that. He'd seen her under entirely different circumstances. It wouldn't come. It was like a half-remembered dream, stuck somewhere in his subconscious.

They reached the asphalt lot, now filled with five or six marked police cruisers and a couple of unmarked patrol cars. A crew in blue coveralls was busy stringing a power cord over from the church, and already three bright lights illuminated the parking area.

"Come on," Smith said. "I'll drive you back to town.''

"Okay.'' Normally he would have insisted on staying at the scene throughout the search to see if anything turned up, but he was tired and his head hurt worse again. He sank into the passenger seat of Smith's big LTD and felt its heat. They rolled down to the street, turned onto Amsterdam Avenue, and accelerated.

"I found out some things about that place," Smith said as he drove. "That clearing, with the grave marker and everything, it's called 'Mary's grave' and the story is, it's haunted.''

"Sure,'' Kelso murmured.

"I didn't say I bought it, Kelso, I'm just passing on the information I got, okay? One of the uniformed guys told me. He says there's this broad named Mary Carter—that was the name on the stone, right?—and supposedly she died back at the turn of the century from pneumonia and complications. She was visiting from Georgia or someplace like that. Well, the relatives she was staying with buried her behind their house for some reason, and that made her spirit restless because she wanted to be planted in Georgia where she was from. So the story is that her body's still there and her ghost is, too, and it's been seen down there by lots of people.''

"That's very interesting,'' Kelso said, as they turned a corner and approached the downtown sector, "but I don't see what it's got to do with anything.''

"Maybe nothing. Just thought you might be interested.''

"Maybe Mary's ghost grabbed somebody,'' Kelso said, trying to be sarcastic. "Maybe it got annoyed at somebody for trespassing on her grave, and grabbed them and whacked off their hand.''

"Talk like that gives me the creeps.'' Smith stopped for a light. There was some traffic in this area, even a few pedestrians. Bars and restaurants were open here and there.

"Don't tell me you believe in ghosts,'' Kelso said.

"Of course not.'' Smith accelerated across the intersection as the light turned green. "Well, I don't know. I do and I don't. Kelso, didn't you ever see anything you couldn't explain? Something at night, in the dark, something moving for example?''

"Not since I was a child.''

"There are things in this world that people don't completely understand.''

"I know.'' Kelso sighed. "But we found a real hand. I saw a real girl. And somebody hit me over the head with a real solid object.''

"Hey,'' Smith said suddenly, and glanced at Kelso. In the car's dim interior the whites of his eyes were bright.

"Kelso, what if that wasn't a real girl you saw? What if it was her?"

"Her who?"

"Mary's ghost." He said it perfectly deadpan, without the slightest hint of humor, then looked back at the street and drove the rest of the way to the Municipal Building in silence.

Apparently somebody had notified Susan Overstreet about Kelso's incident, because when he sat down at his desk in the duty room a sheet of notepaper lay on his blotter bearing words in red ink: KELSO—CALL SUSAN AT ONCE!

Sighing, he reached for the phone. Smith wandered in, removed his blue suit-coat, put his revolver in a drawer, and got out a magazine. Broom wasn't in the room. Maybe he was in the men's room again.

The phone rang in Kelso's ear, worsening the pounding, and he fumbled in his desk for the bottle of aspirin as someone answered, "Hello?"

"It's me," he said.

"George. Are you all right? I've been calling for an hour. They said you got hit on the head in a grave. Did you get it X-rayed?"

"Relax." Smith was watching him with clinical interest, listening. "I wasn't in a grave, and it wasn't much of anything."

"You could have a concussion. Get it X-rayed, okay?"

"Sure."

Susan worked on the social-work staff of a large hospital and always overreacted to anything that happened to Kelso. He knew she'd calm down faster if he acted unconcerned, so he cleared his throat and asked gruffly, "You ever been to Mary's grave?"

"Yes, as a matter of fact. I used to attend St. Luke's."

"Is that the big Episcopal church on Amsterdam?"

"That's the one. I didn't know that's where you were, they just said in a grave. I think I talked to Broom. Someone with a cold. When I was in high school all the kids went down there a lot and told scary stories and made out."

"Who'd *you* make out with?" he asked.

"None of your business. Aunt Eleanor's gone for the night, visiting her sister in Pittsburgh. Why don't you come over and I'll make you a hot drink and rub your back."

Kelso knew where Susan's back-rubs would lead. But too much had happened tonight and he only wanted to go home and get into his own bed and sleep.

"Do you know anything else about the grave?" he asked.

"You're changing the subject, but I'll answer it anyway. Yes, as a matter of fact I do. Stories I've heard. There's a blue light up in the trees. Uh . . . Mary doesn't like cigarettes; she'll knock them out of your hands. She likes pearls and steals them. And, oh yes, the people in the house are insane."

"What house?"

"God, George, don't you know anything? That path from the parking lot continues at the other side of the clearing and goes up through the woods to the rear of a huge house. The people living there are the descendants of the people Mary stayed with, back in the beginning of the century, and they're supposedly all insane."

"Where do you get this stuff?" he asked.

"Around. So are you coming over or not?"

"Look, it's after eleven-thirty. I've got to get some sleep."

"Are you assigned to the murder?"

"There's no murder yet. Just a hand. And I'm assigned to it. By the way, you don't happen to know a girl, about twenty, dark hair, dark eyes, thin face, a kind of strange smirking smile, do you?"

"Are you kidding, George?"

"No. Why?"

"That's a pretty good description of Mary," Susan said. When he didn't reply, she said, "Promise me you'll be careful. And get your damn head X-rayed."

"I will. You worry too much."

"Get X-rayed. I love you. Call me tomorrow."

"Good night." He hung up, wondering why he felt so irritable and nervous. A bang on the head will do that, he told himself.

"These broads are immoral," Smith said, flipping the

pages of another magazine. "Kelso, what would you do if Susan were to pose for one of these things?"

"Buy up all the copies I could find."

"I'm serious, Kelso."

"So am I."

"Are you leaving now?"

"Yes." Kelso swallowed two aspirin, pocketed his pipe, wadded up the message and tossed it into a wastecan, and went to the door. "See you, Smith."

"Look out for those ghosts," Smith said, without looking up.

He pulled up in front of his apartment at midnight and unlocked his door with a bitter wind biting at him from the north. Inside, the big yellow cat waited in the hall, its green eyes glaring up at him accusingly.

"I know, I didn't come back to give you your dinner. Look at you, you're almost as fat as I am. Here, eat this and shut up." He spooned tuna-flavored something from a can into the cat's bowl and patted its head. "You're an eating machine," he told it, and went upstairs.

The apartment was a two-bedroom townhouse. In the back of his mind he admitted that the place was big enough for someone who might move in with him, but the single life had grown on him, fitting him more and more comfortably with the passing years, like a good pair of shoes. In the shower he wondered about the severed hand and its owner. Finally, lying in the dark in his bed, he visualized the grave and what Susan had said. The girl he'd seen fit the description of Mary's ghost. Fortunately, he didn't believe in ghosts.

He jumped when something hit the bed, but it was only the cat.

Kelso liked sleeping in a cold room; one window was partly open to the night air and off in the distance he heard a train whistle, the faint barking of a dog, and a truck grinding its way through many gears out on the main road. The cat began its nightly ritual bath, and its licking became the lap of water against a pier jutting out into a lake, then the rattle of leaves along the path down to Mary's grave. Kelso slept, and dreamed disturbing dreams.

Chapter Five

The Priest

The next morning he awoke before the alarm. Wednesday, October 29, two days before Halloween. He fed the cat, ate a breakfast of raisin toast, cold bran flakes, juice, and a banana, then drove the VW downtown to the Municipal building, arriving at the Detective Section at five before eight. Meyer and Smith were in the duty room; they looked up as he entered.

"Hello," Smith said. "How's your head?"

"It's fine. Everybody was worried about nothing."

"The lab has the hand," Smith said. "We should have a report soon. Menwhile Leill has put Meyer in charge of the investigation." He said it blandly, but Kelso thought the blond detective might be irked. Relations between the two were less than perfect.

"Okay," Kelso replied, nodding.

Meyer scowled. "Leill put me in charge as punishment. Why else would he stick me with it? It's a hopeless case. How are we going to find out who took that hand?"

"I don't know," Kelso said.

"Leill knows it's hopeless, why else would he have assigned me to it?" Meyer shook his head, his heavy black brows knotted over his nose. "It must be because I refused to attend the picnic last month. God, I think I've got more important things to do with my time than attend office picnics. What does he want from me? Okay, that church out there must have a priest. So we need to find him, ask him some questions, see if he was with the women who met there last night. We need to find the woman who called in about the scream and question her. None of this

25

will do us the slightest bit of good, but I can't think of any other way to proceed so that's what we'll do.'' He lit a cigarette and tossed the match angrily into an ashtray, puffed hard, and added, ''I've got to talk to the pathology people this morning. Kelso, you and Smith go out to the church and find that priest and the woman who made the call and see if they know anything useful. That should waste a couple of hours. I hope it makes Leill happy. He must be nuts.''

''The thing's got to be investigated,'' Smith said calmly. ''What are you so upset about? A crime has been committed.''

''Yeah, I suppose so.'' Meyer shrugged his narrow shoulders. ''Okay, get going.''

Kelso hadn't bothered to remove the heavy jacket he was wearing. He took out his pipe and shoved it between his teeth, not filling or lighting it, and waited for Smith. Somewhere back in the remote past, Smith was related to the Germans—probably he'd been Schmidt once—and it seemed to Kelso that when he spoke to Meyer he sometimes affected a very slight German accent. He wondered if Smith did it consciously, just as a way of further annoying Meyer. Smith was not anti-Semitic, but he seemed to take a perverse interest in finding ways to irritate certain persons.

As they opened the door to the hall Meyer said gruffly, ''Kelso, if your head bothers you I'll put someone else on this.''

''There's nothing wrong with my head,'' Kelso said. It was true, but even if he'd felt poorly he wouldn't have admitted it, mainly because he wanted to stay on the case. Overnight, it had become an obsession.

''I'll drive,'' Smith said, as they walked outside into a gray, overcast morning that threatened rain. During the night clouds had moved in on a hard wind and there had been no frost, but the temperature was only in the upper thirties, more like November than October. They climbed into the LTD and Smith adjusted the car's heater fan.

''Sleep okay last night?'' he asked.

"I had a few nightmares, but otherwise it wasn't too bad." Kelso tamped tobacco into the bowl of his pipe.

"Nightmares, huh? What about? The grave and the hand?"

"Not exactly. More like things chasing me in the woods. Things sneaking up behind me. I had this feeling that something was gong to grab me and chop my arm off."

"It's obviously because of the hand," Smith said. "I read a book about dreams, and what's happened is that you've got all these fears piled up in your mind and when you sleep they come out. The hand frightened you on some deep level, so you relate to its owner by imagining the same thing is happening to you. In other words, you identify with the victim."

"So what?" Kelso didn't particularly like dream analysis.

"So nothing. I'm just telling you why you dreamed about someone chasing you with a chopper."

"It's pretty obvious," Kelso said, striking a match and touching its flame to the tobacco. "By the way, I found out some more about the grave last night. There's a kind of myth surrounding it. There's supposed to be a ghost there, and kids visit the place all the time to make out and scare each other."

"Making out never scared me," Smith commented, accelerating to make a yellow light. "Maybe the hand belongs to one of the stupid kids messing around down there. Serve 'em right. Kids these days have no respect for other people's property."

"Are you on another anti-kid kick?"

"I don't like kids. But you're not one to talk, Kelso. You and Susan aren't exactly filling up the maternity wards."

"We're not married."

"Exactly my point. If you liked kids, you'd be married. That's the only real reason people marry, to bring snot-nosed little brats into the world, many of whom will grow up to take their places in our jails and insane asylums."

Kelso said nothing. Smith had a strange way of joking which often bordered on serious feelings of hostility, especially when he was in a bad mood. It could be the case. The hand and its implications had everyone on edge.

They turned into Amsterdam Avenue, a wide street lined with towering trees that shielded large expensive-looking homes. As they crossed the intersection with Wilhelm Drive and approached the church, Kelso's pipe went out and he fumbled for his matches. There might have been a grain of truth to Smith's comment about the kids. He himself had wondered if the hand could belong to one of the high school students who frequented the grave, but it didn't really make sense. Kids going down there would surely be in groups; besides which, they'd found no evidence of violence actually at the grave.

"What did the search last night turn up?" he asked.

"Not a thing." Smith pulled into the parking lot and stopped, killing the engine. "They finally gave up sometime around 2 A.M. Well, there were a lot of cigarette butts, some empty bottles and beer cans, some used condoms, the kind of junk you'd expect to find in a secluded area where lower-class people congregate to drink and screw around, but none of it will turn out to have any significance." Smith sounded very sure. "You want to know what I think?"

"What do you think?" Kelso asked, getting out of the car and knocking out ashes against one palm and then shoving his pipe into a jacket pocket.

"I think it's a hoax. I think that hand's going to turn out to be from some corpse. Probably someone who works in a morgue or an emergency room took it down there and left it, just to scare people."

"Even if it were true," Kelso said, "it would still be a crime. You can't just cut off a dead body's hand and carry it away. And who'd do a thing like that? You'd almost have to be insane."

They walked toward the church. It had started to rain very lightly and felt even colder than before. At the edge of the lot a paved walk led across the extensive lawn to the main entrance.

"I knew a guy who worked in a morgue," Smith said as they walked hunched over in the rain. "He was a real weirdo, let me tell you. I think he might've done something like that, if he'd thought about it. One Halloween he stole a corpse and left it in a chair on someone's front porch. Caused quite an uproar."

Kelso grimaced. "What happened to him?"

"He was arrested, then committed to an institution. The shrinks said he was schizophrenic, but that's what they always say. Well, I hope the priest is in—maybe we can get some coffee." They had reached two massive oaken doors and Smith pulled one open. Kelso followed him inside.

It was dark and quiet in the vestibule. At one end a door stood open to an office, but no one was visible inside it. Opposite them were two doors, several feet apart, both open and both leading into the sanctuary. They wandered through one door and stood looking down a long aisle at rows of pews, their backs lined with prayer books and hymnals in little racks. At the far end was an altar, surrounded by a wooden railing and crimson cushions for kneeling. High up on the wall behind the altar hung a huge wooden cross. Along either side of the room the pale light of day filtered in through stained-glass windows whose colors were intense.

"These places make me nervous," Smith said in a hushed tone.

"Did you ever go to church often?"

"When I was a kid in grade school. My parents were Lutheran."

"Why did you stop?" Kelso asked.

"When I was in the fourth grade a girl in my class was shot by a burglar. A guy broke into her house one evening when she was at home alone, waiting for her parents to get back from a party. I suppose they thought that, at the age of nine, she was old enough to stay home alone." Smith shrugged. "It wouldn't have mattered. The bastard had a shotgun, and for some reason he chose to use it on her. Later he tried to say he hadn't meant to, that it had been an accident. Nobody believed him."

"What happened?" Kelso asked, almost in a whisper.

"The word about what happened was all over school the next morning. I'd been especially fond of her, you might say. I left school without permission and went to the church. All morning I sat on a pew and prayed that she'd live. When I went home at noon, I found out she'd died the night before, in the emergency room. Not only that, but I was punished for staying away from school.'' Smith shrugged. "I never went back to church."

"I think somebody's coming."

A small door to the right of the altar opened and a man entered, dressed in a black suit and a clerical collar. He smiled and walked up the aisle toward them. He was tall, slender, and bald, with a black fringe of hair around the sides of his head. Probably not over forty-five, Kelso thought. There was a pleasant look to his small dark brown eyes.

"Good morning, gentlemen. May I help you, or have you come to pray?"

"Morning," Smith said.

"Father Ullman." The priest held out a hand, smiling. They both shook it.

"Sergeant Kelso, city police, Father." Kelso showed him his I.D. "This is Detective Smith."

The priest's face went serious, as if he were trying to think, then a look of concern came into his eyes.

"It must be about that business last night. Would you like to come back to my office?"

"You know about it?" Kelso asked.

"Certainly, if you mean the hand. I heard about it on the news."

"Well, that's why we're here, Father."

"All right. I don't think I can help much, but come on back and we'll see." He turned and led the way down toward the door. "Has the hand been identified yet?"

"Not yet," Smith said. "We're working on it."

They followed Ullman through the door, along a short corridor, and into a comfortable office, its walls lined with books, a large wooden desk and leather chair to the left, two upholstered armchairs to the right. It smelled of paper and leather and pipe smoke. Father Ullman sat down behind his desk and gestured for them to sit.

"I have a girl who helps me out part-time. Would you care for some coffee? I think she's just made a new pot."

"Sounds good to me," Kelso said, wondering if there was food but too polite to ask.

"I'll have a cup," Smith said. He seemed nervous.

The priest got up, went to the door, and called out into the hall, "Rosemary? Would you bring three coffees, please?"

As the priest took his seat again, Kelso pictured a gray-haired old lady, stooped and wrinkled, scurrying tiredly somewhere in the church. But Ullman had referred to her as a girl. He watched the door, interested.

The priest lit a pipe and puffed thick clouds of acrid smoke. Speaking around the pipe stem, he said, "Rosemary's been with me for two years. She's the daughter of a friend of mine. Born with some kind of brain damage. Retarded, never progressed much beyond the sixth grade. Also she has a few emotional problems. She spends several hours a week here doing odd jobs, cleaning, making coffee, even doing some light typing. A psychologist told me she's mentally about twelve years old. Ah, here she is."

The hall door opened and a young girl entered carrying a tray. Kelso stared. She had neck-length black hair, very dark eyes, a narrow face. She was probably about twenty. There was something not quite right about her. He'd seen it before in mentally retarded persons—a faintly blank expression, the facial features not exactly normal, as if someone had attempted to draw a human face but without a sense of the right proportion. And on her lips, a vague smile, a turning up at one corner to form a slight enigmatic smirk, similar to the Mona Lisa. Kelso gripped the arms of his chair, frowning.

He was sure it was the girl he'd seen down in the woods, standing in the darkness near Mary's grave, just before he'd been hit over the head.

She was wearing faded blue jeans and a green wool sweater, dark socks, leather shoes, and was extremely busty. Not making eye contact with anyone, she set the tray down on the priest's desk, returned to the door, and started out.

"Thank you, Rosemary," the priest said.

"You're welcome." The words came rather thickly. The door closed.

"Help yourselves, gentlemen," Ullman said.

On the tray were three cups filled with steaming black coffee, a bowl of individual sugar packets, and several plastic containers of cream, along with spoons and paper napkins. When everyone had taken a cup and Kelso was stirring two sugars and some cream into his, Ullman sipped his coffee and smiled politely.

"Now we can get down to business, gentlemen. I assume you have some questions for me?"

Yes, Kelso thought emphatically. He did have some questions. Such as, who that girl was and where she'd been the previous evening at about 10 P.M.

"We understand there was some sort of meeting here last night," he said.

"Yes, there was. Choir practice. And I happened to be here, though normally I wouldn't have been. I came along to introduce one of our new church members to the choir director. However, I left early, so I wasn't here when the, er, event occurred."

"What time did you leave, Father?" Smith wanted to know. He was not smiling.

"Let's see. They began about seven, and I believe I left a couple of minutes after that. Five past seven at the latest."

"You actually left the church, or you came here to your office?"

"I went home."

"Do you know who telephoned about hearing a scream?" Kelso asked. It irritated him that the dispatcher, someone recently hired, had failed to obtain the caller's name and address.

"As a matter of fact, I do. Just a little before nine-thirty one of the ladies in the choir telephoned me to say she'd heard a terrible scream. It was Mrs. Hutchinson, and she was pretty upset." Father Ullman smiled. "Mrs. Hutchinson's an older lady, somewhere in her late sixties, and in my opinion she's prone to imagining things, so frankly at the time I didn't think too much about it. Well, you can imagine how I felt this morning when I saw the news about the hand." He paused to sip loudly from his mug.

"What exactly did this Mrs. Hutchinson say, Father?"

Kelso had gotten out a notebook and pen and was jotting down some notes. He always suspected everyone, even priests, though from a gut-reaction point of view he'd mostly written the priest off. He wrote: *Mrs. Hutchinson—imagines things—called re scream.*

"Well, she said she and another lady, Mrs. Kramer, were in the parking lot, just getting into their car, when they heard a scream from down in the woods. Mrs. Hutchinson was certain it must've come from Mary's grave—Uh, you gentlemen know about that, I suppose? Yes. Well, it came from the grave, she said, because Mrs. Kramer heard it also and they both agreed on the direction." The priest hesitated and looked slightly embarrassed. "She said it was Mary's ghost screaming, and wanted to know if she should pray."

"Mary's ghost," Kelso murmured, and entered it in his notebook.

"I'm not criticizing her," Ullman said. "But it does strike me as a little ironic. I mean, here we are in the middle of an existence that's problematic at best, and Mrs. Hutchinson wants to know if she should pray for a ghost. I told her as kindly as I could that in my opinion she should pray for an end to nuclear proliferation, a cure for psychosis, victims of AIDS, the blacks in South Africa, the poor, the sick—" He shrugged. "But that if she wanted to add a couple of prayers for Mary's ghost, it was all right with me."

"Father," Smith said, "did Mrs. Hutchinson tell you anything else besides about the scream? Did she see anything or anybody unusual?"

"I'm sorry I can't be more help. She heard a scream." Ullman shrugged again and puffed at his pipe, which continued to exude thick clouds of smoke. The light from a lamp glinted from the surface of his bald head. His eyes were bright with intelligence.

"How many screams?" Kelso asked. "One, or more than one?"

"I believe she said two."

"Have you talked to anybody else who heard the screams?"

"No, I haven't. As a matter of fact, when I saw the news about the hand I got pretty upset. I came straight here to my office, and the only one I've seen or talked to this morning is Rosemary.''

"What about that grave?" Smith asked. "Is somebody actually buried there?"

"The grave." Ullman sipped, eyeing Smith as if deciding on an answer, something Kelso would have regarded with suspicion in another man. "The grave's been a local legend in this area for a long time, but I never go down there myself. I don't know why. Maybe it's like I was saying before, that to me the living are more cause for my concern than the dead. I've heard all the usual stories, as I'm sure you gentlemen have. Strange blue lights, something about cigarettes and pearls, various tales. I don't know. As for a body, there's no way I could either confirm or deny that something is buried there.''

One of the priest's long fingers began tapping on the rim of his coffee mug, another possible indication of nerves, sometimes an indication of guilt. The priest's dark brown eyes met Kelso's briefly, held them, the finger stopped tapping, everything was frozen in time. Then the priest looked at Smith and the spell was broken.

"Father," Smith said, "does your church have an official position on the issue of ghosts?"

Kelso suppressed a smile, but Father Ullman nodded and replied seriously, "Well, I suppose you're referring to the Episcopal church, which is in fact the American version of the Anglican church. An official position on ghosts? Spirits of the departed, you mean? Life after death?"

Smith nodded but said nothing.

"Obviously, a fundamental of any Christian faith is the so-called life everlasting. The soul, if you will. If you're asking me if I believe the spirit of a girl named Mary Carter for some reason frequents that grave down there and makes herself visible occasionally, well, as a rational man I'd have to say it's probably rumor and myth and the power of suggestion. But as a priest I'd have to remind myself that the disciples saw Christ after the crucifixion.''
A very faint smile played at the corners of the priest's lips and he stuck his pipe in his mouth, almost as if to stop the smile. Around the pipe stem he said, "If a Christian

man came to me today and swore he'd seen the spirit of Mary down there, I wouldn't be able to call him a liar.''

A slight chill crept up Kelso's spine to his neck and spread quickly up the sides of his face to his scalp. He shifted his position in the armchair and downed the rest of his coffee, then replaced the cup on its saucer with a loud clink.

''Is it possible for us to talk to Mrs. Hutchinson?'' he asked, relieved to hear his voice coming out low and steady but embarrassed at having to cover up his anxiety with a stupid question. Of course it was possible. He was a police detective, he didn't need the priest's permission. It had been the first thing to pop into his head. He frowned.

''Surely,'' Father Ullman replied, setting down his pipe in an ashtray and pulling open a drawer of his desk. He took out a small address book and flipped it open. 'Here, I'll give you her number and address, and Mrs. Kramer's also.'' He scribbled on a notepad, tore off the sheet, and handed it across to Kelso. ''Here you are. Mrs. Hutchinson's a widow. I'm sure you can catch her at home during the day. Mrs. Kramer works some mornings, I think. I'm not sure where.''

''Okay.'' Kelso took the paper, folded it, stuck it into his pocket, and stood up. ''Thanks for your time, Father Ullman.''

''Not at all. I'm sorry I couldn't be of any more help. By the way—it wasn't mentioned on the morning news— was a body ever found?''

''Not yet.'' Smith replied, also standing up.

They all looked glum for a moment; then Ullman stood and led them out through the hall and into the hushed sanctuary again. He turned and shook hands.

''Well,'' he said in a low voice, ''good-bye, gentlemen. I hope this thing gets cleared up soon. I'll say a few prayers for you and the victim and especially for the poor soul who did it.''

Smith said nothing. Kelso said, ''Thank you,'' then added, ''By the way, can you tell me Rosemary's last name and her address?''

''McAllister is her last name,'' the priest said. A strange

look covered his long face, guarded, a little worried. "She lives around on Wilhelm Drive, about the fourth or fifth house. I don't know the address without looking it up. But I don't think she'll be of much help to you."

"Just for our notes," Kelso said, putting away his notebook and pen. "Thanks again."

"Not at all." Father Ullman seemed about to say something else, then his lips pressed together and he turned and hurried down the aisle. He disappeared through the small door and it closed firmly. The light coming in through the stained-glass windows seemed faded.

Kelso followed Smith out of the church through the heavy oak doors. It was still raining outside, in a cold steady drizzle. Cursing himself for not bringing a hat and umbrella, he ran for the LTD in the parking lot. In it, he slammed the door, sneezed, and reached for a Kleenex. Smith climbed in and cranked the engine.

"What do you think, Kelso?" Smith turned the car and they headed out of the lot onto Amsterdam Avenue.

"I don't know. There's something strange about the priest. I can't put my finger on it."

"You think he's lying about something?"

"Maybe. I'm not sure. But I do know one thing."

"What's that?"

"Rosemary's the girl I saw down at the grave, the one who smiled at me just before I got whacked over the head."

"You're kidding."

"Yes, I'm kidding. I always kid and make stuff up when I'm investigating a maiming and possible homicide."

"I was only asking."

"Well, I'm not kidding."

They drove in silence then, the rain slanting into the windshield, the wipers clicking back and forth, everything as gray and bleak as one of Kelso's nightmares.

Chapter Six

Two Witnesses

Mrs. Dorothy Hutchinson lived at 521 Mapletree Crescent, a small older neighborhood north of the business district, with narrow streets, two-story frame houses, and huge ancient trees. The streets ran up and down hills; nothing was level. As the morning progressed the sun stayed hidden behind thick somber clouds and rain fell unceasingly, so that the pavement was black and shiny. Between masses of sopping leaves the gutters ran with water.

Smith parked the LTD in front of the house and he and Kelso, under an umbrella, trudged up to the front porch. A few minutes after they pressed the bell button the door opened inward on a safety chain and a thin pale-faced woman in her sixties peered out with wide gray eyes. Her nose was short and very thin, there were thick bags under her eyes, her cheeks sagged inward. She wore heavy black eyeliner, too much rouge on her gaunt cheeks, and she'd dyed her hair jet black as if to emphasize what was left of it.

"Good morning, ma'am," Kelso said politely, seeking to disarm her; she was looking at them as if they'd come to carry her off. He produced his police I.D. "I'm Sergeant Kelso and this is Detective Smith."

"Oh yes?" Her voice was slightly quavery but loud enough.

"Yes, ma'am. We'd like to ask you a few questions about what you heard last night."

"At the church," Smith said. "Father Ullman sent us."

"Oh, he did?"

"Well, he didn't exactly send us." Kelso glanced at Smith. "We just spoke to him, and he told us that you and a Mrs. Kramer heard screams and telephoned the police last night."

The woman's face registered sudden comprehension. She raised her black eyebrows, as artificial-looking as her hair, and said, "Oh, the *screams*. You've come about the *screams.*" She closed the door. There was the sound of the chain being unhooked, then the door opened wide and she stepped back to let them in. Tall, Kelso observed, almost his own height of just under five ten, and frail, in a long purplish dress of some silken material which hung robelike down to her brown leather slippers. There was the sudden heavy odor of cheap perfume as they stepped into the house.

"I wondered if anyone would come about that," she said, and led them through a dim hallway and into a living room crowded to overflowing with furniture, tables, lamps, paintings from a discount store, thin curtains, snapshots, scatter rugs, books, newspapers, magazines, TV set, ashtrays full of cigarette butts. On one armchair a gray tabby slept soundly.

"I *collect* things, you see, all kinds of things." The woman lifted a pile of magazines from the sofa and deposited them on the floor. "Here, sit on the couch. I won't apologise about the mess. Like to read, but I'm always behind. Living alone is a bother, I've got to have my reading, don't you know? Would either of you like some tea? I can boil the water."

"No thanks," Kelso said, sitting next to Smith on the sofa. "We'd just like to ask you a few questions, if it's all right." He was trying to form an impression of her. Was she reliable, for example? Was she a good observer? She would tell them a story and Kelso would have to decide whether or not to believe it, or how much of it to believe. Sometimes he met a witness who had a mind like a newspaper reporter—the facts came out all hard and thoughtful, instantly and obviously correct. Other witnesses told the wrong story over and over again, an endlessly repeating lie. Most had bits and pieces of the truth mixed in with belief, opinion, mistake, and rumor. Mrs. Hutchinson looked like the usual. Bits and pieces of the truth.

"I don't know much," she said, picking up a burning cigarette from an ashtray and puffing at it hurriedly, "but I'll try." She coughed smoke. "What would you like to know?"

"What time did you leave the church last night?" Smith asked.

"It was right at nine." She nodded. "Yes, it was nine, because I looked at my watch on the way out to see if Mr. Wiggins—that's the choir director—had kept us over again, but he hadn't *this* time. Sometimes he keeps us till nearly nine-thirty, and it gets you home so *late*, don't you know? But it was nine—"

"Excuse me," Kelso put in, "but when you left the church, when did you actually hear the scream? Were you inside your car?"

"Well, no, we weren't in the car yet. Helen and I, that's my friend Helen Kramer, we got to the car and I had just put out my hand to open the door when the scream came. It was *chilling*, I tell you. I said a little prayer right then and there, thinking that something terrible was happening." She paused to glance back and forth at the detectives, then raised her overly black eyebrows and continued. "Well, Helen got into the car at once, but I opened my door and then I think I stood there for a minute, you know, maybe several seconds, just listening. Because by then I wasn't so sure what I'd heard. So then the scream came again, and that's when I got into my car and locked my door and told Helen we had to go and call the police because either Mary was screaming down there or else somebody was being *murdered.*"

"Mary," Smith said, a skeptical glower on his pale features.

"Mary's ghost," Mrs. Hutchinson said, as if that settled it.

"So you heard two screams." Kelso was noting it down.

"Yes, that's right. Two screams."

"And by then it was a minute or so after nine?" He didn't know why he cared. There was something about

Mrs. Hutchinson he disliked. It had nothing to do with the clutter or the cheap paintings hanging from the wall or the terrible reek of perfume; it was something in her attitude, her demeanor, a kind of subtle presumptuousness, as if she were talking down to them. She seemed too sure of herself. He could swear she was making an effort to sound slightly British, and she'd offered them tea. He didn't like her. But apparently she'd heard a couple of screams, so he would have to listen.

"My car doesn't have a clock," she said. "I mean, it *does*, but it hasn't worked in months and I just haven't gotten around to having it fixed. They want so much to fix anything these days. But I should calculate it was, yes, two minutes after nine when we drove out of the church lot."

"So you didn't call the police right away?"

"Not right away, no. I mean, neither of us was going to get out of the car in that parking lot and go back to the church, with somebody screaming and the only light burned out. I drove toward my home, and I was thinking that if somebody was getting murdered down there the police would want to know as soon as possible, so we stopped at a drugstore and I telephoned from a booth inside."

"What time?" Smith asked.

"It was a quarter past," she replied, "because I looked at my watch again just before I dialed the number, to see how long it had been since I'd heard those screams. I remember thinking, nine-fifteen now, screams at nine— fifteen minutes. And then I thought, somebody could be murdered *several* times in fifteen minutes. But I called anyway."

"We're glad you did," Kelso told her. The perfume hung in the room like a cloud, as if someone had recently fumigated. Perhaps someone had. It must have been eighty degrees in there, and no ventilation. The scent had permeated every piece of furniture, the carpets, the curtains, the wallpaper. When he shifted his weight on the sofa he could smell it wafting up from the upholstery. He disliked her, but her words had the ring of absolute truth. It irritated him all the more. "Did you see or hear anything else in the parking lot, Mrs. Hutchinson? Anything suspicious? Anybody you didn't know, for example, or maybe a car you didn't recognize?"

"Let me think." Mrs. Hutchinson narrowed her darkly lined eyes. She stabbed out her cigarette and pulled another from a pack next to the ashtray, lit it with a Zippo, and puffed hard. Kelso noted that she was smoking Parliament Lights and he could just make out the rectangular box with the warning: SURGEON GENERAL'S WARNING: Smoking by Pregnant Women May Result in Fetal Injury, Premature Birth, and Low Birth Weight. He supposed that Mrs. Hutchinson no longer was worried about that aspect of her health.

Finally she replied, "No, I honestly can't recall anything like *that*. Nothing unusual. It was so dark, don't you know, and after hearing those screams all I wanted was to get away from there. Helen and I were about the first ones out from choir, and you see other cars but you don't think about them. You know, if you see a strange one you know it belongs to one of those teenagers who're always playing down at the grave. Honestly, it's disgraceful, if you ask me, and I've spoken about it to Father Ullman, but he says it's off the church *property* and kids will be kids."

There was a silence. Then Smith stood up and said, "We've got to go, Mrs. Hutchinson." He brought out a card and handed it to her. "Would you call this number if you think of anything else?"

"Oh yes, you can be sure I will." She peered closely at it. "Although I'm fairly certain I won't think of anything. But I *will* call if I do. Are you sure you wouldn't like tea?"

"No, thanks," Kelso said quickly, standing up. "We really have to go. But thanks for your help."

"You're very welcome." Mrs. Hutchinson got up and walked them to the front door, opened it, and smiled. "I'm sorry I couldn't help you more. One's not prepared for something like this, so when it happens, you don't always know what to *do*, don't you know?"

"We know," Kelso told her, moving out onto the porch.

The fresh cold air was like food to a starving man; he took in large gulps of it.

"By the way," Smith said, "I don't suppose you've ever been down to Mary's grave, have you?"

"You couldn't *pay* me to go down there," she said. "For one thing, I'd be afraid of being attacked by one of those boys who go there just to find *women*. For another, I'm a Christian, and Father Ullman will vouch for me on that, but I believe in Satan as much as I believe in our Lord, and I can tell you that things go on down at Mary's grave that smack of the devil himself. Why tempt fate, is how I look at it."

"You think there's a ghost down there?" Smith asked blandly.

"*Something's* down there. Call it a ghost or a spirit or a manifestation of evil, I'm leaving it *alone*, that's all I'm saying." Mrs. Hutchinson seemed to be getting upset.

"Well, thank you," Kelso said. "Sorry to have bothered you."

"Good-bye." She watched them wide-eyed.

"Come on, Smith."

They hurried back through the rain to the LTD. As Smith started it up and pulled away from the curb, Kelso saw the woman close her front door. He caught another whiff of her perfume and scowled; probably it had gotten into his corduroys and now he'd smell it the rest of the day.

"Strange old lady," Smith said. "Reminds me of an aunt I had."

"What'd you do, disown her?"

"She died.'

"Oh."

"Anyway, she dressed like that, long silk things, wore her slippers all day in the house, had her living room all piled up with junk just like this one."

"I didn't like her a bit," Kelso said morosely. "She got on my nerves. There was something fake about her. But she must've been telling the truth about the screams."

"I guess. Well, what now? On to Helen Kramer's place?"

"Might as well. This is getting us nowhere, but I suppose it's got to be done. They heard two screams and drove to a phone booth. So what?" He sighed and stared out at the drab streets through running rivulets of water. "I just hope Mrs. Kramer doesn't use that much perfume."

Smith lit a cigarette from the dash lighter and lowered his window a couple of inches. "This is the work of a cop," he said. "I always wanted to be Dick Tracy when I grew up. Somehow, I don't feel like Dick Tracy." He glanced sideways. "Have you got a dream, Kelso?"

"Sure. I want to get out of the police department."

"Be serious."

"I am serious. I've been taking night classes at the university, in psychology. I'm getting out, eventually, and into something where I can help people. Nothing we do helps anybody."

"Bullshit, Kelso. You're addicted to police work. I know you."

"Maybe." Kelso had his notebook out. "Turn here. She lives around the corner on Mulberry. Look out for that dog."

"I see the dog. I can drive, after all."

"Just pointing it out to you, in case."

A large brown and white hound loped across the street in front of them, on its way somewhere, shining wet. On Mulberry they parked on a steep uphill slant and walked in the rain, sharing the umbrella, up a cracked uneven cement walk to a wide porch, Smith holding the umbrella on account of his height. At the door Kelso knocked loudly and after a time it was opened by a slender middle-aged woman with short blond hair and intense blue-gray eyes. The line of her jaw was smooth and it was obvious that at one time she'd been extremely attractive; now, at the age of forty or so, she still wasn't bad. She was wearing a brown sweater, tan wool slacks, and slippers, and her figure was still good. She spoke in a rather low quiet voice. "Yes?"

"Mrs. Kramer?"

"Yes?"

"Sergeant Kelso, ma'am." He brought out the leather folder. "This is Detective Smith."

"Is it about the scream?"

"Yes, ma'am."

"I can't tell you very much, but you can come in if you want to."

"Thank you." Kelso went in, with Smith behind him. They entered directly into a small neat living room—the opposite of Mrs. Hutchinson's—uncluttered, as if she'd been expecting company. Kelso caught the smell of lemon-scented dust remover and relaxed. Mrs. Kramer was looking at him with a little smile, and he thought she looked tired. Under her eyes were hints of shadows. Her house was spotless; he could tell that every day she went through a fixed routine of dusting, cleaning, moping, straightening, like an obsessive person compelled to wash her hands again and again. In one corner a TV was on with the sound just audible. On the screen a nurse was peering into the eyes of a man in a white medical coat. Without asking them to sit, Mrs. Kramer turned and folded her arms across her breasts.

"What can I tell you?" she asked.

"We understand you went to choir practice last night," Kelso said, feeling almost guilty about interrupting the quiet rigidity of her life with something as messy as a crime. "And afterward you left with your friend, Mrs. Hutchinson."

"Yes?"

"Well, when you got outside to her car, did you hear a scream?"

"Oh, that." Mrs. Kramer blinked once. "Yes, there was a scream. I assumed it was . . ." She paused, not wanting to say. But it was the police, she could tell them. She decided. "I assumed it was some girl down at the grave, with her boyfriend."

"Somebody being molested?" Smith was smiling slightly; he'd gotten the point.

"Yes."

"How many screams did you hear, Mrs. Kramer?" Kelso asked.

"I believe there were two."

"Did you see anything suspicious in the parking lot? Anyone you didn't know, or a car you didn't recognize?"

"I'm sorry," she said suddenly, "would you like to sit down?"

"No, thanks." Kelso shook his head. "We won't be long." He felt vaguely attracted to her, not only physically but also on some other level, and then with a shock he realized what it was. He could very easily imagine that this lady was a middle-aged Susan Overstreet, this was how she'd look in another fifteen years or so. Suddenly Mrs. Kramer wasn't so attractive after all; he noticed wrinkles at the corners of her eyes and at the sides of her mouth, her upper arms were a little flabby, the slacks doubtless hid some veins that were beginning to show. Mrs. Kelso, he thought, and shuddered.

"As a matter of fact," she said, "there was a car. A red sports car of some kind, but I didn't pay much attention to it. High school kids go down there a lot, I just assumed it was one of theirs. It seemed to fit in with the screaming."

"Red sports car," Kelso said, writing it down. "Convertible?"

"No." She was nervous, ill at ease. Kelso considered the possibilities that she was hiding something. Perhaps her teenaged daughter had been down there and had screamed. In polite society it was an embarrassment if your daughter got into sexual trouble. She wouldn't want to admit it. Or maybe it had been her son, trying to have his way with a cheerleader, and again Mrs. Kramer wouldn't want to admit it. Or maybe she was just a tense nervous housewife.

"Hardtop," Kelso said. He looked at her. "Are you married, Mrs. Kramer?"

"Divorced."

"Children?"

"I don't see what this has . . . well, I have a son, Phillip. He goes to Ohio State." Her blue-gray eyes seemed to flicker and she added, hastily, "That's where he is, now."

"Ohio State," Smith said. "That's in Columbus, right?"

"Yes."

"Has he been home recently?" Kelso asked. He felt like an inquisitor, or one of those witch-hunt judges; he didn't really believe her son was involved, but he wanted to poke a little and see if he could find a sensitive spot.

"Not since two weekends ago. But sometimes he . . ."

"He what?" Smith asked. He sounded irritated.

"Sometimes he comes to town without telling me and stays with friends." She said it very quietly. "I have no way of knowing if he was here last night, if that's what you're thinking."

"We aren't thinking anything," Kelso said. He felt sorry for her in a way. She was like so many mothers—she'd brought up this thing called her son without really thinking much about it one way or the other until it was too late; she'd fed him the right food and bought him clothes and sent him to school; and now he was a stranger, more or less, going and coming without telling her, and she was faced with the possibility that he'd cut off a girl's hand. He had the impression of a dark well, and was reluctant to shine his light down into it unless it became absolutely necessary.

"I have to ask you something, Sergeant," she said. "Can you tell me what happened down there last night? Was somebody raped? Or murdered?"

"We found a hand," he replied. "That's all, ma'am. Just a hand. We don't have any evidence of anything else yet." He put away his notebook. "We'll be going now. Thanks for your time, Mrs. Kramer."

"You're welcome. I'm sorry I can't tell you anything more." She went with them to the door and opened it as he handed her one of their cards.

"Would you give us a call if you happen to remember anything else?"

"Of course."

"You don't know anybody who owns a car like that, do you?" Smith asked.

"No. I've been in the choir for years. I know what the

others drive and what the priest drives. It must have been one of the high school kids.''

"Okay," Smith said, too lightly, and a sharp look passed between them. Mrs. Kramer's eyes were like flint, and suddenly Kelso thought she'd been playing with him, manipulating him, letting him feel sympathy for her. Probably she'd used her husband that way and he'd left her. She'd used her son, too, and it made it harder for her, knowing he was out there somewhere beyond her grasp, beyond her pouts and sighs, not feeling guilty.

When the door closed he said, "We'd better have her son checked out."

"It's a dead end," Smith said, putting up the umbrella. They walked toward the car.

"Maybe. But she was putting on some sort of act."

"Nah. It's the motherhood syndrome, haven't you seen it before? Her kid is the most important thing in the world to her, so whatever happens it has to be him. A scholarship, an award, or making a girl scream."

"We should check out the red sports car. Check the other choir members and the surrounding neighborhood."

"You want to start now?"

"No. My feet are wet and I'm hungry."

"It's only eleven," Smith said, unlocking the LTD's doors.

"I don't care. I want something to eat."

"Okay." They got in and Smith started the car. "If it was up to me," he said, "I'd arrest her and take her downtown and question her in one of those little rooms. You think she's really covering up for her kid?"

"Not really," Kelso replied, trying to light his pipe. "I just think she's a neurotic divorced mother. Remind me never to get married, okay?"

"Sure."

They drove back to town and Kelso gazed out at the rain, watching leaves clog the storm sewers and thinking about a maniac with a meat cleaver hiding in the woods behind Mary's grave until the church choir was letting out, then committing an unspeakable act. Until now he hadn't thought of the criminal as having a mother. He tried to see the maniac as the son of Helen Kramer, but it seemed all wrong. He didn't think it had been Mrs. Kramer's son who had lurked around in the dark wet woods, then gone sneaking back up to the parking lot to speed away in a fast red car, leaving behind a hand for the police to find.

Chapter Seven

The Hand

They lunched at a downtown restaurant specializing in home-cooked food. Smith ate broccoli with mustard sauce, boiled potatoes, and carrot cake; Kelso had two pieces of fried chicken—extra crisp—with mashed potatoes and gravy, lima beans, buttered rolls, a huge slice of coconut-cream pie, and several cups of coffee.

"You're going to kill yourself eating like that," Kelso said.

"What?"

"All those vegetables. They're bad for you."

"Huh."

Back at headquarters Kelso found a note on his desk. SEE LEILL. He crossed the room, knocked at the door, heard the irritable-sounding "Come in," and entered.

Lieutenant Leill sat behind his desk, leaning back in his swivel chair, one large hand resting at the edge of his green desk blotter, the other holding a cigarette. His hard gray eyes observed Kelso without blinking.

"You wanted to see me, sir?"

"I wanted to see you." Leill leaned forward. "Tell me what happened last night, Kelso."

"I wrote a report—"

"Stop." He held up one big palm like a traffic cop in an intersection. "No. Not written reports. I'd like to hear this verbally, Kelso. Straight from your lips to my ears. Something about ghosts, is that it? Something about graves? Someone hitting you over the head while you were on duty?"

"Yes, sir." Kelso hadn't been asked to sit, so he stood

with his hands clasped loosely at his back, as if he were back in the Army. He had never had a good relationship with his boss. He told him about the night before in a straightforward manner, professionally, with no personal details. When he finished the lieutenant leaned back and regarded him speculatively.

"There was no light in the parking lot, Kelso?"

"A lady from the church choir says it's been out for a while."

"So it was too dark for you to see much."

"Well, Smith had flashlights in his car."

"And down at the clearing you found this hand, just lying there in the open on a rock?"

"I believe the rock is part of the original gravestone, sir."

"How did you decide to stay there and send Smith for the backup?"

"We, uh, flipped for it."

"Flipped for it. I see." Leill smiled sarcastically. "I get a picture of two courageous detectives. So then a girl came into the clearing and you tried to arrest her?"

"I was afraid she would try to pick up the hand." He paused, feeling suddenly irritated. "This was the scene of a crime, sir. The only reason that girl got as close as she did is because our backup hadn't gotten there yet, otherwise she'd have been stopped at the edge of the clearing and questioned."

"Yes, Kelso, I realize that." Leill nodded thoughtfully, no longer smiling. "It seems to me that the investigation isn't proceeding very well. I've talked to Meyer, and I'm going to talk to Broom and Smith. We have what could be a very sensitive event here, depending on whose hand this turns out to be. Do you understand what I'm getting at, Kelso?"

"No, sir."

"Look." Leill sighed heavily. "That's a rich area of town. Some very influential people live in that area. Jerry Ullman, the priest, eats lunch with some of the people on the city council. A close personal friend of the mayor's lives only a few houses away. We have to proceed carefully, but quickly. I've gotten telephone calls this morning from people who can say a word or two and cost me my job. They want to know why a severed hand has been found over there and what we're doing about it and when we're going to arrest a suspect." Leill stabbed out his cigarette and shrugged. "I've got to press on this, Kelso. I want you to work very hard, you and Smith and the others, and get me a suspect. Do you understand?"

"Yes, sir. We'll work as hard as we can."

"Good." Leill neither looked nor sounded as if he believed it. "Okay, that's all. Go on out there, Kelso, and bring somebody in. Before another hand turns up somewhere."

"Yes, sir."

Kelso left the office. Another hand, he thought. Until now, that hadn't entered his mind. Another hand. He'd been considering the event as isolated, not something that would reoccur. Then people were in danger. He went into the duty room and found that he was alone. Rain streamed down the windows. Sitting down and getting out his pipe, he thought about what Leill had told him. The man was nuts. All he thought about was protecting his job. You couldn't hurry an investigation of this sort. You couldn't create a suspect to please the mayor and his friends.

His phone rang and he answered it with uncharacteristic force. "Hello!"

"Sergeant Kelso?"

"Oh. Hello, Dr. Paul." It was one of the pathologists from the coroner's office, a young competent doctor whom Kelso respected.

"You all right?" asked Dr. Paul.

"Just a little headache." He made himself sound more pleasant. "Is it about the hand?"

"Yes, it is. I'll be sending you a report, but I thought I'd give you some highlights on the phone. Would you like to hear them?"

"Go ahead." Kelso was bolt upright in his chair.

"Here's what we think so far. It's a right hand. The person is young and female, probably around twenty or so. It hasn't done heavy or rough work, but there's a slight flattening of the fingertips that may have come from light typing.''

An image of Rosemary flashed through Kelso's mind: he saw her in an office at the church, seated over a typewriter, smiling faintly as she struck the keys with soft slender fingers. Curious, how the images of Rosemary and the victim had blurred together for a moment. Of course, Rosemary still had both hands.

"Go on, Doctor," he said.

"Her nails are slightly bitten. Sometimes that's an indication of nervousness. Let's see. No particular marks. We're estimating, from the putrefaction and other signs, that the hand had been separated for up to six or seven days, depending on how it had been kept before its discovery, the temperature and humidity, things we don't really know. As for the amputation itself, it wasn't surgically perfect, but it wasn't a butcher job, either. Nobody hacked it off with a dull knife or chopped it off with an ax. In my opinion, it was done with a scalpel by someone who took some pains to make it a relatively neat job, but who was not a skilled surgeon. Had good equipment, though. The bone was apparently done with a modified cast cutter, which is the normal thing to use on bones.''

"Are you saying this was a professional job?"

"That's the curious part, Kelso. It wasn't professional in the usual sense, but it wasn't amateur, either. A medical student comes to mind.''

Kelso made a mental note to find out whether Helen Kramer's son was in medical school.

"What about the state of the victim when it was done?"

"Living or dead?" Dr. Paul's tone was detached. "Clotting and cell trauma are consistent with the victim's being alive at the time of the amputation.''

"Jesus Christ," Kelso muttered. "Okay, let me ask this. If the victim had been given any kind of drug before it happened, would you have found traces of it in the hand?''

"That's difficult to say. Some drugs metabolize more quickly than others. We haven't found anything yet, but the serologists and toxicologists are still doing tests. You have to remember that a negative finding isn't conclusive.

If we don't find any drug, it doesn't prove there wasn't one.''

"I see."

"Well, you'll be getting a full report, and I'll give you a call if we come up with anything else. How's Susan, by the way?"

"She's fine."

"Well, see you later. Have a nice day."

"You too."

They hung up. For a time Kelso sat at his desk and stared at his notepad, not really seeing it, wondering just exactly what it was he was up against. It had been easy to view the hand as abstract before, something rather weird and grotesque but impersonal, almost inhuman. Now it was personal, it had taken on the identity of a young girl with soft hands, a girl who possibly had been alive when someone had rather carefully cut off her right hand. Now it was the event itself that had become inhuman.

He shook himself, lit his pipe, and got up. He walked out to the water fountain in the hall and drank deeply, wondering where the girl was now. He bit down hard on the stem of his pipe and went back inside the duty room. It was ten minutes past twelve on the afternoon of October 29, and outside the windows it was continuing to rain.

Chapter Eight

Strategy Session

With the four of them seated around the table in Conference Room 06-D, Kelso felt much more calm. He felt sane and stable and competent—like a detective again. Strange, he thought, the way he'd let it get to him for a few minutes or so. After all, during his ten years as a cop he'd seen some pretty unsavory sights, experienced some pretty gut-wrenching incidents, all while managing to keep cool; there was no reason why this should be any different. He glanced at his watch. It was 1 P.M.

He used a pipe tool to clean the bowl of his briar. On the opposite side of the table, Meyer smoked a cigarette and sipped coffee from a Styrofoam cup, scowling. On Meyer's left sat Broom—the plump detective who normally was in the men's room—his youthful face bland, one chubby-fingered hand playing with a new pencil. To Kelso's right sat Smith, his ice-cold irises under his eyelids forming little blue half-moons beneath which the whites were visible, giving him a slightly demented look. Smith had brought a large Sprite in with him and every now and then sipped from it with a loud slurping noise.

"The situation so far is this," Meyer said somewhat sullenly. "Two women heard screams when they left choir practice last night at around nine, going to their car in the parking lot of St. Luke's Episcopal Church. One of them thinks she might've noticed a red sports car that didn't belong to anyone she knew. They called the police at nine-twenty. Smith and Kelso got there about nine forty-five and found a clearing in some woods next to the parking lot. In the clearing were chunks of something like a tombstone. Birth and death dates of some broad named Mary Carter are inscribed on one piece. On another stone they spotted a human hand, cut off at the wrist. Smith went to call for a backup. While he was gone, Kelso saw a girl enter the clearing and walk toward the stone with the hand on it, and when he ordered her to turn around she smiled at him and somebody hit him over the head. He was knocked out. When he came to, the girl had gone.''

He paused to crush out his cigarette, scowling as if bored. Broom watched attentively, playing with his pencil by bouncing it on its eraser. Smith sipped Sprite. Kelso cleaned his pipe.

"Kelso talked to Dr. Paul at the lab," Meyer continued. "Paul thinks the hand's from some broad about twenty, and it was cut off of her maybe while she was still alive by somebody who wasn't a surgeon but wasn't a butcher." Meyer held his lighter to another cigarette and glanced at Kelso. "Anything to add?"

After a moment Kelso said, "The girl I saw at the grave looks a lot like Rosemary McAllister, the mentally retarded girl who works at the church."

"McAllister?" Meyer asked. "Barbara McAllister's kid?"

They all looked at him.

"I've heard of her," Smith said. "She's fairly well off, isn't she?"

"That's an understatement." Meyer glared. "She's one of the movers and shakers in this town. Hell, the mayor calls her up to see what color shorts to wear to work. If this case involves her . . ."

Smith said very softly, "If it involves her, then what?"

"If it does," Meyer replied, "then we're in for a hell of a time, that's all."

"Are you saying," Broom asked, trying to balance his pencil on its point, "that she has some kind of influence? That she could affect our investigation?"

"She could probably *cancel* our investigation," Meyer said.

"I find that difficult to believe." Broom began tapping the pencil against the conference table. "I'd like to see her try to influence an investigation of mine. What's she going to do? Call up the mayor and tell him there's a crime she doesn't wish solved, a criminal she'd prefer not to have apprehended?''

"Forget this broad," Smith said. "Let's concentrate on the case. What's the first move, Meyer, since you're in charge?''

"I thought I'd see if you had any suggestions.''

"I have one," Broom said. "I suggest we go back to the crime scene, this so-called Mary's grave, and examine it in full daylight. Even with electric lights nothing looks the same at night. We might discover something important.''

"Somebody ought to talk to that retarded girl," Smith said. "If she's really the one Kelso saw last night, then in my opinion she's got some explaining to do. Like why she was down there in the dark by herself, why she was so interested in that hand, what she knows about it, and who hit Kelso over the head.''

"How the hell are you going to question a mental case?'' Meyer asked.

"She's not a mental case," Kelso said. "She's mildly retarded.''

"If it was up to me," said Smith, "I'd arrest her and interrogate her in one of those little rooms till she confessed.''

"What if she was innocent?''

"They never are.''

Meyer scowled. "It's useless to talk to her.''

"It sounds to me," said Broom, "as if you're worried about her mother.''

"Ah, screw her mother. All I'm saying is, *you* talk to her. Me, I wouldn't waste my time. Besides which, I think we're on the wrong track. We should be looking for a corpse. You can't convince me that whoever did this didn't stash the body around somewhere close to the hand. It'll turn up sooner or later, and then maybe we can get someplace.''

"What if a body never turns up?'' Smith asked.

Meyer glared at him. "One will.''

"The criminal could be holding her somewhere," Broom said, tapping with his pencil again. "He could be deranged."

"I should think he'd have trouble keeping her alive," Smith replied. "Do you know what kind of shock to the body's system that would be? Having a hand chopped off like that? With the combination of shock and loss of blood, she's got to be dead."

"You're assuming one thing, Smith," Kelso said, starting to feel nervous again.

"What's that?'

"You're assuming this wasn't carefully planned by some person with motives we can't even imagine. What if he prepared for it, administered some sort of anesthetic for example, and afterward treated the wound? No one dies automatically of an amputation, not under normal circumstances."

"Normal circumstances don't include leaving the hand on a grave in the middle of the night," Smith retorted.

Meyer sighed and looked at Kelso. "Are you nuts? You think this was done in an operating room? Some refugee from a medical school grabbed this broad and decided to practice Amputation 101 on her?"

"I'm saying I don't see how we can be certain one way or the other, at this point." It seemed to Kelso that they all wanted it to be a random or spontaneous act. The idea that it could have been premeditated seemed to bother them. It bothered him, too, but he was beginning to accept it as a real possibility.

"What about the hand itself?" Broom asked.

"What about it?" Meyer asked.

"I don't really understand why the criminal, no matter what his or her motives for removing the hand in the first place, would have left it down there on that gravestone."

"Maybe the pathologist is wrong," Smith offered, "and the victim was in fact dead. Maybe the murdered chopped her up and left parts of her in various places."

"Be serious," Meyer said.

Smith shrugged and said nothing.

Meyer stood up. "I don't think we can accomplish any

more here. Okay, Broom, you go with me and we'll check out the grave again, in daylight. Kelso, you and Smith go talk to that broad at the church.''

Kelso nodded and pushed his chair back to stand up.

''I guess you realize we're merely putting off the inevitable,'' Broom said, tapping his pencil a couple of times on the table edge and then putting it down.

Meyer glared. ''What's the inevitable, Broom?''

''At some point we're going to be left with that house behind the grave. I've heard it's where her relatives live—you know, the relatives of the people who buried Mary. And I've heard they're all insane.'' He smiled slyly, as if he found some secret humor in this, then added, ''I suppose eventually we'll have to find out for ourselves, don't you think?''

''We'll get to it soon enough,'' Meyer said.

Chapter Nine

Rosemary

At two that afternoon Father Ullman let them into his office again, smiling but not quite so much as before. It was nothing Kelso could pinpoint, merely a vague impression. Maybe the priest was busier this afternoon, maybe he was upset about the hand, or maybe he'd just given comfort to a bereaved or heard a difficult confession. Did Episcopal priests hear confessions? Kelso thought they did.

He and Smith sat in armchairs facing Ullman's desk.

"Can I offer you gentlemen some coffee?" When they shook their heads, he said, "This thing with the hand is causing quite a problem with my congregation. I'm a little disappointed, to tell you the truth. I thought they were a little more level-headed than that. I've been getting phone calls from men and women I'd have sworn were intelligent, asking if I think the devil's gotten loose, if there's a demon in the woods, if it's safe to come to church." He shook his bald head and sighed. "Have you brought me any answers?"

"We don't have any answers yet," Smith said. "But you can take my word for it, it's not demons and devils. A human being did this, and we'll find him. It's just a matter of time, that's all."

"What we'd like," Kelso said, "Is to talk to Rosemary McAllister. Is she here?"

There was a long silence. Father Ullman seemed to examine a spot of dirt on one corner of his desk blotter, rubbing his thumb over it repeatedly and frowning. Finally he looked up, and there was something different in his expression. He was polite, but not especially friendly.

"She's here, but may I ask why?"

"Of course," Kelso said. "It's nothing much, really. Since she's around the church a lot, working here, we wanted to see if she'd seen or heard anything unusual recently. Especially last night." Kelso tried to keep a blank face. Probably priests were as expert as detectives at telling when someone was lying. Could he fool a priest?

Father Ullman spread his hands in a wide gesture. "I don't want to sound difficult, Sergeant, but surely you realize that Rosemary isn't normal. She has the mental capacity of a twelve-year-old, approximately. I don't understand why, out of all the possible witnesses, the entire congregation of my church, you want to question Rosemary."

Kelso looked hard at the priest without seeming to, gazing at him but keeping his eyelids slightly lowered, his expression bland, almost bemused. "It's just routine. I understand what you're saying. But in a case like this we can't afford to ignore anything. Even if Rosemary was in fact a twelve-year-old girl, if she'd been around this area a lot recently we'd still talk to her." There—surely that would satisfy him.

But the priest didn't look satisfied. If anything he frowned harder, and now there was a hard set to the muscles of his jaws, and his lips had become thin and tight. He looked like a man trying to solve a very difficult problem, or trying to figure a way out of a jam.

"Excuse me," he said, "but I don't think you gentlemen entirely understand the situation."

"Okay," Smith said. "What's the situation?"

"I'll tell you." Ullman leaned forward and lowered his voice slightly. "Last week Rosemary was followed. It happens sometimes—a certain type of man thinks a retarded woman is easier, so to speak, than another woman. According to Rosemary's mother, who spoke to me about it on the phone, a man followed her out of the church and across the parking lot last week when she was working late, doing some typing for me. We've never had that problem before, it's always been safe. I blame myself for not going out to the parking lot with her." The priest wiped at his forehead. "Apparently he didn't try to attack her, but offered her money."

"She drives?" Kelso asked.

"No. A friend had come for her. Maybe that's why it wasn't any worse than it was, the presence of the other woman."

"Who was the other woman?" Kelso asked.

"I don't know. Rosemary never said, and now she seems to have forgotten. Anyway, the incident deeply upset her. I talked to her about it for almost an hour the next day, but even now she's not completely over it."

"Does she ever go down to Mary's grave?" Smith asked.

Kelso watched the priest's eyes for some hint of a lie.

"She goes there often," he replied.

"Why would she do that?"

"Remember, she's only a little girl in some ways. Older girls are just as fascinated by it. She's curious. She's always asking me questions—Who's Mary? Why'd she die? Why's she buried down there? Why isn't she in Heaven? Why do people see her ghost? Are there other ghosts? When people die do they hang around their graves or go somewhere else? And so on."

Kelso took a deep breath and asked carefully, "Was Rosemary down there last night? Say, between eight and ten?"

"I'm not sure about that," Ullman answered, a trifle irritably, and Kelso had the impression that the priest was very sure about it. "Let me see." He looked thoughtful, then shrugged and glanced from one to the other of them, frowning. "I don't know. Are you implying that she may have some idea about what happened there last night?"

"Anything's possible," Smith said. "We're investigating a mayhem, maybe a murder. If she was down there we have to follow it up. We have to talk to her, with or without your cooperation."

There was another long silence. Kelso considered saying something to soften the effect of Smith's words, but decided against it. Let the priest know where he stood, especially since he seemed to be keeping something back.

Finally Ullman shrugged; his expression sagged, as if he'd come to a decision he didn't like but had resigned himself to it. He said, "All right. I don't suppose there's anything I can do to prevent it and I don't want to stand in the way of your investigation. But could you do me one favor?"

"What's that?" Smith asked.

"Since the incident I told you about in the parking lot, Rosemary's been very nervous around strange men. What if only one of you questions her?"

"I'll do it," Kelso said. "You and Smith can talk about Mary's ghost." He stood up.

"She's in a room across the hall," Ullman said, rising and coming around his desk. "I'll go over and introduce you."

Out in the hall a door with a frosted-glass window stood slightly ajar and Kelso heard the sound of slow deliberate typing. When Ullman knocked, the typing stopped. He followed the priest inside.

Rosemary sat at a typewriter. The room was small, with one window. There was a metal desk, typing stand, secretary's chair, and a wooden folding chair. Along one wall metal shelves contained books, paper, boxes, and a coffee maker and mugs. She was wearing a blue wool sweater, faded jeans, tennis shoes, and a thin gold bracelet on her left wrist. The sleeves of her sweater were pushed up almost to her elbows, revealing an unusual amount of dark hair on thin forearms. Kelso found himself looking to make sure her right hand was there.

"Rosemary?" Ullman said. "Have you got a minute? There's someone who'd like to talk to you."

"Okay," she said, very low, very quiet.

It occurred to Kelso that it must be difficult to relate to someone both as a grown woman and as a young girl. Suddenly he was uncertain of his ability to carry out the interview.

"This is my friend Sergeant Kelso. He's a policeman. Sergeant, this is Rosemary McAllister."

"Hello," Kelso said. "How are you?"

"Okay," she said faintly, watching him with a faint smile on her lips, the same faint smile he'd seen as she'd turned into his flashlight beam the night before. There was no longer any doubt about it. The same thick dark hair, very dark eyes, thin face; there seemed to be fear in her eyes, but maybe it was just curiosity.

"Sergeant Kelso would like to talk to you for a few minutes. I'll be across the hall in my office with someone else. Okay?"

She nodded. "Okay."

Ullman went to the door. "See you after a bit," he said, and went out, leaving the door open. He crossed the hall and Kelso heard his office door open and close.

Kelso sat down in the wooden folding chair. On the wall behind the desk hung a small cross, and next to it was a framed painting of Jesus kneeling as children and animals approached his outstretched hands. Outside the single window it was gray, and the glass panes were beaded with rain. It felt cold in the room.

He wondered if Rosemary recognized him. She was well-built; he could imagine some pervert being attracted to her. A guy shoving money at her in the parking lot; yes, that must have upset her. And then last night Kelso had aimed his flashlight and revolver at her, ordered her to turn around. Yet, he would swear she hadn't been afraid, had only observed him with ironic calmness, watching whoever had come up behind him. What had she done while he lay unconscious? Simply wandered away without a word?

He looked closely at her. It only made sense if she'd known the person behind him. Maybe his attacker had merely smiled and nodded at the girl in the darkness. Father Ullman?

"Rosemary," he said, "do you go to Mary's grave very often?"

She nodded slowly. Her expression—serious dark eyes and vaguely amused smile—didn't change. "Yes, I go there."

He caught just the trace of an impediment in her speech. Probably something had happened to her at birth. She was sitting facing him in her secretary's chair, hands clasped loosely in her lap, knees together, shoulders slightly slumped. The bulkiness of her sweater did nothing to conceal the heaviness of her bust, something that must have attracted the man who'd offered her money in the parking lot.

"Do you go there alone?"

"Sometimes."

"Were you there last night?"

She seemed to hesitate. Thinking . . . or debating whether to answer with a lie?

"I went there last night," she said, very quietly.

"After dark?"

"Yes."

"Did you have a flashlight?"

"No."

"Why not?"

A quick smile, one corner of her mouth turning up, the other not, as if she suffered one-sided paralysis, and her dark eyes flickered. She shrugged.

"Did you hear anything unusual last night, Rosemary? A shout, maybe, or a scream?" Leading the witness, he thought. But it was okay, she was a child.

"A scream." Rosemary nodded. "Yes. I heard a scream."

"Where were you when you heard the scream?"

"Where?"

"Yes. Where were you? At the grave? Up in the parking lot?"

"Going down," she told him. The smile became faint again.

"Excuse me?"

"Down the path."

"Oh, I see. You were on your way down to the grave."

"Uh huh."

"Did you keep on going then?"

She nodded.

"Did you see anybody?"

"No."

"What happened when you got to the grave?"

She blinked. Shook her head slowly.

Patiently, kindly, Kelso said, "At the grave, was any-body else there? Anybody with you?"

"No. I didn't see anybody."

"Okay. So then what did you do?"

Rosemary shrugged. "I walked in the woods."

"Do you know for how long?"

"No." Almost a whisper. It was, he thought, like talking to some incredibly shy little girl.

"Then what happened. Can you tell me?"

"I don't know. I went back to Mary's grave."

"Did you see anybody there?"

She started to reply, then hesitated. He saw the quick change of her expression, a slight frown, a narrowing of her eyes.

"I saw . . ."

"Yes? You saw?"

"You!" And she smiled abruptly with one side of her mouth. Merriment sparkled in her eyes; wide open, they were a very dark brown, big and childlike. It was as if she'd guessed the right word in a game. "I saw *you*," she said, and gave a brief shy laugh.

"Yes, that's right." Kelso smiled. "Do you remember what I was doing?"

"No." The smile receded partially. "I don't know. You had a flashlight. You told me, 'Turn around. Hands up.' Like TV."

"Like the detective shows?"

"Yes." She nodded. "Mother lets me watch sometimes. I don't know their names." She raised one hand, pointed her index finger, smiling that faintly mocking smile, and said softly, "Hands up."

"Okay," he said. "Now please think, Rosemary. This is important, okay?"

"Okay." She put her hand back in her lap.

"Did you see somebody behind me?"

"Behind you?"

"Yes. When I asked you to turn around, and you did, like on TV, did you see somebody behind me?"

She stared for a very long time, so long that he wondered if she'd lost track of the question and drifted off into some imaginary world of her own. Suddenly she looked a little anxious and said, with a slight tremor in her voice, "I saw a hand on the grave."

"Well."

"I saw a hand on the grave," she said, and got up. Her eyes were black shadows, her face was expressionless. She walked past him and into the hall. He heard a door open and close and knew that it was over. He sat there trying to cling to a shred of hope, but knew there was none.

After a moment the door opened again, footsteps crossed the hall, and Father Ullman entered the office with Smith, blond and grim, behind him.

"Sorry," Ullman said, "but Rosemary's pretty upset. I don't think you'd better talk to her any more just now."

"Yeah, you're right." Kelso got up from the folding chair. "I didn't mean to upset her. She was telling me how she went down to the grave last night, and when she remembered the hand . . ." He shrugged.

"Yes," Ullman said dryly. "I can imagine."

"Well, thanks again for your time. And for Rosemary's. Is she going to be all right?"

"She'll be okay. I'll talk to her." The priest walked them down the hall to the sanctuary, then up the aisle to the vestibule. "Did you find out anything important, Sergeant?"

The question and its tone were faintly sarcastic, implying that he should never have questioned Rosemary in the first place, that nothing important could have been gained from it. Kelso was irritated.

"Yes," he said. "I found out something very important."

With satisfaction he noticed the quick surprise on the priest's features.

"Oh, really? What was it?"

"I'd rather not say yet," Kelso told him, feeling like a heel. After all, it wasn't really the priest's fault, he'd only been trying to take care of his retarded secretary.

"Suit yourself." Ullman was now coldly polite. "Good afternoon, gentlemen. You might give me a call before you come out again, in case I'm in the middle of something."

"Good-bye," Smith said.

The priest hurried away and Kelso followed Smith outside and across to the parking lot. In the LTD, with rain misting lightly on the windows, Smith asked, "So what happened in there? What'd you find out?"

"Nothing, really. I was just giving Ullman a hard time, like he was giving me. I did find out that Rosemary's the girl I saw last night. Smith, I think she recognized whoever hit me over the head."

"No kidding. Are you sure?"

"Ninety-nine percent sure."

"But she wouldn't tell you?" Smith started the car.

"No. That's when she got scared and left the room."

"Huh. I wondered what went on. She came in looking pretty upset. Well, where to now?"

"I was just thinking. Since we're here, why not take a look at the grave?"

Smith glared. "It's raining, Kelso."

"Only a mist. And we've got umbrellas."

"It'll be wet down there."

"I want to see it in daylight," Kelso persisted.

"Broom and Meyer are supposed to do that."

"I know. But I'd like to see it for myself. Come on, it won't take long. Or you can wait here in the car."

"No way. If you get yourself bashed again, they'll only blame me." Smith sighed loudly. "Oh, what the hell, I might as well humor you. Nothing else to do." He turned off the motor again. "Tell me one thing, though. Are you actually onto something now, or just screwing around?"

"I'm curious, and I'd like to see the place."

"Just screwing around," Smith muttered, and got out of the car.

Kelso got out, too. The mist wasn't hard enough for his umbrella, so instead he gripped it in one hand like a club. They stood for a moment hunched over in their raincoats, glancing around uneasily at the empty black parking area, the looming stone church, and the surrounding black and yellow trees. Then Kelso led the way onto the sodden leaf-covered path.

They descended, pushing past glistening wet foliage and sharply stabbing limbs, twisting and turning their way down and down into the dense soaking woods to Mary's grave.

Chapter Ten

Unseen Things

The clearing looked different in daylight, even the drab anemic light filtering down from leaden clouds through the canopy of dripping tree limbs and dying leaves. It looked bigger, for one thing—a trick of the light, no doubt. Kelso stood in the middle and turned slowly to get the full effect, watching the edges where the trees grew closely together, the dirt floor strewn with dead leaves, the pieces of broken stone lying here and there. The growth was so thick that nothing could be seen through it; they might have been in the middle of an Amazon rain forest with nothing around for miles. Kelso shook off the feeling that eyes were watching him, peering from the shadows beyond the edge of the clearing, and fumbled for his pipe and tobacco.

"Mary doesn't like smokers," Smith said. "You'd better look out."

"I heard it was cigarettes she didn't like," Kelso replied rather hotly.

"Cigarettes, huh?" Smith reached inside his raincoat and got out a Kent, lit it with a match, tossed the match to the ground. "Let's see about that." He walked over to the monument base on which they'd found the hand, sat down on one edge of it, and puffed hard. "Okay, Mary," he said, exhaling smoke. "Here I am, right on top of you, and I'm smoking a cigarette. Well, Mary, what are you going to do about it?"

Kelso glared at Smith for a moment, wondering if he was serious, then shrugged and looked away. He bent over slightly and began examining the clearing floor, poking with the toes of his crepe-soled shoes at various sticks, leaves, and rocks, looking for something, anything. An object out of place, something which seemed to blend in with its surroundings but which, at second glance, didn't really belong. He found nothing. Smith chuckled, and Kelso looked at him again. The lean blond detective still sat perched on the slab of limestone that might have been part of the original monument, puffing out a cloud of blue smoke and holding his cigarette a few inches from his face, smiling wryly.

"Mary's a fake," Smith said. "A fake and a fraud."

"Having a good time?"

"Sure."

Kelso tamped tobacco into the bowl of his pipe but refrained from lighting up, content for now to carry the pipe in one hand, rubbing its smooth briar bowl with his thumb. He smelled the wet dead leaves, the soaked bark, and the rain.

"She's a fraud," Smith said. "See? I've smoked half of it already, sitting right on top of her grave, and nothing. Absolutely nothing." Smith brought the cigarette toward his lips for another drag. "See? Hey!"

Kelso stared. The cigarette left Smith's fingers and arced upward, as if knocked from his hand by an invisible force. It fell behind him. He stepped slowly to the ground—tall and thin and pale, his ice-cold eyes not smiling—and frowned. One of his shoes went out and stamped the butt into the leaves and mud. Then he looked at Kelso, the whites of his eyes showing beneath the blue half-circles of his irises.

"Son of a bitch," he said softly.

Kelso watched him, feeling weird. Things like this did not happen in real life. They happened in comic books, late-night TV shows, old movies—but not in real life. He forced himself not to shiver. "What happened?" he asked carefully.

"What *happened?*" Smith stood motionless, hands thrust into the pockets of his raincoat. "Didn't you see that? I was getting ready to take a puff, and something knocked the damned thing right out of my fingers. Didn't you *see* it?"

"Yeah." Kelso nodded. "I guess I did. I saw the cigarette leave your hand."

"I didn't drop it," Smith said testily.

"I didn't say you did."

"You saw it, didn't you? I didn't just drop it. It flew out of my fingers, Kelso. It flew right over my shoulder."

"I know."

"Man, I don't like this at all. Not at *all.*"

Kelso didn't know what to say. He stood a little forlornly and scanned the edges of the clearing. Suddenly it no longer seemed safe here, despite the daylight and the fact that both of them were armed. He tried to concentrate on the weight of the .38 in its holster at his hip, but it made him feel no better. You can't shoot what you can't see, he thought. You can't shoot a ghost. He made himself breathe deeply several times. At the sides of the clearing the thick woods seemed to press inward threateningly and the rain came a little harder, changing from a mist to a thin drizzle, wetting his hair and the shoulders of his raincoat. He opened his umbrella and heard the drops thump against it; the drops made a rustling noise as they splattered against leaves, for some reason reminding him of dripping blood. He looked at Smith.

"I don't believe in ghosts."

"Neither do I." Smith opened his umbrella. "But something hit my hand."

In front of Kelso, at about the center of the clearing, was the portion of the stone he'd examined the night before. He could read the engraved words easily now. HERE LIES MARY CARTER. Born November 1, 1897. Died July 10, 1916. An eighteen-year-old girl, almost nineteen. Was she buried here? Was there, against all logic and science and all that Kelso had grown to believe, some unnatural, preternatural *thing* here, something capable of knocking a cigarette from a living human hand? And, if so, of what else was this thing capable? Severing a hand from its arm?

No, he would refuse to believe it. It was absolutely impossible.

Smith stood solemnly, quietly, one hand holding his

umbrella at a slight angle, the other dangling loosely at his side, cold blue eyes watching. It occurred to Kelso that he and Smith now stood in almost the exact position he and the strangely smiling girl had occupied the night before, when she'd turned to look mockingly just before something or someone had struck him from behind.

Suddenly he had the chilling feeling that it was happening again, that someone was sneaking up behind him, unseen.

"Don't move," Smith said in a loud whisper.

"What?" Kelso jumped slightly, already cringing from the expected blow.

"Shut up! Listen!"

He shot a glance over his shoulder. Nothing. Looked back at Smith. The cold blue eyes were narrowed, the blond head tilted slightly. Kelso held his breath. He heard rain spattering against the nylon of his umbrella and wind rustling the leaves that still clung desperately to their black shining branches. Then he heard something else, and froze.

A heavier noise, off in the woods. The unmistakable rustle of shoes slogging through the undergrowth only a few yards off. A twig snapped like gunfire. The rustling quickened, as if the unseen intruder had panicked and begun to run.

"Somebody's spying on us," Smith muttered. "Come on, let's get the son of a bitch."

"Okay," Kelso agreed. Furling his umbrella and securing its snap, he gripped it in one hand and made his way across the clearing, into the woods. The path seemed to disappear; branches stabbed and lashed at him from every side, tripping him as he tried to move each foot.

"Over here," Smith said. "Here's the damn path again."

Kelso followed. Yes, now they had the path back. Like the one from the parking lot, it wound upward, away from the clearing, its uneven surface zigzagging this way and that. Sometimes what looked like a clump of wet leaves was a hard mound of dirt, a thick rock, or a heavy root; other times it really was a clump of leaves. Once, it was a hole. Kelso twisted his ankles, banged his shins, scratched his hands and face on things that slapped out at him before he could see and avoid them.

They seemed to be gaining slightly on the running feet just ahead, then the path made another sudden turn and they came out of the woods abruptly and stopped, breathing hard.

In front of them was a wide expansive yard, leaf-bare, the width of a football field. On the other side a stone Tudor house rose up brown and gray from the rain and grass like some ancient castle. There was no one in the yard, and the sound of hurrying footsteps had ceased.

Kelso felt silly, gripping his umbrella in one hand, his unlit pipe in the other, standing at the edge of someone's private yard with drizzle running down his forehead and slapping a tattoo on the shoulders of his raincoat.

"Where'd he go?" he asked, realizing the futility of the question even as it left his lips.

"Beats the hell out of me," Smith replied sullenly, and opened his umbrella again.

They huddled in the rain, a cold wind pressing wetness against their faces and tugging at their clothes, and gazed at the house.

Chapter Eleven

Another Girl

Everything was faded and washed out, like a French impressionist painting in one of Susan Overstreet's art books. The expansive lawn, without so much as a single tree, spread between them and the rear of the house like a barrier, its well-cut grass clashing oddly with the surrounding leaf-filled woods. Flat stone walls loomed three stories high. Rows of impassive windows stared bleakly. At the ground level was a single closed door without a porch. Trees at either side towered taller than the house, their dying leaves swirling down from their branches. The whole thing reminded Kelso of some of his dreams, from which he sometimes awoke sweating and trembling. He had the impression that unseen eyes watched from every window.

"What do you think we ought to do?" Smith asked. He sounded impatient and rather disgusted.

"I don't know." Kelso's words came out gruff. "This is getting us nowhere."

"Somebody was just ahead of us in the woods. He must have come out here."

"Maybe. But these woods are big; he might've ducked back in another direction."

"We didn't hear it, if he did."

"I know." Kelso was cold. His shoes were wet, and water had begun to seep through to his socks. "Maybe it was somebody who beat us to that door." He pointed. "We were running through unfamiliar territory. Time gets messed up under those conditions. Maybe he got out of the woods and across the yard to the door before we got here."

"That's hard to believe." Smith stuck his umbrella under one arm to light a cigarette and tossed the spent match onto the ground. Seeing Kelso's look, he glared. "The hell with 'em. Let somebody come out here and accuse me of littering, and I'll let them explain why they've been playing hide-and-seek with us."

"It didn't have to be anyone in the house," Kelso said. "Maybe it was a ghost and it simply disappeared."

Smith didn't reply, just stood scowling at the house and puffing at his cigarette, holding his umbrella over his head again because the rain once more was falling steadily. After a moment he asked, without much enthusiasm, "You want to go knock at that door?"

"Not especially." Kelso, too, raised his umbrella. "No, wait. On second thought, it'd be interesting to see if someone answered the door with wet shoes."

"Wet shoes wouldn't prove a damn thing. They might've just come in from the front."

"Still, there's nothing to lose, and I don't feel like standing here forever." Kelso started forward. "Let's try it."

They trudged across the wide empty yard, tilting their umbrellas against the slanting downpour, which seemed to intensify with each step. The yard was soaked, it was like walking through a swamp, their shoes sank ankle-deep into water and spongy mush. At the back door Kelso raised his fist and knocked.

For a while nothing happened. He shivered in a gust of cold wet wind and raised his hand to knock again. Then the door opened suddenly, quickly, moving inward about halfway, its knob held by a frowning woman in a rather formal purple dress of some silky material, high-heeled shoes, pearls at her throat and ears, black hair pulled tightly back. She was middle-aged, with very pale skin, heavy black brows, unfriendly yellow-brown eyes.

"Yes?" she asked, putting a lot of anger and impatience into the one word, as if he and Smith were waifs begging for handouts.

Kelso hadn't actually expected anyone to answer. He stared for a second, then brought out his leather police folder and let her see it. "Sergeant Kelso," he said. "This is my partner, Detective Smith."

The woman squinted at the official card and shield, then frowned harder and spoke with even more impatience. "Well? What is it you want?"

"You weren't in those woods back there just now, were you?" Smith asked, evidently unwilling to play games. His tone was very close to accusing.

The woman's eyes widened slightly, then narrowed. "In the first place, Detective, they are *my* woods, and I go in or out of them as I please. In the second place, I don't see what business it is of yours. In the third place—"

"Excuse me," Kelso said, forcing himself to sound polite, forcing his voice to come out low and calm. "Ma'am, we're investigating a crime that may have occurred down in the woods. It's just routine." He'd already noticed that the woman's shoes were dry. Of course, she might have just changed. "We'd like to ask you a few questions, if it's convenient. Or we could come back some other time. But we'll have to ask the questions sooner or later."

"Why are you here at the back?" The woman stared from Kelso to Smith and back again. "Why didn't you come to the front?"

"We were down at the grave, ma'am, and we heard somebody running. We followed and came out here, at the edge of the woods."

"Someone running? You chased someone to the house?" She seemed suddenly apprehensive. "Where are they now?"

"We don't know," Smith said. "But you might."

"I don't like your attitude," she snapped.

"He only means," Kelso said, "that we thought you might have seen or heard something."

"Nothing at all. Now if you'll excuse me, I've got things to do. I'm very busy."

Kelso lowered his umbrella and hung it over his arm. Instantly the rain began soaking his head. He got out a notebook and a ballpoint pen and blinked water from his eyes. "Could I have your name, please?"

"What for?"

"Just routine, ma'am."

"This isn't my house. I live here, but I don't own the place. You'll have to speak to the owner. I can't presume to say anything else about this."

"Maybe you'd like to go downtown and answer some questions there," Smith said testily.

"You bring an arrest warrant with my name on it and I'll go downtown with you," she snapped. "Then I'll notify my attorney to initiate proceedings against you for false arrest, malicious prosecution, harassment—"

"Ma'am," Kelso interjected, "all I want is your name."

"I would have given it to you, Sergeant, but not now. Now you'll have to get a court order. Good day to both of you." She started to shut the door. Then a wide figure loomed behind her, and a low resonant voice spoke.

"What's the trouble, Margaret? Ah, we have visitors. And you were about to turn them away in this weather?"

"We can't let them in," she said, almost hissing, looking over her shoulder. The man behind her was dimly visible, like a shadow in the dark recesses of the house. "Police," she said, trying to whisper.

"Yes, Margaret, it's all right. I'll take care of it. You go on and give Harold a hand, won't you?" She said something Kelso couldn't hear, and the man's tone went slightly hard. "I said, I'll take care of it."

She stepped backward and disappeared from view. At the same time, the figure moved into the doorway and looked out at them, an extremely obese man in a black three-piece suit, white shirt, maroon silk tie, black shoes. The shoes were dry. His suit jacket was unbuttoned, emphasizing the bulk of his paunch. He had a round face, heavy jowls, and small dark eyes.

"Gentlemen, please come in. I apologize for my sister, she tends to be a little antisocial these days. Quite understandable, when you consider it. Come in. There's fresh coffee. You are the police? I'm at your disposal."

Kelso didn't hesitate. It was wet and cold outside; inside it looked dry and warm. He stepped in quickly, with Smith following. The door closed. They stood in a small carpeted hall, without furniture except for a three-legged table against one wall and, over it, a tall mirror which reflected the rear of the fat man.

"Dr. Leslie Winthrop," he said, holding out a massive hand and beaming.

"Sergeant Kelso." They shook. The man's hand gripped Kelso's firmly; it felt slightly moist. "This is my partner. Detective Smith."

"How are you?" Smith said. "Medical doctor?"

"Psychiatrist," Winthrop said. "Detectives, eh? Glad to know you. Criminology is an interest of mine. Please, come into the living room and we'll try to get you dried and warmed. If you see or hear anything unusual, don't worry about it. This house is haunted, as you probably know, but most of the manifestations are harmless. This way, gentlemen." Winthrop led them down the hall, pulled open a door at the end, and ushered them through. The house smelled of furniture polish. There was a faint echo, giving Kelso an impression of vastness. Of *course* the house is haunted, he thought. Someone had told him the people who lived here were nuts. Yes, he thought, it must be true.

Glancing at Smith, he followed along after the fat man.

The door opened onto a much longer hall, papered in a faded pinkish red with faint gold lines. The carpet was equally faded, in an Oriental design. No furniture, paintings, or mirrors. Once Kelso glanced back; Smith followed a few feet behind, looking grim. Their umbrella left a trail of water on the carpet.

After a while they reached another door and Winthrop opened it and stood aside for them to pass. It was a large room in dark tones of tan, red, and purple. Heavy drapes, wallpaper, Oriental carpeting, overstuffed furniture, a round wooden table in the center with nothing on it but an empty ashtray and a small china cup containing several cigarettes. The drapes were parted over gauzy white curtains, but as not much light came in, the room seemed drab and lifeless. At the far end a mantelpiece ran along the wall over a stone fireplace in which two logs blazed.

"Sit down, sit down." Winthrop came into the room,

closing the door behind him. No other doors were visible. "Would either of you like some coffee, or tea? A little brandy?"

"I'll take coffee," Smith said flatly. "Black."

Winthrop made a slight bow. "And you, sir?"

"Coffee," Kelso said. "With cream and sugar, please."

"Of course." The man clapped his hands together twice, loudly, making two gunshots in the quiet room. Unbelievably, the hall door opened and a thin young girl stood there in a black dress and white apron, holding her hands behind her and staring straight ahead. She must have been about twenty. Her face was pale and her eyes were expressionless. She wore heavy black shoes, very clean and dry.

"Two coffees, Charlotte. One black, one white with sugar. I'll have my usual."

Charlotte nodded without speaking and left the room. Winthrop beamed, lowering himself into a chair. Kelso and Smith sat at either end of a sofa.

"So, gentlemen," Winthrop said, "what brings you to my house? It *is* mine, by the way. I own it. I inherited it from my father, who is now dead. Police business. I don't read the papers or watch much television, but no one has broken into my house or I would have known it. So what is your business?"

The man was theatrical but not melodramatic. He seemed to be putting on the jolly-host bit too thickly, though. Kelso frowned. Eccentric, probably. That was a lot different from insane. He was no expert, he'd only taken a couple of psychology courses at the university's evening division, but he thought he could tell the difference between someone merely eccentric and someone overtly psychotic. Of course, psychotics didn't always exhibit their bizarre behavior openly; sometimes they seemed almost normal, then something happened and they were off.

"You don't know about the hand?" Kelso asked. He'd considered probing to see if the man knew, but decided against it. He didn't feel like playing games. Either Winthrop knew or he didn't. In either case, Kelso wanted to get on with things as quickly and directly as possible.

"The hand?" Winthrop's eyebrows went up.

"A hand was found down in the woods behind your house," Smith said, with a dangerous accusatory tone to his voice. "Lying on top of a chunk of limestone that's supposedly part of something called Mary's grave."

"Indeed!" Winthrop gazed blandly at Smith. It was impossible to tell what he might have been thinking. If he'd chopped or whacked that hand from someone's body himself, a surge of guilty memory must have shot through his brain at that instant, but he looked as innocent as a babe. "Just a hand? Nothing more? Are you referring to an actual hand, a human hand, or . . ." His low voice trailed away as the hall door opened and the young maid, if that's what she was, hurried in carrying a metal serving tray. She brought it over to Kelso and waited quietly while he removed a mug of coffee and added sugar and cream. He tried to catch her eye but she stared away from him at nothing. She moved to Smith, then to Winthrop, who took something amber in a small glass. Brandy, apparently.

"Thank you, Charlotte. That will be all for now."

She nodded expressionlessly and left the room. Kelso noted that she had both hands. The door closed softly.

"I suppose you noticed," Winthrop said, "the family resemblance."

"Excuse me?" Actually, Kelso hadn't looked for one.

"She's my niece, the daughter of my sister Margaret, whom you met briefly."

"I see. Is she in school?"

"No, sir. And she hasn't been, not since the third grade. Childhood schizophrenia was the original diagnosis. Now it's just schizophrenia. I know what you must be thinking, that she didn't look psychotic."

That wasn't what Kelso had been thinking, but he kept quiet.

"In fact," Winthrop said, sipping at his drink, "she is heavily medicated most of the time. Trilafon, currently. It is the only way she can exist normally. She's incapable of employment or education. I don't sound grief-stricken,

Sergeant, because I have learned to live with my curses. Charlotte is one of them. The ghost is another, though it wouldn't be if only I could communicate with it. The one that inhabits this house, not Mary's ghost.'' He smiled. ''My niece is able to prepare refreshments for guests and to feed herself, dress herself, though once or twice a month she relapses—decompensates, we psychiatrists say—and goes into fits of rage, screaming, throwing things, biting. She has to be restrained.''

''Are you her psychiatrist,'' Smith asked, ''or does she see someone else?''

''I'm her psychiatrist. After receiving my M.D. I did a residency in psychiatry, and then I spent seven years at the Loffer Kleinschmidt Institute for Psychoanalysis. Perhaps you've heard of it. No? Well, no matter. So I've been in the private practice of psychoanalysis for the past twenty years. In 1980 my mother died, and the following year my father joined her. He left me this house, which now serves both as my home and my office. I'm sorry, I've gotten off the point of your visit. Something about a hand?''

''A hand,'' Kelso said, trying the coffee and finding it too strong. He added sugar from a packet he'd taken from the tray. ''What we'd like to know, Dr. Winthrop, is whether you've seen or heard anything unusual or suspicious down around Mary's grave, especially yesterday evening.''

It sounded like such an absurd question now, on the heels of Winthrop's eccentric behavior, his schizophrenic daughter—no, niece—and the weird woman who'd answered the door. But it had to be asked.

''Sorry, Sergeant. I can't help you. I like to assist the police whenever possible. Criminal behavior fascinates me, it is one of the most interesting and, obviously, most problematic of the forms of abnormal behavior. But in this case . . .'' He shrugged massive shoulders.

''What does a psychoanalyst do?'' Smith asked. There was an edge to his voice.

Winthrop blinked. ''I provide therapy for the mentally disturbed,'' he replied. ''Primarily for neurosis, as did Freud, but occasionally for treatable cases of certain personality disorders, depression, and even schizophrenia, which isn't an entirely organic psychosis despite the arguments of the neurobiologists. And in addition to my clientele, there is my research, sir. My research.''

"What kind of research?''

"Various kinds. I am investigating a problem in melancholia, which is a severe aspect of depression. Also, I am studying the relationship of the ego defense mechanisms to hysteria and the dissociative disorders, such as, for example, fugue states.''

There was a silence, then Smith said, "I took psychology in high school.''

Winthrop smiled benevolently, and Kelso felt embarrassed.

"It's a little more than that, sir. And, in addition, I am conducting, quite on my own, some investigations into the greatest problem of them all. The paranormal. In other words, death.''

"Ghosts?'' Smith asked.

"How eloquently you dive to the crux of the matter,'' Winthrop said, beaming. "Yes, it includes ghosts. After all, since I have one in my house, I might as well investigate it.''

"Dr. Winthrop,'' Kelso said, "can you tell us if in fact anyone is buried down there? Is there a Mary Carter in a grave in the clearing?''

"As far as I know, Sergeant, there is. I am related to the people who owned this house at the turn of the century when a young girl named Mary Carter came here from Georgia to visit. She died of pneumonia and was buried down there. I don't know why. There is a story that she was disturbed, that she saw visions and heard voices. Insanity runs in families, you know. A combination of genetics and the environment. Maybe she was afflicted in the same way as my niece. She died, and was buried down there. It's said that her spirit was seen by the people in this house from time to time. Supposedly it drove some of them insane, but I can't vouch for that.''

"You've never seen her ghost?'' Smith asked. His smile was sardonic.

"Not yet," the psychiatrist answered, unruffled.

"Who lives here in the house with you, Dr. Winthrop?" Kelso asked.

"My, my, a little like the census, isn't it? Well, if you are investigating a crime . . ." He shrugged again. "There are myself, my niece Charlotte, my sister Margaret whom you met at the door. I apologize for her rudeness, she's not used to strangers."

"Anything the matter with *her?*" Smith asked.

Winthrop turned small dark eyes on the detective and seemed to appraise him the way someone looks over a piece of steak. "No," he said, very quietly, "there is nothing the matter with my sister." He looked back at Kelso. "And then there is Harold, our cook."

"That's all?" Kelso asked.

"Yes, that's all."

"Awfully big place," Smith pointed out, "for no more people than that."

Winthrop smiled amiably and sipped at his brandy.

"Heard any screams around here lately?" Smith asked. "Anybody running through the woods?"

"I don't go out much at night, and I don't go down into the woods at all. Sometimes when I'm in the back yard I hear people in the woods, but I ignore them. As you probably know, children are prone to visit the place, for their various purposes. Children do run and scream, don't they?"

"Why don't you go in the woods?" Smith wanted to know.

Winthrop glanced at him. "I have no reason. Besides, we are having a problem with the church, St. Luke's, about the property line. Until it is settled I am not even certain how much of the woods I own." He seemed suddenly impatient, and even pulled up the sleeve of his jacket to glance at a gold watch. "Any more questions, gentlemen?"

"We've taken up enough of your time," Kelso said, putting his coffee mug down on a side table and standing. "We appreciate it."

Winthrop raised his enormous bulk from his chair. "Not

at all. As I said, always happy to help the police, though I don't suppose I've been much help. Tell me, Sergeant, did you really find a human hand down there?''

''Yes.''

''Whose was it? Any idea?''

''No. At this point it's unidentified.''

''Male or female?'' the fat man asked quietly.

''I'm sorry,'' Kelso said, ''I don't want to discuss the details until we know more. By the way, do you happen to know Father Ullman, the priest at St. Luke's?''

Something flickered in Winthrop's eyes, making them darker. ''I don't attend church, Sergeant, and I don't know any priest, either socially or otherwise.''

''He has a part-time secretary. Young girl, slightly retarded, helps him out afternoons. Do you happen to know her?''

''No.'' The word came out emphatic and hard. ''This way, gentlemen. . . .'' Winthrop led them across the room to the hall door and opened it. As Kelso went through, he saw the girl, Charlotte, standing a few feet away in the hall. It was impossible to tell how long she might've been there and how much she might have heard. He smiled at her but she looked through him as if he were a ghost. He was struck, suddenly, by her physical resemblance to Rosemary.

''Charlotte,'' Dr. Winthrop said in a low tone, ''show these gentlemen out, please. Uh, would you prefer the front or the rear, Sergeant?''

''The rear, if it's all right. I think we'll go back through the woods, if you don't mind.''

''Not at all. Nice to have met you, Sergeant Kelso.'' He bowed formally. ''Detective Smith.''

''Thanks for the coffee,'' Smith said.

''You're entirely welcome.''

The fat man turned back into his living room and closed the door, leaving them alone with Charlotte. Without a word she set off down the hall, walking rapidly, hands clasped in front, reminding Kelso of a nun in her long black dress and heavy shoes. He and Smith followed, shrugging into their raincoats and getting their umbrellas ready. Kelso looked left and right as they went, hoping for a glimpse of anything else interesting, but he saw nothing.

The girl led them through the connecting door into the short hallway at the rear, then pulled open the outer door and stood to one side, like a proper maid, not meeting their eyes. Her expression was sullen. Even her face was similar to Rosemary's.

Smith walked past her. Cold damp air came into the hall. Kelso started to leave, then stopped even with Charlotte and looked directly into her eyes.

"Excuse me," he said softly, "would you mind keeping my card and giving me a call if there's ever anything you'd like to tell me?" He got out one of the white cards with his name and number and handed it to her.

Slowly, she turned her face upward and regarded him with eyes that were dark, unsure, frightened. Her lips moved. "I can't," she said, almost in a whisper. "I can't."

"Sure you can. Here, just take it. It's only a card."

"I can't." Her eyes filled with tears, making them bright. Then she turned quickly and hurried away down the hall. She went through the connecting door and it closed with a click.

Kelso pocketed the card and stepped outside into the cold wet afternoon, closing the door to the house. A few feet away Smith looked disgusted, a freshly lit cigarette in his lips. The rain had stopped for the time being. The wind gusted.

"Bunch of nuts," Smith said.

Kelso didn't answer. As they crossed the water-filled lawn to the woods and made their way back along the winding path to the grave, he frowned hard and wondered at the coincidence of two young dark-haired girls existing on either side of the place where the hand had been discovered. It was 3 P.M., two days before Halloween.

Chapter Twelve

The Thing in the Grave

"Schizophrenia," Smith said, when they had come out into the clearing again. "That's split personality, right?"

"No." Kelso stood near the engraved stone, holding his umbrella in one hand. "It's what they call a thought disorder, the worst kind of psychosis. Schizophrenics have trouble thinking clearly, their feelings and emotions don't go along with their thoughts and perceptions. They have delusions and hallucinations, too. There are several varieties."

"How come you know so much about it?"

"I don't really. I just finished a course in abnormal psychology, that's all."

Smith lit a Kent with one hand. "That girl was having hallucinations?"

"She didn't act like it," Kelso said. "But they have medicines for it that pretty much control the symptoms. They don't cure the disease, though."

"What was all that bullshit about a ghost?" Smith sounded indignant. "Or was he just trying to scare us?"

"I thought he sounded serious," Kelso said. "But maybe the whole thing was a big con. Who knows?" He glared around at the dripping trees. "I need some dry clothes. My feet are soaked. Let's go change and get something to eat, huh?"

"Fine."

They wound their way back up the other path and crossed the parking lot to Smith's LTD. The rain became a light mist again. It was still heavily overcast and the wind continued to gust. Smith drove down the drive and turned into Amsterdam Avenue, toward town. After a few minutes the heat came up and Kelso felt a little better.

"What do you think so far?" Smith asked.

"It doesn't make any sense to me." Kelso sighed and held a match to his pipe. "A human hand is found on Mary's grave, after two women hear screams. The hand apparently came from a young girl. No young girls are missing. I see Rosemary McAllister at the grave, she smiles, somebody bashes me over the head, and when I wake up she's gone. Rosemary's retarded and doesn't seem to know anything, but on the other hand she admits seeing me at the grave. On the other side of the woods is a big house where a fat eccentric psychiatrist lives with his weird sister and her schizophrenic daughter. The fat man is obsessed with ghosts but never goes into the woods. And there's a cook named Harold, but we didn't see him." He sighed. "Nothing makes any sense."

"If that fat guy is into ghosts so much, I don't understand why he doesn't spend more time at the grave. Seems to me like that'd be the perfect place for it."

"Maybe he was lying. Maybe he goes there all the time."

"That broad Rosemary," Smith said. "She must've seen whoever hit you."

"Yeah."

"By the way, do schizophrenics ever commit murder?"

"Not usually. Except maybe for paranoids. And don't ask me if Charlotte's paranoid. I'm no expert."

"Is Charlotte paranoid?" Smith asked.

"Very funny."

"According to the stories, that whole bunch in the house are supposed to be nuts. Maybe they chopped off some girl's hand because they're nuts." He turned left and headed toward Kelso's apartment.

"Maybe they did," Kelso said. "But what did they do with the rest of her body?"

"Maybe it's still in the house."

The car stopped. Kelso got out and peered in at Smith. "Pick me up in half an hour. I'll be ready to go eat something." The car moved off.

He got out his keys and went into his apartment. He was cold and wet and in a foul mood. The case was depressing. Nothing fit. Somewhere there was a young woman missing her right hand, and the police were no closer to finding her than they'd been at the outset. He went up and took a hot shower, changed into dry clothes, felt slightly better. He fed his big yellow cat and made a cup of instant coffee, stood sipping it by the front door. The retarded girl, Rosemary, had both hands. So did Winthrop's sister Margaret. So did Margaret's daughter Charlotte.

He went into the living room and turned on the TV set. It was nearly 4 P.M. He turned to the weather channel and watched the forecast. The rain was part of a large low-pressure area that would linger for awhile. Someone rang the bell and he turned the TV off. At the door, Smith was waiting for him.

Something occurred to Kelso, and he thought about it in silence as they drove across town to a coffee shop. Inside, sipping coffee and waiting for their orders to be brought, he said, "I've got an idea."

"Okay."

"Suppose a couple of people killed a girl and chopped off her hand. Suppose they did it in the woods a few yards from Mary's grave."

"Okay. I'll suppose that."

"What if they then carried the body into the clearing and dumped it into a grave, one they'd already dug."

Smith eyed him skeptically. "We didn't find a fresh grave, Kelso."

"I know. But there's a place we never looked."

"Where?"

"Under the monument."

Their food arrived. Smith ate a prune Danish, Kelso had three yeast donuts.

"It's an idea," Smith said at last. "Kind of nutty. But it's an idea."

"Want to go check it out?"

"I guess so. After all, we don't have anything better to do." He said it sarcastically.

By the time they got back to Mary's grave it was a quarter to five and already gloomy. There was no rain at the moment, but they could hear thunder rumbling disagreeably off in the distance and the clouds seemed darker and faster. The air smelled cold and wet. They stood in the clearing, the trees blowing around them and wet leaves fluttering groundward, and looked at the stone on which someone had left a girl's severed hand. Smith carried a large shovel, Kelso held a spade.

"You pry on that end," Smith said. "I'll pry on this end."

They stooped to their task, grunting with effort. Kelso's hands slipped on the spade's handle. The stone was heavy, but gradually they got their tools underneath and raised it high off the ground.

"So much for that," Smith said glumly. "Any other theories?"

Kelso frowned. The ground was hard and flat; it hadn't been turned in a long time. Maybe years. Worms and beetles tried to get away from the sudden light.

"No one's dug here recently," Kelso said thickly. "Let it down."

They lowered the stone and stood panting, glaring at it.

"In ten minutes we're off duty," Smith said. "Let's go back to the office and see if Meyer and Broom came up with anything. There's obviously nothing here." He started toward the path.

"Wait a minute." Kelso turned.

"What the hell for? It was a good idea, but you were wrong."

"There's another stone," he said, pointing.

Smith looked. Kelso was indicating the large enscribed chunk in the center of the clearing. It was almost the size of the one they'd just looked beneath. Red and yellow leaves flew in the air, covering the ground and resting wetly on top of the stone.

"Okay," Smith said. "Once more and then we'll go. Right?"

"Right." Kelso stooped with his spade.

Again they grunted and struggled. This one seemed heavier, or maybe they were already tired. It came up finally, and they held it, peering into the shadow it made. The dirt was packed from the stone's weight, but even a glance told them it was loose. There were many clots, it was all rough and uneven, and leaves were mixed in with the dirt. Colored leaves, from the turning trees around the edges of the clearing. Fresh leaves.

"Somebody's dug this up very recently," Kelso said, feeling enthused for the first time since they'd found the hand.

"Son of a bitch," Smith murmured. "Well, let's get this thing over to one side and see what's here."

They swung the stone around, dropped it, then set to work. The area was a rectangle a couple or so feet wide and a little over four feet long—not the size of a real grave, but large enough to hold a body. They dug, and the loosely packed earth came up easily. After a few minutes the tip of Smith's shovel struck something hard with a loud clang. He bent down to scrape dirt away, then looked up.

"It's a crate of some sort. Now what?"

"Can we get it out?"

"I don't know," Smith said. "I'm no expert on digging up crates."

"Let's radio for help," Kelso said.

"Toss to see who stays behind?"

"Nuts. I'll stay, and this time I'll be careful."

"Okay. But don't say I didn't warn you." Smith put down his shovel and started up the path for the parking lot. "Yell if you need anything," he said.

"Just hurry it up," Kelso told him.

Smith's footsteps faded into the woods. Kelso looked around. Thunder rumbled. It was easy to imagine eyes peering out from the surrounding woods again, easy to imagine the footsteps of someone sneaking up behind him again. He drew his .38 and stood by the hole, the one somebody had dug before them, and scanned the line of trees and underbrush. After about five minutes he heard someone coming down the path, then Smith appeared, grinning.

"Don't shoot, Kelso. It's me."

"Well?" Kelso put his gun away.

"They'll he here pronto. Anything happen while I was gone?"

"No."

Ten minutes later several cops arrived, wearing blue police coveralls and boots. They brought shovels and some other gear, and were followed into the clearing by the small dark-suited form of Detective-Sergeant Meyer, who glared around and then came up to Kelso.

"Was this Smith's idea?"

"No, it was mine."

"Oh." Meyer watched the proceedings. "I was just on my way home," he said, as if to blame Kelso.

"A policeman's work is never done," Smith commented.

The men dug quickly and came up with the wooden crate. At Meyer's nod, the top was loosened and opened. One of them looked inside, paled, and turned away. Meyer walked over to the box. It was about two feet high and as wide, maybe four feet long. Like a crude small casket. The wood was heavy and unfinished. Meyer looked inside. The expression on his face didn't change from its usual sullenness. He squared his narrow shoulders, turned away, and squinted at Kelso.

"Well, I guess you'd better see it."

Kelso took a breath and let it out. Knowing what to expect was never preparation enough. He stepped over to the container, glanced at Smith, and looked.

She was probably about seventeen or eighteen, twenty at the most. Very pale, making her thick black hair contrast sharply with her body. Her eyes were closed. Someone had more or less stuffed her inside the crate and folded her arms mummylike across her breasts, with her knees drawn up, so she would fit. She was completely nude. The only obvious sign of violence was her right arm, which ended at the wrist with reddish folds of skin.

Her right hand was missing.

Kelso walked over to an edge of the clearing and for a moment stared up at the trees, their dying leaves rattling in the chill October wind.

Chapter Thirteen

The Body

For the second time in two days the clearing became a crime scene as the area was roped off and searched. Kelso sat in Smith's car up in the church parking lot, the window rolled down about an inch, listening to the rain on the metal roof and watching the windshield fog up while he thought about things.

Someone has cut off a girl's hand and then killed her. They had deposited the hand on what was popularly supposed to be Mary Carter's grave, and at some point—either before or after disposing of the hand—had dug a shallow grave beneath a large broken portion of the tombstone and placed the girl's body there, stuffed inside a wooden crate. The implication was that they didn't care whether or not the hand was found, but they hadn't wanted the body found.

Kelso lowered the window another inch or two and felt rain splash onto his face. Why had they hidden the body but flaunted the hand? They must have been confident that no one would be able to identify the hand. Still most murderers didn't leave parts of their victims' bodies lying around as a sort of challenge for the police.

He sighed, fingering his unlit pipe. The only conclusion seemed to be that the hand had been cut off and left on the grave for some particular purpose. Kelso thought that if only he could discover this purpose, he might be a long way along toward figuring out who had killed the girl and why.

Someone came up into the lot from the woods and approached the car. Kelso rolled the window down some more and Meyer glared in at him, his dark blue official raincoat soaked, his black hair soaked. Meyer hated hats and never seemed to have an umbrella.

"Did you find anything?" Kelso asked.

"Not a damn thing. I didn't expect to, since we already searched it once." Meyer regarded Kelso with narrowed eyes. "Are you nice and dry?"

"Yeah."

"Good for you." Meyer shoved a manila envelope through the window opening. "Here. Copies for you and Smith." Then he turned without waiting for a reply and strode toward his own car.

Kelso opened the envelope, not feeling guilty. There was no reason for him to be down there now, since the crime-scene investigators were perfectly capable of searching the clearing without his help. He preferred to waste his time in the dryness of his car rather than messing about in the downpour, getting in the way. He opened the envelope wider, stuck his hand inside, and pulled out the contents. Polaroid shots of the girl's body, including two close-ups of her face and some of her right wrist. Grimacing, he shoved them back inside the envelope.

Smith emerged from the woods and hurried toward the car. He climbed in, tossed his umbrella into the back, and closed the door. His raincoat, too, was soaked, and he smelled of dirt and leaves. The windshield fogged considerably more.

"Well, she definitely wasn't murdered by any damned ghost," Smith said.

"What do you mean?"

"She's got a bullet hole in the back of her head."

"Oh." Kelso hadn't foreseen that. In his way of looking at the case, it changed things. The situation was now slightly different. "I'm glad to hear it," he said.

Smith stared briefly. "Huh?"

"I mean, before this we were dealing with something mysterious, something that haunted graves and ran invisibly through the woods and jerked cigarettes out of your hand. Now we're dealing with an ordinary murderer, somebody who loads a gun and points it at the back of somebody's head and pulls the trigger. I can comprehend that.''

"Don't forget," Smith said, "if a ghost could knock my cigarette away, it could do other physical things. Pull the trigger on a gun, for instance.''

"Bull," Kelso muttered. "I don't believe in ghosts, and even if I did, this isn't a supernatural event. It's plain murder.''

"Suit yourself." Smith started up the LTD and pulled out of the lot, the windshield wipers click-clacking back and forth. "But I'm not placing bets either way. Not yet. I sat on that grave and something knocked my cigarette out of my hand, and I say there's something damned weird about that place. Where to, by the way?''

"Let's get something to eat." Kelso's stomach was rumbling.

"You sound awfully grumpy.''

"I'm just depressed." In the back of his mind was the idea that the hand itself had been somehow separate and alone, a thing detached. It had been intriguing, but by itself it hadn't meant much. He'd found it difficult to visualize it as part of a real body. It was a kind of mystery. Now that its body had been dug up, the crime had become both irritating and depressing. Now he could see the girl herself. He could conceive of what had happened, though not why. The dead girl with the skin folded over her wrist was too real and the crime too vicious. He had the uncomfortable feeling that he was dealing with something abnormal.

"Do you believe in evil?" he asked Smith as they pulled into the parking lot of a Pancake House.

"What the hell kind of question is that?''

"I don't know.''

They got out and hurried through the rain to the entrance. Inside, a hostess seated them in a booth along a wall, where they could stare out the windows. Between two buildings across the street the sun was setting, peering through a gap in the clouds to suggest possible clearing. The streetlights were on, along with signs and lamps in various windows and storefronts. In the streets cars crowded bumper to bumper, headlights glaring. Secretaries hurried down the sidewalk toward bus stops while an old man, his eyes watery in a face gray with stubble, hawked the evening paper.

"So what's all this about evil?" Smith asked, lighting a cigarette.

"I've got a strange feeling about this case."

"Because of the hand?"

A waitress set down two coffee mugs. Kelso stirred in sugar and cream. "No," he said, "not just that. It's a feeling about the crime itself. Well, maybe it's the hand. I don't know, it's not normal."

"Nobody said it was."

"Normal people don't amputate someone's hand before killing them. I just think we're dealing with a really warped mind, somebody who doesn't have the slightest sense of morality, someone totally amoral."

Smith sipped his coffee. His cold blue eyes gazed out at the street. "Well, I don't see how you can consider any murderer either sane or moral, no matter how they commit the crime. How can you judge? Three kids, all under seventeen, stab an old lady to death for ten bucks. A husband hires a professional murderer to kill his wife. Somebody shoots a political figure in the belief that he was called upon to rid the world of Satan. They're all nuts, and they're all amoral. I don't see the difference."

"I suppose," Kelso muttered.

"And what's evil, anyway? Evil is a social convention. Incest isn't evil in a society that approves it. In this country, it's not evil to burn a guy in a chair hooked up to a few thousand volts or stick a needle in him and stand around gawking while government-approved poison is pumped into him. It's okay to flush a psychotic from a low-rent apartment building and then fire fifteen or twenty rounds of ammo into him when he waves a butcher knife. Evil's a relative term, Kelso."

The waitress brought a vegetable omelette for Smith and buttermilk pancakes with sausage links for Kelso. They ate.

"Once when I was in the fifth grade," Kelso said, "I

saw three little girls surround a boy they didn't like and kick him for several minutes. It was during recess. He lay on the ground in the dirt, and they just stood there kicking him while he bawled and screamed and tried to get away.''

"Jesus Christ. What'd you do?"

"I ran over to my teacher and told her three girls had this kid down on the ground and were kicking him. And you know what she said?"

"What?"

"She said, 'Well, George, as long as they don't kill him.' Can you imagine that? 'As long as they don't kill him.' Well, in my book those three little girls were evil, I don't care of they *were* only fifth-graders. And so was that teacher."

"But that's my point," Smith said. "To you it was a terrible thing. But obviously it was socially approved behavior at that school, on that playground, in that fifth-grade class."

"It wasn't socially approved by that little boy," Kelso replied hotly.

"Yeah. By the way, why were they picking on him?"

"I don't remember."

"You saw only one side of it, Kelso. Suppose he'd been pestering them for weeks. Suppose he'd hit them and shoved them and pulled up their dresses? Suppose he'd put live worms in their sandwiches and spiders in their milk?"

"Are you defending him?"

"I'm just saying that evil's a relative term."

"I know that people act out of various emotions and drives," Kelso said. "But in this case, I've got a bad feeling. I don't think we're dealing with the usual murderer, somebody with a rational motive like greed or revenge."

"So now you're defining evil as something you can't understand."

"Forget it." Kelso felt angry. Things were all turned around. Normally it was Smith who saw everything in black and white and Kelso who understood the world as a continuum, but now they seemed to have switched roles. It's this damned case, he thought.

"Don't worry," Smith said. "When we find the killer,

all this stuff about evil won't mean a thing. He'll be arrested and tried and convicted and wind up as just another number in a prison cell."

"I guess so."

As they were about to drive away from the Pancake House, Smith radioed headquarters to check in, and the dispatcher forwarded a message for Kelso to contact the coroner's office. He went back inside the restaurant and used a pay phone.

"Dr. Paul? This is Kelso."

"Hi. I've got some information for you on the body you dug up."

"Yes?" He glanced around. Several waitresses he knew smiled or waved at him, unaware that he was discussing a girl who had been shot and buried under a gravestone after her hand had been cut off.

"The girl is indeed the owner of the hand," Dr. Paul said. "There's no question. And I can now confirm that the amputation was performed while she was still alive."

"That's terrible," Kelso muttered.

"We found large amounts of Pentothal and morphine in her system. Probably she was kept heavily sedated after the surgery, until she was killed."

"How long ago was she killed?"

"Right now I'm estimating two days ago. Let's say on the twenty-seventh, midnight plus or minus six hours. The amputation was probably done five or six days prior to that."

"I see."

"The cause of death was a gunshot directly to the back of her head, with a .32 caliber weapon. The range was close, about six inches. The bullet struck some bone and then lodged in her brain. She died instantly."

Dr. Paul said good-bye and hung up. Feeling grim, Kelso went back out to the car.

"I'm sure nobody expected us to dig her up," he told Smith as they drove away. "Now that she's been found, her killer's going to feel threatened. It could change things. Maybe he'll make a mistake now, do something to give himself away."

"Maybe," Smith said. "You got any theories about it?"

"Not really." He tried to think. His mind was a jumble, as if he were trying to wake up from a dream. He felt that already he'd overlooked some important fact, something he'd seen and not recognized for what it was. Some vital clue was staring him in the face and he was ignoring it, looking right through it. "Let's talk to Father Ullman again," he said without much enthusiasm. "There are a couple more questions I'd like to ask him."

"I think we should arrest that retarded girl," Smith said. "After all, she watched you get bashed over the head and she messes around down at the grave all the time. I think she knows something."

Kelso didn't answer. He was trying not to think about the girl, because he had a feeling she was going to wind up involved, and it bothered him. What's evil? he wondered. A mentally retarded girl who shoots someone without understanding what shooting means? A retarded girl who cuts off her victim's hand without comprehending what amputation means? But how could a retarded girl have the skill to sever a hand or to administer an anesthetic? No, if Rosemary was involved, she wasn't alone. Someone was using her.

He recalled the strange smile with which she'd regarded him just before someone hit him over the head, and involuntarily he pictured her smiling in just that way as she gazed down at a young girl whose hand was about to be severed by a person Kelso couldn't visualize. Someone evil.

Remembering the priest's admonition, he made Smith pull into a parking lot and used a pay phone to call the church. Ullman was in and agreed, reluctantly, to see them. They drove up Amsterdam Avenue through the rain and darkness. In the warm steamy confines of the front seat Kelso watched red and orange leaves fall through the headlight beams, listened to the hiss of the tires on wet pavement, and shuddered, fighting to rid himself of the terrible images diving and swirling in his mind like scenes from a nightmare.

Chapter Fourteen

The Bald Man

It was almost seven-fifteen when Father Ullman once again led them into his office. The more they approached him the colder he seemed; Kelso wondered if this was because he was busy or because he was hiding something. Each successive visit by the police often made it more difficult for a guilty man to keep himself from blurting out the truth.

In his office, Ullman sat back in his chair with the light glinting from his bald head, puffed hard at his pipe, and watched them with a blank expression, the way a bank officer looks at someone whose loan application he is about to turn down.

"We've uncovered the owner of the hand," Kelso said after a silence, not unaware that he was making a pun. When Ullman merely nodded, he added, "She was buried about two feet down in a crate, under a piece of the monument near Mary's grave."

"I see."

"Her right hand was missing, and the hand we found is hers."

"I'll pray for her soul," the priest said in a low voice. Kelso couldn't tell for sure if he was being serious or ironic. "Has she been identified?"

"Not yet. There wasn't anything with her, no clothing or identification. But her prints and dental records are being checked, and we're searching through all recent reports of missing girls fitting her description. Her picture will be circulated, and maybe something will break. By the way, would you mind taking a look to see if you know her?''

"I'd rather not,'' Ullman said, so softly that it was difficult to make out the words. He had a mug of coffee on his desk and Kelso could smell its aroma; it made him want some, but he was too polite to ask unless the priest offered.

Kelso smiled gently. People reacted in different ways to being asked to view a photograph of a dead person, for many different reasons. But Ullman was a professional, he'd attended the dying and buried the dead and, surely, looked at photos of them. He would get over his reluctance quickly. Unless he had another, darker reason.

"I'd like you to look at it,'' Kelso said. "It'd help us out. There's a chance you might have known her.''

"No girls from my church are missing.'' Ullman frowned slightly. He seemed agitated but in control.

"Look at it anyway,'' Smith said bluntly. "After all, this is a murder investigation.''

Father Ullman shrugged impatiently. "Oh, all right, but I don't think it'll do you any good. Here, let's see it.''

Kelso handed it across to the priest. It was the close-up of the girl's face, snapped with the camera held directly over her head. He watched Ullman examine the snapshot. The priest's expression grew slightly intense, as though he were encountering something disagreeable—such as a bug in his coffee—and his jaw hardened. Then he frowned harder and returned the photo to Kelso. Taking his pipe from his mouth, he poked at its bowl with a wooden match and spoke without looking up.

"I've never seen her before.''

"Are you sure?''

Ullman's eyes came up, then, and met Kelso's directly, without flinching or blinking. "Of course I'm sure.''

"Well, we had to ask.''

"I know.'' He cleared his throat loudly and lit his pipe, got it going, then glanced at Smith and Kelso. "There's something you might like to know about Mary's grave.''

"What's that?'' Smith said flatly.

"This may be important to you or it may have no bear-

ing at all," said the priest. "But I suppose you can be the
judges of that. Well, about a month ago, it was sometime
back in September, I was working late here in my office,
alone. I locked up around nine and walked out into the
lot. It was a warm night, almost like late August instead
of September. As I was about to get in my car I heard a
noise from down in the woods." He paused to glance at
the door, which was closed, as if he thought someone
might be listening at the other side, then continued. "It
sounded like chanting."

"Chanting?" Smith said.

"Yes. So out of curiosity I went a little way down the
path, toward the clearing. There was a bright moon, almost full. Ten or twelve yards from the clearing I stopped
so whoever was there couldn't see me."

"Who was there?"

"I'm coming to that. I stood and listened for several
minutes. It was chanting, coming from the clearing. A
very definite kind of chanting."

Again he paused, and Kelso got the impression that he
wasn't trying to be dramatic, that he was having trouble
telling it. He waited patiently, hoping Smith would keep
quiet, and after a moment the priest spoke again.

"Somebody was calling on various demons," he said.
"They were reciting some Latin that I couldn't understand, but there was English interspersed with it and the
English part was beseeching various of Satan's compan-
ions to appear. And several times I heard them mention
the name Mary. I assumed they were referring to Mary
Carter."

"So what are you trying to say?" Smith asked heavily.
"You've got some devil-worshippers down there, is that
it? What's that got to do with the murder?"

"Do you think," Kelso asked, keeping his voice pleasant, "that this girl we found was killed by someone as
part of a devil-worship rite?"

"Your guesses are as good as mine, gentlemen. Look."
He leaned forward and rested his elbows on his desktop.
"Personally, I don't believe in a literal devil. In my ver-
sion of life and death, Satan is a metaphor for universal

suffering and universal aloneness, the state of man in the absence of hope and faith and striving. I don't believe these people I heard were actually communicating with any kind of devils or demons. But even so, it irritates me. Maybe they believed in what they were doing, or maybe they were only joking around, but it irritates me to have human beings that close to my church standing over some poor woman's grave and praying to everything that's dark and evil. The reason I'm telling you this is because you've got a pretty gruesome murder on your hands. Someone who's as lost as a human can be has cut a girl's hand from her arm and then killed her. Maybe there's no connection at all. But if there's a chance of a connection, then it seems to me that you should know about it.''

"Did you recognize any voices?" Smith asked, slightly less forcefully.

"No."

"You didn't see anyone?"

"I didn't see them at all. After I'd listened to their chanting for a while, I felt very depressed and I went back up to my car and drove home."

"And what about since then?" Kelso asked. "Have you heard the same thing again?"

"I haven't been back down there since then. And I don't plan to."

Kelso put his hand in his jacket pocket and felt the square of the photograph. He was reluctant to ask the next question because he thought he could predict the answer, but he asked anyway.

"Is Rosemary here right now?"

The priest was busy with his pipe again. "Hmm? Oh, yes. Rosemary. I suppose she is. She's working late to-night on something. Would you like some coffee? Sorry I didn't think of it—"

"No, no," Kelso said. "Not that. I'd like to, uh, have her look at the picture."

"It's out of the question," the priest said.

"It's possible she knew the murdered girl. We don't have a lot of ways of identifying her, and we don't have a lot of time."

"Absolutely not."

"What are you afraid of?" Smith asked.

The priest frowned. "I'm not afraid of anything, except upsetting a girl whose mind isn't completely balanced anyway. I'm responsible for her while she's here with me."

"I appreciate that, Father," Kelso said, "but just because she's retarded, she—"

"You don't understand. She has emotional problems as well. Something like this could throw her completely off balance."

This was going to be tricky. The priest seemed rigid, but his reasons made no sense. Surely he was hiding something. What was his real purpose in keeping the photograph from Rosemary? The possibility that she would recognize the dead girl? And did that mean that Ullman had recognized her? Or had Ullman, in fact, murdered her?

"I'm sorry you feel that way," Kelso said. "But Rosemary's involved in this thing, one way or another. She was down at Mary's grave last night, and she witnessed someone hitting me over the head." Kelso kept his tone low. "I'm not trying to be a bad guy, Father Ullman. But Smith and I've got a job to do. We can get a court order, but if Rosemary's legally an adult then of course we don't even need that. Since she lives with her mother, I don't think you have any status as her guardian, and your rights as her employer don't extend to keeping us from talking to her. I don't want to be mean, and I promise I'll be careful. But one way or the other, she's got to see this photograph."

Ullman sighed. "All right. I don't like it, but you can show her the picture, here in my office, in my presence." He went over to the door and called out, "Rosemary? Would you mind coming in for a minute?"

They waited. The door opened and Rosemary entered quietly. She glanced quickly at Kelso and Smith, then looked questioningly at the priest.

"Rosemary, these two men—Uh, you remember Sergeant Kelso and Detective Smith?"

She nodded.

"Well, they have something they'd like you to look at."
His voice was gruff. "If you don't mind."

"Okay."

Kelso got the photo out of his pocket and handed it to
her. She took it in both hands and peered closely for a
while. He watched her face. She looked solemn, intense,
as if studying. Still staring hard at the likeness, she asked,
"Why are her eyes closed?" When she spoke, she hesitated a little between each word.

"She's asleep," Smith said.

"Rosemary," Kelso said gently, "do you know who it
is?"

Rosemary frowned slightly, then returned the picture to
Kelso. Now the frown faded, and he saw the faint smile
grow on her lips, that strange half-smile he'd seen down
at the grave.

"Mary," she murmured.

"Excuse me?" Kelso wasn't certain he'd heard correctly. "I'm not—"

"Mary's ghost looks like that," she said haltingly. Still
she smiled.

It was quiet in the office. The priest looked worried.
Kelso had the impression that something was about to happen, that they were under a spell, but that if he did or said
the wrong thing the spell would be broken and everything
would be lost. It reminded him of the way he often felt
when coming awake from a pleasant dream as he lay trying to retain its details, only to have it fade from his mind
even as he thought about it. Be careful, he told himself.

"Rosemary," he said, "have you seen a girl who looks
like this?"

She nodded.

"You have?"

"Yes."

"Sergeant Kelso," the priest began sharply, but Kelso
stopped him with a look.

"You saw a girl like this," he said softly. "Can you tell
me where you saw her?"

"Yes."

"Where did you see her?"

"Down at the grave. Mary's grave."

"Mary's grave," Kelso repeated. "Can you tell me when it was?"

"When?"

"Yes. When did you see her?"

"It was . . ."

Come on, he thought. Come on, you can do it. You can remember.

"It was . . . Monday."

"Rosemary, that's very good," Kelso said, trying to remember that she had the mind of a fourteen-year-old, trying to pretend that he was speaking to a normal girl of that age. Emotional problems, too, the priest had said. "Monday? You mean two days ago?"

She shrugged. Nodded slightly.

Kelso thought quickly. Two days ago, before the discovery of the hand, before the screams. According to Dr. Paul the time of death was between 6 P.M. on Monday and 6 A.M. Tuesday. Rosemary must have seen her shortly before the murder.

"Do you remember what time on Monday you saw her?"

She shook her head, but then replied, "I went home from here. I went through the woods. And I saw her."

Kelso glanced at the priest, who frowned and murmured, "That would've been about four-thirty in the afternoon."

"When you saw her," Kelso asked, "was she alone?"

Rosemary smiled vaguely. "No."

"She was with someone?"

Very softly: "Yes."

"Can you tell me who it was?"

She hesitated. The light seemed to go out of her eyes. Kelso went cold. Then the light came back and his heart beat faster. He realized he was making his hands into fists.

"Do you know who she was with?" he asked, very gently.

"Tall," Rosemary said. "He was tall." She smiled her lopsided, strange Mona Lisa smile. "Nothing here." One hand went to the top of her head.

"Bald? He was bald?"

"Yes. Tall and bald. A tall bald man." Slowly, she spoke so slowly. "They were . . . at the grave. They went away."

"Can you tell me which way they went, Rosemary?"

"Into the woods."

"Here? To the church?"

"No." She shook her head. "Away from the church."

That would be, he realized, toward the house. He had one more question, but he was afraid the girl would clam up at any moment. Her face would go blank, the smile would disappear, the light in her eyes would dim. Keeping his voice soft and patient and friendly, he spoke again.

"Rosemary, I've got one more thing to ask you about. Is that okay?"

"Okay." The smile faded a little, but not completely.

"When you saw this girl in the woods on Monday, did you notice her hands?"

"Sergeant," the priest said again, sounding angry.

"Please." Kelso held up his hand to silence him, watching the girl. "Did you see her hands?"

"Yes. I guess so."

"Both hands? Her left and her right?" Kelso held up his own, palms out.

"I don't know. I don't remember."

He'd have to let it pass. Much more, and she'd become upset. But a final question remained. He took a deep breath. Her eyes were on him.

"When you saw me in the woods last night—Do you remember that? You saw me, and someone came up behind me, and you saw who it was?"

"Yes." Uncertainly.

"Was it one of the people you saw on Monday? The girl, or the man?"

He read confusion in her eyes. She said nothing.

"You saw who hit me," Kelso said, at the limits of his patience, grinding his fingernails into his palms. "Was it the girl who looked like Mary?" He held up the photograph again for her to see. "This girl?"

Slowly, she shook her head. "No."

"Was it the man? The tall bald man?"

She just looked at him. Nothing. No words. Too late, he thought. But then the side of her mouth twisted upward in that eerie smile and she spoke.

"Yes. The bald man."

"The man who hit me last night, that was the man you saw with this girl?"

"Yes." She nodded. "The tall bald man." She kept smiling with one side of her mouth, as if she knew a private joke.

Kelso looked at the priest then. There was a hard look in Father Ullman's eyes . . . and he was tall, and bald.

Chapter Fifteen

Going Off Duty

It had quit raining, and this time it seemed that it might actually clear up for a while. A few stars peeped out between fast-moving clouds. In the LTD, Kelso opened his window a little to let in some fresh air, trying to figure out the answer to the maiming and murder. He looked at his pipe and stuck a finger into its bowl. It needed cleaning.

"So where's that get us?" Smith asked, as if they'd been right in the middle of a conversation. In fact, neither detective had spoken a word since leaving the church. After Rosemary's statement about having seen a tall bald man, she'd gone back across the hall, leaving Father Ullman to show them out rather moodily, not really smiling and only saying good-bye in a low, distracted tone of voice.

"If you're referring to what Rosemary said," Kelso replied, "it gets us a suspect. The dead girl was seen shortly before her murder down at the grave with a tall bald guy, and they left the clearing and went into the woods toward Winthrop's house. So we've got a connection between the murder and the house, and maybe with a bald guy in the house. Or, on the other hand, it could've been Ullman."

"I say we arrest the retarded girl and the priest." Smith turned the wheel sharply to avoid a woman in a Cadillac who swerved suddenly into their lane, cutting them off. Smith slammed on his brakes, hit the horn, and growled, "Stupid old bitch. If I wasn't so tired I'd pull her over and write her up!" He roared around the Caddy with his hand on the horn. "Stupid old biddy," he said. "As I was about to say, you seem to think this solves everything."

108

"I didn't say that."

"Actually, it doesn't solve anything at all. I mean, first off you've only got the word of a mental case—"

"She's not a mental case. She'd mildly retarded and may have a few emotional problems, but you can say the same about most of the politicians we've had lately."

"All the same, just assume everything she told you is accurate."

"I'm assuming exactly that."

"Okay, okay. Point is, that still doesn't get you anywhere. A guy with no hair. What the hell's that? We only know one suspect with no hair, that priest, and you don't have a thing on him."

"Dr. Winthrop said there was a cook named Harold," Kelso said stubbornly. "I think it'd be interesting to find out if Harold happens to be tall, thin, and bald."

"I suppose so."

Kelso stared out at the city's business district. A young woman, the wind catching her long hair and tugging at her skirt, stood waiting for a traffic light to change. Looking at her, he wished he were ten years younger. At thirty-six, he felt over the hill. Already he had a paunch and a receding hairline. Waitresses had recently started calling him "sir." It was very depressing. He thought instead about the bald man.

Was it remotely possible that Rosemary McAllister had actually glimpsed the murdered girl and her killer together shortly before the crime? And if Ullman was the killer, would she have told him, would she have described a tall bald man right there in front of Ullman? Perhaps the priest had some sort of power over the girl. He sighed. Nothing really fit together properly.

At the Municipal Building they rode the elevator up to three. Four other detectives were in the duty room, having come up on the rotating night-duty roster. It was now 8 P.M. and outside the windows everything was black, the panes serving only to reflect the room's brightness back at them.

"I think there's a supernatural element to this case," Smith said, perching on the edge of Kelso's desk and lighting a Kent. Kelso sat down and leaned back in his chair, unzipping his jacket but leaving it on. It was cold in the room. On his desk were some official forms, a few letters, a memo about an escaped arsonist, a wanted poster for a convicted rapist who was out on parole and already had raped three women in three weeks, a jar of instant coffee and a box of sugar packets, a can of pipe tobacco, and a *Psychology Today* magazine.

"Be serious," Kelso said. Smith, the calm, unemotional, rational skeptic—"a supernatural element?"

"I *am* serious." Smith looked annoyed. "This whole thing is centered around a grave which may or may not be haunted. I sat on that grave myself with a lighted cigarette, which Mary's ghost is supposed to dislike, and you yourself saw it flung from my hand by some invisible force."

Kelso tried to think of an appropriate disclaimer, but couldn't. So instead he said, "There's a note here from Meyer."

"Has he resigned or anything?"

"No." Kelso picked it up and looked at it. "He says the dead girl is still unidentified. Her fingerprints aren't on file locally or with the state, so they're waiting to hear from the FBI."

"That won't do any good," Smith said. "We already ran the prints from the hand."

"I know. Let's see. . . ." He frowned at the note, scrawled in Meyer's peculiar handwriting. "No missing persons reports match up with her. No reports of runaways. Some detectives are checking the houses in the area along Amsterdam and Wilhelm, showing the residents the girl's picture. And they're checking with the university." He put down the note. "Well, I'm calling it a day. We've already put in three more hours than we get paid for."

His telephone rang.

"Hello?"

"Sergeant Kelso, please." The voice was female, unfamiliar to him.

"Speaking."

"This is Barbara McAllister, Sergeant."

"Yes, ma'am?"

"I understand you've been talking to my daughter Rosemary."

"That's right. We—"

"I want you to stop it, do you understand?"

Kelso grimaced at Smith, who raised his eyebrows.

"Do you hear me, Sergeant?"

"Yes, ma'am," he said.

"Leave my daughter alone."

"Ma'am, we're investigating a crime. You'll have to speak to my boss, Lieutenant Leill, if you've got a complaint—"

"Don't give me that crap, Sergeant. I've talked to the mayor. The mayor is a friend of mine. If you so much as go near my daughter again, I'll have your job. Do you understand that, Sergeant Kelso?"

"Yes, ma'am."

"Good. See that you remember it. Good-bye, Sergeant." She hung up before Kelso could say good-bye.

He slammed down the receiver and stood up. "Fucking bitch," he said.

Smith chuckled. "You don't usually say stuff like that. Somebody insult your girl friend?"

"That was Rosemary's mother. Barbara McAllister. She was calling to warn me not to talk to her daughter again, or she and the mayor will have my job."

"Oh Jesus Christ," Smith muttered, scowling in disgust. "You're not going to take that seriously, are you?"

"What am I supposed to do? How am I supposed to take it?"

"Ignore it. You had it right the first time. She's a fucking bitch."

"Nevertheless, if she can take my job—"

"Let Leill worry about that. I don't think she's as powerful as they say. Look at it this way, if she was really that powerful, why call you up personally, why not get the mayor to call you, or have the mayor call Leill?"

"I don't know." Kelso shrugged. His phone rang again. He didn't want to answer it; then he thought, what the hell, and picked it up. "Yes?"

"Boy, do *you* sound grim."

"Hi." It was Susan. "I *am* grim."

"Aunt Eleanor made peach cobbler and left to play bridge. There's enough for both of us, if you want to come over. I thought you were going to call me after work today."

"I was. I forgot."

"Did you ever do anything about your head?"

"Look," he told her, "Smith and I were just on our way to talk to a witness. Then I'll be over, okay?"

"It's a little late to be talking to witnesses, isn't it?"

"Not when you're trying to solve a murder."

"Well, I'll be here."

"Okay." He hung up. Smith eyed him speculatively.

"Lying to your best girl?"

"I'm just not in the mood for social chat," he said gruffly, zipping up his jacket again and pocketing his pipe. "Are you eating tonight?"

"Yeah. I thought I might have a bite. The omelette didn't fill me up."

"Want to grab something with me?" Kelso asked.

"I guess so."

"If you've got plans—"

"I don't have anything planned. You don't have to feel sorry for me, Kelso. I don't mind eating by myself."

"I'm not feeling sorry for you. As a matter of fact, it's purely selfish. I thought we could talk about the case."

"As long as you put it that way," Smith said.

Outside, a cold wind tossed parts of the afternoon newspaper along the cement past their shoes and out into the street. They got into Smith's LTD again, which was parked next to Kelso's VW in the police lot. It was dark, with not much traffic. An ambulance wailed its way along the street, not bothering to pause at intersections.

"Listen," Kelso said. "I want to know something. Were you really serious when you said you thought there was a supernatural element to this case?"

"You asked me that before."

"What's the answer? Without bullshit."

"To tell you the honest truth, Kelso, I'm perfectly serious."

Kelso peered at Smith in the car's dim interior to see if he was being kidded. "I find that hard to believe."

"Anything ever touch you when you're lying in bed at night, Kelso? Don't look like that. I mean when you're alone. Anything ever make a noise in the darkness when you're climbing the stairs on your way up to bed? You ever wake up in the middle of the night and get the feeling something's there in the bedroom with you? You ever go to a funeral?"

"Things don't bother me in the dark. I've been to a couple of funerals. So what?"

"Funerals are the last unsolved mystery, Kelso. What happens when you die? I mean, have you ever really asked yourself that? Or do you just shrug it off like everybody else and hope you don't have to find out for a long time?"

Kelso considered it. He had to admit that he tried not to think about it. It was too disturbing.

"How about it, Kelso? What happens when you die? Nobody has an answer for that, except maybe the atheists."

"I suppose not."

"What if there's a spirit? A soul? What if there's something that continues to exist after the body dies? Maybe it's possible that sometimes we can see a spirit, or hear one, or feel one."

In the cold confines of the LTD—Smith had neglected to turn on the heat—Kelso shivered. Coincidentally, at that particular moment a hearse came into the next intersection, made a turn, and passed them in the opposite direction. Kelso shivered again.

"You believe in ghosts, Smith?"

"I thought I'd made that obvious. Of course I do."

"Turn here," Kelso said. "There's a good restaurant a block down this street."

"Listen, after we eat are you doing anything?"

"I'll probably go over to Susan's for a while."

"What about after that?"

"Nothing. Just home. Why?"

"There's something I'd like you to see," Smith said. "Have you ever heard of the blue angel?"

"What's that. A topless bar?"

"No, it's a real angel. It guards a mausoleum. After you leave Susan's place, why don't I pick you up and take you to see her."

Hunter's was one of those no-nonsense places Kelso thought of as plain-food restaurants. It reminded him of small-town coffee shops back in the fifties, but with a unique flavor resulting from the combination of "down home" and downtown. Now, with darkness outside, the atmosphere was sharply tinny, a little gloomy, a little melancholy. The blackness outside its plate-glass windows seemed to drain the light from the flourescent tubes in the ceiling fixtures and accented the clank of flatware against dishes. The conversations of the other customers were hushed, as if their words were evaporating as soon as they were uttered.

Kelso and Smith sat at a Formica-topped table along one wall and looked over the menus. A plump blonde in a low-cut waitress uniform took their orders.

"Grilled cheese sandwich," Kelso said. "And some mashed potatoes on the side. Coffee."

"You, sir?"

Smith, who had been ogling her chest, forced his eyes to the menu. "I'll just have the vegetable soup," he said. "And some milk."

"Back in a jiff." She hurried away, hips swinging.

"I'd like to see *her* in a *Penthouse* spread," Smith said. "How old would you say she is, Kelso?"

"Late twenties. Thirty, tops."

"That's what I thought. Just right for me. I'm thirty-two."

"I thought the girls in those magazines were immoral?"

"She's not in a magazine, she's a waitress. I only said I'd like to see her in one. There's a difference, you know." Smith got out a Kent. "Maybe she'll go out with me.

"She probably will."

Smith's eyes narrowed. "Is that a crack?"

Kelso smiled. The waitress returned with a mug of coffee and a tall glass of milk. As she set them down, she leaned over in Smith's direction—as if she knew he liked seeing the faint V of her cleavage and didn't mind showing it to him—and smiled.

"I'm Florine. Need anything else, just give me a yell. Food'll be out in a few minutes. Is that enough cream, sir?"

"Sure." Kelso grimaced at the word "sir."

"Stopped raining out there?"

"Just cold and clear now," Smith said. "Probably frost tonight."

"Frost on the pumpkin." She laughed, turning away.

"Excuse me," Kelso said. She looked back at him with wide blue eyes. "Have you ever heard of a place around here called Mary's grave?"

"Mary's grave? Sure. It's up by that big Episcopal church, isn't it? St. Luke's? I've been there a few times. Why?"

"We were just wondering if it was worth seeing."

Florine stepped closer. "Listen, I'll tell you something about Mary's grave. There's something there, and you can laugh at me if you want to, but I've seen it. First there's this blue light up in the trees. Then you hear breathing. And if you light a cigarette, she'll snatch it right out of your hand. You guys believe in ghosts?"

"*I* do," Smith said, implying that Kelso did not.

"Well, honey, I'd take my prayer book if I was you. Scared the you-know-what right out of me. I almost had to get myself a dry pair of jeans."

"You wouldn't be afraid to go down there with me, would you?" Smith asked, deadpan.

The waitress seemed to look at him for the first time. She tilted her head a little to one side, smiled, and patted Smith's shoulder good-naturedly. "Honey, you call me up sometime, and we'll go check out the ghosts. Got an order up." She trotted away.

"Why'd you ask her about Mary's grave, Kelso?"

"Just to make a point." He sipped his coffee. "Just to show you the kind of person who takes those things seriously."

"The kind of person? Jesus, Kelso. Sometimes you're an awful snob, you know that?"

"You think she's a genius?"

"That's not the point."

Kelso shrugged. "Well, maybe you should ask her out. She seems to want to give you her number."

"Maybe I will." Smith sounded petulant.

The food arrived. When they finished, Florine came back and showed Smith her cleavage again. "You guys like anything else?"

"That can be interpreted in more than one way," Smith said.

"I know."

They smirked at each other for a moment, making Kelso feel very old.

"I'll have a beer," he said.

"Same here," Smith told her.

"Two beers." She went away.

"You're too old for her," Kelso said. "I've revised my estimate of her age, downward."

"I'm not too old for anyone out of puberty, Kelso. Besides, she's cute. Besides, I'll bet she's not more than five years younger than me."

"I don't think she's over twenty-five."

"So what?" Smith lit a cigarette. There were only a dozen other people in the place. Faint music played, an instrumental. "It's not fair," he said. "Life is such a piece of shit in so many ways. Life's for the young. You can eat and drink what you want when you're young, cigarettes don't make you wake up every morning coughing, you can date young girls. There's a waitress at a bar I go to, Kelso. She looks like a young Sophia Loren. She doesn't wear a bra under her T-shirt, and she doesn't sag, not even a little. Her waist looks like you could put your hands all the way around it. And her ass, in her tight jeans—"

"You're only making yourself miserable," Kelso told him. "What you need is somebody mature, somebody down-to-earth."

Florine brought the beers.

"You ought to get married and settle down," Kelso said. He sipped the beer; it was icy cold.

"Like Broom?" Smith made a wry face and poured

beer into a glass, then scrutinized the label on the bottle as though he'd never seen it before. "Just like Broom. You've met his wife, I suppose? Is that what it's all about, Kelso, an obese bitch who whines and nags and makes you miserable for the rest of your life?"

"There are better marriages than his."

"No there aren't. Marriage simply doesn't work. Look at you, for example. You and Susan. Are you planning to marry her? How long have you been dating her now? You're thirty-six, and she's what, thirty? This has been going on for three years. You get along really well, I suppose?"

"We get along pretty well most of the time. Sometimes I think about asking her to get married. But then—" He shrugged. Normally he didn't discuss personal things with anyone. "I think about the changes it would make in my life. I've gotten used to living alone. Suddenly I'd have somebody with me all the time, everything would get all feminine and frilly, I wouldn't have any privacy."

"Marriage is sharing," Smith said wryly.

"If I was lucky," Kelso said, "I might have a den to keep the way I liked, but otherwise everything would be hers. The living room, bath, bedroom, all frilly and feminine. Then we'd have to talk about kids, and probably she'd decide how many and when. I don't know. It just doesn't appeal to me. My life wouldn't be mine anymore."

"Two more," Smith said, holding up his empty bottle as Florine went by.

Kelso realized he'd finished his first already. Normally he had only one, and never more than two.

"Shouldn't we go? I've got to get over to Susan's."

"See?" Smith said. "It's started already. And if you married her, it'd get worse fast. Suppose you wanted to have a drink, like this, one night after work. Well, you'd have to get her permission. That's what Broom has to do. And you know what?"

"No. What?"

Smith chuckled. "Broom's wife always says no."

"Really?"

"Owning you, my friend. That's what marriage is about. Owning you."

Two more beers arrived.

"And another thing," Smith said, filling his glass. "Suppose, after you and Susan tied the knot, suppose you were to run into some staggering sexual creature like the one in the bar I was telling you about, and it popped into your head that you'd like to get to know her better. I guess I don't have to tell you what you'd decide."

"I know." Kelso sipped. "I've thought about that, too."

"Of course, if you were like Broom, you wouldn't have to decide. It'd already be decided for you." Smith belched softly. "By his pig of a wife."

"There are pros and cons," Kelso said, feeling light-headed.

"Another thing—"

"I wanted to talk about the case."

"Oh yeah. The case. Okay. What about it?"

"Do you think a priest could murder someone?"

"You mean Ullman?" Smith swallowed more beer and appeared to reflect. "Hell, I don't know. What's a priest, anyway, when you come right down to it? A guy who went to school and studied religion and how to serve wine. I don't know."

"He's tall and bald," Kelso said. "Rosemary saw a guy like that hit me, and she saw a guy like that with the murdered girl on Monday."

"But if it was Ullman, surely she wouldn't have said that."

"Yeah, that's what I keep telling myself. But it might work to his advantage, by making us eliminate him as a suspect. You know: let Rosemary describe a bald guy, he appears to object, we reason that she's got to be describing somebody else."

"Why not just ask her flat out?" Smith said. "Just ask her if it was Ullman?"

"I might do that."

They drained their beers and went outside. It was cold and starry. A huge moon was rising over one of the department stores; it had been full the previous night. Mary's ghost was suddenly very far away. A severed hand and the nude body of a handless girl seemed unreal, like some weird nightmare had in the wee hours and forgotten at dawn.

Kelso's head buzzed as they climbed into the LTD and the cold seeped into his clothing like water, making him shiver and thrust his fists into his jacket pockets. Smith started the engine and said gruffly, "Susan's place? Or the police lot."

"The lot. I'll drive myself."

It took fifteen minutes to cross town and reach the Municipal Building, and neither spoke during that time. They pulled to the curb and Kelso opened his door to get out.

"I still think something unnatural's going on at that grave," Smith said. "I think we ought to be careful."

Kelso glanced at him for a moment. Smith's ice-blue eyes were level, serious, unblinking, in the dome light. "We'll be careful."

"You still want to see the blue angel tonight?"

"Oh, I forgot." He looked at his watch. "It's already quarter till ten."

"So?"

"I'll probably be at Susan's for at least an hour."

"So?"

"Okay. I'll meet you. Where is it?"

"Park Lawn Cemetery," Smith said. "I'll be outside the main gates at eleven-thirty."

Smith drove away and Kelso unlocked his VW and got in, thinking that he was crazy, ghosts didn't murder people, Susan wouldn't turn into a nag like Broom's wife, priests didn't cut off girls' hands and shoot them, and he wasn't really going to meet Smith at a cemetery shortly before midnight when he had to get up the next morning and go back to work.

Before shutting the door he checked to make sure no one, and nothing, was lurking in the darkness of the back-seat.

Chapter Sixteen

Susan

The streets were virtually deserted, eerie and spectral, the occasional streetlamp only serving to emphasize the darkness. The houses in this neighborhood were dark and brooding; their empty black windows observed Kelso with silent cunning like monster eyes, daring him to stop just once and try to get past on foot. He drove hurriedly and pulled into Susan's driveway at ten o'clock. He got out, went up the curving walk to the porch, and pressed the button.

Susan Overstreet opened the door.

"It's about time," she said, and let him in.

"I didn't know I was on a schedule." He removed his jacket and tossed it on a chair. A fire blazed in the living-room hearth, adding to the sudden heat. Susan lived with an elderly aunt who couldn't tolerate temperatures below eighty. He rolled up his sleeves. "Got any iced tea?"

She kissed his cheek and sat opposite him as he sank into an armchair. She was looking good. She had on a tan sweater, a beige skirt, hose, and gold at her ears and one wrist. At some point she'd discarded her shoes. Her hair was thick, rather short, blond, and her eyes were brown. She was three inches shorter than Kelso, though her slenderness made her seem taller.

"How are things at the hospital?" he asked, getting out his pipe.

"Today was hectic." Susan worked as a psychiatric social worker at a large downtown hospital. "A woman came in with fifty snakes. Not real ones, but they were real to her. She had names for all fifty and she kept reciting them, over and over. She'd recite forty-nine names and then get hysterical because she couldn't remember the fiftieth, she'd think it had gotten lost and she'd get down on her hands and knees and look for it, screaming that we'd taken it away from her.''

"What'd you do with her?''

"Dr. Neumeier saw her and they're doing a temporary commitment. And it was like that all day. What's happening with the case?''

"Nothing. It's very depressing.''

"Did you ever get X-rayed?''

"No, and I'm not going to, either.''

He could hear Susan's aunt in the kitchen, her heels tapping on the tiles. After a while she came in, a short elderly woman with white hair in a bun, wire-framed glasses, a nightgown. She was carrying a tray.

"Hello, George,'' she said in her deep quavering voice. "I made some fresh coffee for you. How are you feeling?''

"I'm fine, Eleanor. Thank you.'' He took a steaming mug off the tray and set it on a side table to cool. "Are you all right?''

"My bones ache and I have to take medicine for my stomach, but I'm still alive.'' She handed Susan a mug, then took one for herself and sat on the sofa. "Now that you're here, we can have a séance.''

Kelso glanced at Susan, who said, "I don't think George is interested in that, Aunt Eleanor.''

"Aren't you, George? My, my, I would've thought so, the way you go exploring in graveyards.'' She chuckled. Her voice was so low that it was almost masculine. "No harm in trying to contact the other side, you know. We're all bound for there, may as well try getting some information about it before we go. Isn't that so, George?''

"George has had a long day,'' Susan said politely. She smiled at Kelso. "Eleanor thinks we should try to communicate with that dead girl's spirit and maybe she'd tell us who cut off her hand and killed her.''

He tried to think of a diplomatic way to tell the old lady what he thought about séances. He shrugged.

"Maybe some other time, I'm not really in the mood for it tonight," he said, sounding a little gruff.

"Let me tell you something that happened to me once, George." Eleanor sipped her coffee loudly and lit a cigarette. She chain-smoked from breakfast till bedtime. She blew a puff of smoke to one side and went on. "When I was about twelve, my Uncle Mortimer died. He was always my favorite because he'd bring me some little present every Sunday when he came for dinner. Once he brought me a watch chain he'd worn. Another time it was a doll. For some reason he seemed to like me the best, better than my other sisters." She paused to cough dryly.

Kelso shifted in the armchair and lit his pipe, wondering if this was going to be a long tale. Susan caught his eye and smiled knowingly.

"Anyway," the old lady said, "my sisters and I decided to hold a séance when Uncle Mortimer died, to see if we could contact his spirit. So we went up to the attic and sat around a little table with a candle on top, and they decided I should be the medium because I'd been his favorite. He'd left a brown hat one day, by mistake, and never bothered to get it because he bought a new one right away, and that hat was there in the attic. So I put it on, and I put on the watch chain he'd given me, and we burned a piece of paper in the candle flame and I smeared the ashes under my nose to look like my uncle's mustache." She gave another low chuckle. "Then we all chanted: 'Mortimer, Mortimer, come to us.' "

Only one lamp was on in the room and the fire was beginning to die down, leaving flickering shadows in the corners. The mood was eerie. Kelso wiped his palms on his pants and puffed at his pipe to keep it going. He looked at Susan, but it was impossible to tell what she thought from her nonchalant gaze.

Eleanor had a far-away look in her eyes. She folded her withered hands, holding her cigarette in a corner of her lips, and rubbed her fingers together with a sound like sandpaper against wood, making Kelso grimace. Then she took the cigarette out of her mouth and continued.

"I don't remember what happened next. The next thing

I knew, I was sitting bolt upright with the candle burned halfway down. My sisters said I'd gone into a trance and they'd heard Uncle Mortimer's voice coming from my lips, which had opened but not moved. He said he'd found peace, that the next world was painless and beautiful. He told us to have faith and live our lives as best we could." She coughed. "To this day, I've kept his brown hat and his watch chain. Well, it's getting late." She stood up slowly, put out her cigarette, picked up her coffee mug, and grinned. "Time for an old lady like me to hit the sack. I don't think I'd have been able to last through a séance tonight, anyhow. Nice to see you, George. You take care of that head of yours, now."

"Yes, ma'am. I will. Thanks for the coffee."

"Oh, pshaw, don't thank *me*. You're one of the family here." She chuckled. "See you tomorrow, Susan."

"Good night, Aunt Eleanor."

The old lady left the room and her heels clicked down the hall. A door opened and shut. She could be heard climbing the stairs and then clomping around overhead.

"I didn't know Eleanor was superstitious," Kelso said.

"Oh, she's not, really. Not in the usual sense. She just happens to believe in séances. You know, she doesn't go around tossing salt over her shoulders or reading her astrology chart. It's just that one thing, and it's probably more religious than anything else."

"What's the difference between religion and superstition?"

Susan lit a cigarette, one of the four or five she would smoke during an entire day, and crossed one leg over the other at her knees, causing the skirt to ride up. "I suppose religion and superstition are the same thing," she replied. "But don't tell a religious person that. Tell me about the case. Do you have any leads? Any suspects?"

He told her what they had so far.

"I've got it figured out," Susan said.

"Sure you do."

"No, I really do."

"All right. Tell me the answer."

"Look. Rosemary McAllister saw a bald man with a

dark-haired girl who looks like the murdered girl's picture. And later she saw the same bald man hit you over the head down at Mary's grave. Here's what I think, George. Father Ullman is a priest, and everybody knows priests have trouble suppressing their sexual drives. So he was having an affair with some young girl he probably met in a coffee shop, one of those girls who left home and was making her way across the country, maybe working as a waitress, with no family or friends to miss her. He got her pregnant and she tried to blackmail him, so he killed her.''

"What about the hand?"

"Simple. All priests have tremendous guilt complexes. They have to feel guilty about everything they do. Now, this was a terrible sin, and he couldn't go through life hiding it. He cut off the girl's hand and left it on the grave, where it would be sure to be found, because he wants an investigation started. He wants you to look for him. Only by getting caught can he rid himself of his terrible burden of guilt.''

Kelso shook his head. "What an incredible imagination you've got, Susan. First of all, I think someone told me Ullman's married.''

"So what? His wife's probably frigid. Anyway, who says a priest can't cheat on his wife?''

"In the second place, the girl's hand seems to have been cut off before she was killed.''

"Hmmm. That one's tougher. But he could've poisoned her and cut off her hand while she was unconscious.''

"No way. Dr. Paul says her hand was probably amputated five or six days before the murder. And she wasn't poisoned, she was shot.'' Susan shrugged. "Well, so much for that. What do *you* think happened?''

"I don't have any idea.'' Actually, something was beginning to nag at him. Something Eleanor had said about her séance. He tried to think what it was, but he was tired, and the room was too warm. Susan got up and came over to his chair, sat down on his lap, and whatever he'd been thinking went away completely. Her skirt rode farther up, exposing her thighs, as she put her arms around his neck. He caught the pleasant aroma of Chanel No. 5.

"Did you know," he said, "that I've got an amazing coincidence in my life? Every girl I've ever dated seriously has worn Chanel No. 5."

"No kidding? What other girls have you dated seriously? You never mentioned them before, George."

"There are so many," he said, "I've forgotten their names."

"You smell like pipe smoke." She did something to his ear with her tongue and he began pulling up her sweater. She wasn't wearing a bra. "Let's lie down on the sofa," she murmured.

"Are you still on pills?"

"No, I've decided to become secretly pregnant and force you to marry me. Come on." She pulled him up and they moved to the couch. He lay on his back and she tossed the pillows to the floor and began taking off her hose.

"We can't do this," Kelso said. "I've got to meet Smith pretty soon and besides, your aunt's here."

"Smith can wait," Susan said. "And Aunt Eleanor is probably already asleep. Yes, I'm sure she is, I can hear her snoring." She reached for his belt buckle as she bent her head to kiss him.

"I don't think—"

"Shut up, George," she said softly and her tongue darted into his mouth. She lay pressed against him and he stopped resisting.

"I have to go now," he said.

They were dressed and sitting next to each other on the couch. She was smoking a cigarette. She put it out and stood up, helped him on with his jacket and zipped it up. They went to the front door and out onto the porch.

"You'd better go in," he told her. "You'll get pneumonia."

"I love you," she said, huddling with her arms folded across her breasts.

"Thanks for the coffee."

"You're so romantic."

"I'm not the romantic type."

"At least you aren't frigid," she said, shivering.

"Men aren't frigid, women are."

"Not me."

"Yes, you are," Kelso said. "You're freezing."

"Call me tomorrow. Let me know how the case goes."

"I will."

"Father Ullman did it," she said, opening the door and stepping inside.

"In the dining room with the wrench," he said.

"I love you, George."

"Me too."

"You're impossible." She closed the door.

He stood there for a minute, seeing his breath, feeling a little strange, then hurried around the walk to his VW. He got in, whistling a tune from a musical, the name of which he had forgotten, started up the engine, and backed into the street. Everything was dark and empty. His watch read only eleven o'clock, so he drove aimlessly for a while feeling warm but slightly uneasy, before heading for the cemetery.

Chapter Seventeen

The Blue Angel

When he pulled up to the big main gates of Park Lawn at eleven-thirty, Smith was already parked across the street and he could see the faint red glow of a cigarette through the LTD's windshield. Washington Avenue at this point was bounded on either side by a high brick wall topped with wrought iron. Kelso pulled up behind Smith, cut the VW's engine, got out and went up to the LTD's driver's-side window, which was partway down. Smith's cold blue eyes looked out at him.

"Hello," Kelso said. "Is this the bus to the guardian angel?"

"Blue angel," Smith said. "Get in."

Kelso went around and got in. Smith crushed out his cigarette and immediately lit another. Kelso caught the first sweet aroma that always came from a freshly lit cigarette.

"If there was really a god," he said, "cigarettes would be good for your health."

"There is a god," Smith said. "He's weird and vengeful. Probably it wasn't fruit in the Garden of Eden, it was tobacco."

"They didn't have fire back then," Kelso pointed out.

"That was the serpent's job." Smith started the car and pulled across Washington Avenue to the cemetery entrance. "It had matches." He glanced at Kelso. "You look like the cat that ate the canary, only with a guilt complex."

"Huh?"

"How was Susan?"

128 MALCOLM MCCLINTICK

Kelso felt his face go hot. "Oh. She was okay."

"I'll bet." Smith drove slowly into a narrow lane bordered by row after row of tombstones, white near the headlights and fading into darkness.

"What's this all about, anyway?" Kelso asked gruffly.

"There's a story about it. Some rich guy named Eades had a little dog. They were both old and sick. Eades knew he was going to die soon, and the dog was in bad shape." He paused to flick his cigarette out the window. "Ashes to ashes," he said and chuckled.

"Very funny."

"Anyway, he had one of those big mausoleums built for himself and told the Park Lawn officials that he wanted to be buried in it with his dog. They said no way. No animals in the cemetery, it was reserved for the rotting carcasses of two-legged things, not four-legged."

"What a nice way you have of putting things," Kelso said.

"Thanks. Anyway, Eades was pissed. So the day before the cement for the mausoleum's floor was poured he had his dog put to sleep and that night he buried it there. When they poured the cement the next day, the deed was done. A couple of weeks later Eades died and was buried there."

"And the point is," Kelso prompted.

"And the point is, ever since then the place has been guarded at night by this blue angel, to keep anybody from digging up the dog."

"Bull. It sounds like something a high school kid would make up."

"Nope. I've seen it myself."

"No, you haven't."

"Yes, I have." Smith turned onto a side drive. The only light was from the car's headlamps, cutting twin swaths ahead. It was eerie. On either side tall trees rose up, clawing at them, and the neatly ordered rows of white stones marched away into the blackness.

"All those bodies," Kelso said. "It gives me the creeps. Have you ever considered how really bizarre this human habit is, Smith? This habit we have of taking corpses and sticking them into the ground in expensive boxes?"

"I've thought about it."

"How long will it be before the whole world is just one big cemetery?"

"Archaeologists will dig them up after so many years," Smith pointed out. "As long as they dig them up faster than they're buried, we'll be okay." The headlight beams swung around again as they turned into a still more narrow lane. "The Eades mausoleum is directly ahead."

"Where?"

"When we get within a few yards, you'll see the angel. There. Look at that, Kelso."

Smith braked the LTD to a halt. They sat motionless, listening to the engine idling, gazing straight ahead. Just at the limit of the high beams the mausoleum rose up in the darkness, and something or someone appeared to stand before it. A bluish white figure in a flowing robe, with wings and maybe a halo.

Kelso's voice came low. "This is weird. What the hell is it?"

"I told you. It's the blue angel." Smith cut the engine but left the lights on. "Come on, I'll show you."

"I think I'll stay in the car," Kelso said. He didn't believe it was an angel. There was no such thing. But he didn't feel like getting out. Cemeteries always affected him the same way.

"Suit yourself," Smith told him, opening his door so that the dome light came on. "I'm going up there. Jesus, you look pale. Are you all right?"

"I'm fine. Leave me alone."

The door shut with a loud bang and he watched Smith walk toward the mausoleum. It had nothing to do with the supernatural. All his life he'd steadfastly avoided funerals, anything to do with death. Ironically, his professional role of police detective brought him into constant contact with such things, but in that capacity he was somehow able to maintain an impersonal attitude. At all other times, however, he preferred to ignore the absurdity of nonexistence, as he had come to think of it. Where had he read that? In college, something about existentialism. That French guy, Sartre. He shrugged in the darkness of the car. Smith was nearing the mausoleum. Grimacing, Kelso made himself get out of the car.

Inside the structure Eades and his dog rested. Supposedly. The blue angel with its upraised wings stood at the entrance. I'm not afraid, he told himself, letting his right hand touch the handle of the .38 at his hip. He'd forgotten to leave it at the office. He remembered an incident three weeks ago when he'd chased two armed hoods down an alley after they'd shot a bank guard. There had been no question of fear or bravery at the time, he'd simply done what had to be done. They'd fired shots at him, and he'd returned fire, ducking behind one of those large steel garbage dumpsters with bullets whining around his head. The hoods had come to a dead end and surrendered, terrified that Kelso might kill them. Ghosts can't shoot, he thought angrily, and glared defiantly at Smith, who had now reached the structure and was gesturing at him.

"Come on, Kelso," he called.

Kelso marched himself forward, his footsteps loud in his ears. A few feet from Smith he stopped. There was no angel now, only some marks on the double doors of the mausoleum. He moved closer and peered at them.

"It's tarnish," Smith said. "And these little windows at the top of the doors. See how the headlights reflect on the tarnish and glass?"

It was the reflection that produced the glowing shape of something that could be imagined as the figure of an angel with robe, wings, and halo.

"You set me up, Smith."

"I just wanted to make a point."

"What point? I feel like a damn fool."

"That's because you are. Sorry. I only wanted to show you how easy it is to believe in the supernatural. You thought you'd see a blue angel, so you did. Same thing happened to me, first time I came here. Only I was with a girl." He smirked. "She was worth it."

"What a lousy thing to do," Kelso muttered. He walked up to the doors. By standing on tiptoe he could bring his eyes to window level, but the interior was black. He turned away. "Let's go. I hate this place."

"Okay."

They returned to the car and drove out of the cemetery.

"Don't ever do anything like that to me again, Smith."

"Oh, hell, Kelso, I didn't do anything to you. You did it to yourself."

"Did you make up that stuff about the old man and his dog?"

"It's just a story I've heard. I don't have the slightest idea if it's true or not." They pulled up behind Kelso's VW. "Listen, as long as we're out, let's go check Mary's grave again."

Kelso stared. "Are you crazy?"

"No. I'd like to see if anybody's around this late."

"Like who?"

"I don't know. Bald men, maybe. Devil worshippers. Who knows? If you'd rather not, I'll go alone."

"I don't want Leill and Meyer jumping all over me when you get bashed over the head. What the hell, I'll go with you." He felt that he had to go, that it was the only way to redeem his self-respect. "I'll follow you."

There were no other cars in the parking lot of St. Luke's Church. Smith got two flashlights from the trunk of his LTD and handed one to Kelso. It was cold, the wind had died, the sky was sprinkled with stars.

"Let's go," Kelso said. "I don't want to hang around here all night."

"We won't."

They entered the woods and made their way down to the clearing. This time the twisting path seemed more familiar. Their shoes sounded uncomfortably loud on the leaves; anyone within half a mile could hear them approaching. Kelso wondered if anyone from the house was lurking nearby in the dark, maybe a bald man named Harold, waiting for some unsuspecting girl to come along. No, he thought. Not this late. No girl in her right mind would visit Mary's grave at midnight, after a severed hand and a dead body had been discovered there.

As soon as he thought "no girl in her right mind" he

immediately thought of Rosemary McAllister and Dr. Winthrop's schizophrenic niece Charlotte.

"Here we are," Smith said, stepping out into the clearing and shining his light around. It was empty of people. "Just us and the ghosts. Hail, Mary, wherever you are."

"Funny," Kelso muttered. He, too, let his light move around the edges of the clearing, making shadows move. Something in the trees made a constant rasping noise— crickets or frogs, he wasn't sure. The smell was strong, rotting leaves and smoke from burning wood. The whole city was thick with smoke in October.

"Reminds me of Scout camp," Smith said. "You ever go to camp, Kelso?"

"Yeah, I did." And church camp, too. But he didn't say it.

"Listen."

Car doors slammed from the direction of the parking lot.

"Somebody else is here," Smith said. "Sort of late for it."

"Here they come," Kelso said. And now they could hear clearly the crunch of leaves on the path. "Let's hide and see who it is."

"Have you got your gun?"

"Yeah."

Now a light flickered high up through the trees. The footsteps were louder.

Kelso turned and followed Smith into the woods on the far side of the clearing. He stood behind a tree and watched Smith disappear into the shadows a few feet away. They waited, surrounded by cold, woods, and midnight blackness, listening and watching as the crunching footsteps came louder and the flickering light bobbed its way into the clearing.

Chapter Eighteen

Two Witnesses

Kelso's eyes had begun to adapt, so that at the last minute, as the footsteps and light entered the clearing, he could see rather clearly. It was a young couple. The guy held a flashlight, casting its beam all around, and said something to the girl in a tone so low he couldn't catch the words. The girl kept whispering and giggling. Almost immediately they went over to the monument base and the guy held his light on it for a moment. Then the light winked out and the couple came to stand in the center of the area.

"There's nobody down here but us, Elaine," the guy said. "I told you it'd be all right." He spoke in a normal voice now, and from the sound of it Kelso guessed he was in his teens.

"But what about those cars in the lot?" the girl said.

"Must've been somebody at the church. Who knows? But there's nobody here."

"Are you sure?"

"Of course I'm sure. If anybody was here, we'd see 'em. Trust me, Elaine."

Kelso wondered if he and Smith had caught their killer, quite by accident, just as he was preparing to make this girl his next victim. He stood still, breathing carefully, listening to the things in the trees, and let his right hand rest on the handle of his .38. He waited, straining to see better. Fortunately the moon was up now. The couple stood close together with their arms around each other, and there was the unmistakable sound of a kiss. It annoyed him. He felt like a voyeur. But he had to wait and make certain they were what they seemed to be before he made a move.

They'd gone directly to the stone where the hand had been found. That rang in his head like an alarm bell. Maybe the guy had left the hand, and was checking to see if it was still there.

"What if somebody's hiding in the woods?" the girl said. "How could those cars be someone at the church this late?"

"Come on, Elaine." The guy sounded impatient. "Nobody's hiding in the woods."

Yes, we are, thought Kelso.

The boy switched on his light again and the beam made a quick circle around the clearing, illuminating the trees at about chest level. "Hey, all you zombies out there," the guy called in a mocking tone, "come out, come out, wherever you are." The girl giggled. He turned out the light. "See? There's nobody here but us. And the living dead. Wooo . . ."

"Stop it, Bill." She laughed nervously.

"Mary's ghost is coming to get you," he said. "You better hold me tight, here she comes!"

"Bill . . ." The girl laughed in protest and it was quiet again. They embraced.

Once again Kelso heard the sounds of smooching. He sighed to himself. Now what was he supposed to do? They might stand there making out for an hour. If he and Smith tried to sneak away through the woods, the couple would hear them immediately. But he wasn't going to stand here behind this tree all night, listening to a couple of horny teenagers going at it.

He peered out from around his tree again, hoping the cold might drive them back up to their car. Actually, there were a couple of questions he'd like to ask this kid, such as why he'd gone directly to Mary's gravestone when he'd entered the clearing. He could see them; they were only a few feet away, the girl's arms were around the guy's neck and his arms were around her waist. In the stillness he could hear their breathing becoming heavy. Then the zipper of the girl's jacket made a loud noise as the boy opened it and unbuttoned her white blouse. His other hand went beneath her skirt and their gasps became harsher.

He moved completely behind his tree again, embarrassed and irritated. But there was nothing he could think of to do.

"Let's lie down," he heard the boy say.

"My dress'll get dirty."

"We'll take it off," he said.

She began uttering little moaning sounds.

This had gone far enough. Kelso stooped, felt around on the ground, and found a small stone. He picked it up and tossed it into the woods, in the direction of the house. For a second or two there was nothing, then came the faint crunch as the stone landed several yards away.

Instantly the girl's voice came in a half whisper, high and frightened. "Bill! What was *that*?"

"What the hell . . ."

"Did you hear that?"

Kelso tossed a larger stone in the same direction, not quite as far. It landed with a louder noise.

"Bill, somebody's coming!"

"Jesus, Elaine . . ."

The sound of a zipper going up, then another.

"We'd better get out of here," the boy said, sounding angry and afraid.

Then they were plunging onto the path to the lot, the flashlight bobbing again, making no attempt at stealth. When the light could no longer be seen Smith's voice came in a hiss. "Kelso?"

"Yeah?"

"What the hell's happening? Is somebody coming?"

"No. I threw a couple of rocks."

A shadow split off from a nearby tree and became Smith. "What'd you do that for?"

"It was getting embarrassing. Come on, I want to ask that guy a couple of questions." Kelso turned on his light and made for the path.

"What a damned prude you are, Kelso. Just when it was getting interesting."

"Come on, or we'll lose them."

He made his way as quickly as possible up the zigzagging path, tripping on roots and vines, fighting off fingerlike branches, and broke out into the open just as the boy was closing the passenger door of a red Trans Am. His date was already inside. Red sports car, Kelso thought, as the boy came around and reached for the driver's door. The new light on the parking-lot pole bathed the area.

"Hold on," Kelso called, trotting toward the car. "Wait a minute."

The boy's head jerked around. Fear showed clearly on his young face. "Get away from me!" His hand grabbed for the door handle.

"Police," Kelso said, holding up his leather folder.

"Police!" The boy stared, hesitant. "What for? I haven't done anything."

"I know you haven't," Kelso replied, catching his breath. He was aware that Smith had come up alongside him. "I just want to ask you and your friend a couple of questions."

The girl leaned across to the driver's window of the Trans Am and looked out at them, wide-eyed. She was younger than he'd thought, probably no more than fourteen, with a thin, delicately featured face, large dark eyes, and long soft hair. The guy was tall, heavily built, broad shouldered, and his cheeks and the tip of his nose were red. About seventeen, Kelso guessed.

"Bill," the girl called. "What's happening? What's wrong?"

"Nothing," he snapped, sounding disgusted. "Stay in the car, Elaine."

Smith said, "You could be in a lot of trouble, kid. This is private property. You ever hear of trespassing?"

"Listen, Bill," Kelso said. "That's your name, right? Bill?"

"Bill Riley." His tone went sullen, defensive. "I'm a senior at North High. I'm on the football team. And I haven't done anything wrong, officer."

"All I want is some information, Bill. Were you and your friend here last night?"

The boy was confused. He didn't see what this had to

do with anything. He'd just been down at Mary's grave with his girl, making out with her and maybe planning to go further than that, when suddenly things had fallen apart and now he was being questioned by the cops. Probably he wasn't sure if he was being arrested for feeling up his girl, or for trespassing, or maybe for possession of whatever he might happen to have in the glove box of his Trans Am. And now there was a question about last night.

On the other hand, he was driving a red sports car, which Helen Kramer had spotted upon leaving choir practice when she and her friend had heard the screams. Maybe she'd spotted the kid's Trans Am. And he'd gone right to the stone on which the murdered girl's hand had been found, as if he'd maybe put it there himself.

"He asked you a question," Smith said, playing it tough. "Were you here last night?"

"Why?" the boy asked. As if to stall for time. He was chewing his lip.

He's nervous, Kelso thought. He knows something. I'll find out.

"It's just a routine investigation," he said. "Were you here?"

The kid's eyes narrowed. He'd decided to be difficult, now that the initial shock had worn off. After all, his parents were probably well off, his dad had popped for the new Trans Am, he was on the football team, and he couldn't lose face in front of this obviously nice girl, the kind of girl who was a cheerleader, made good grades, went to church on Sunday, and went down to Mary's grave at midnight during the week and let football players reach under her skirt. The kid looked stubborn and said nothing.

"Let's take him downtown and book him," Smith said.

"You can't take me downtown," the boy said.

"I can't, huh?" Smith stepped up to him. The kid was almost as tall as Smith, and looked strong, but Smith was bigger and heavier and stronger. He leered. "Listen, you little piece of shit. You've got two choices. You can start answering questions right now, without any goddamned lip, or we can take both you and your pretty little broad downtown and call your parents to come bail you out. And

before they come to bail you out, you'll be charged with
trespassing and resisting arrest and other things I'll think
of on the way down, and you'll be printed and stripped
and searched and put in a holding cell with some people
that'll make me look like the Easter bunny. Either way
you want it.'' Smith brought out his handcuffs and held
them up for the boy to see. ''What's it going to be?''

''I know my rights,'' the kid said, but his voice was
shaking.

''Go check his glove compartment, Kelso, while I read
him the rights he already knows.''

''Wait!'' It was the girl. ''Bill, tell them!'' She looked
at Kelso, a frightened little girl with big eyes. ''We were
here last night, sir. I'm Elaine Rogers. We didn't do anything wrong.''

''Okay, Elaine,'' Kelso said kindly. ''What time were
you here?''

''It was about nine.''

''Did you see or hear anything unusual?''

''We didn't have anything to do with it,'' Bill blurted.
''Nothing.''

''Nothing to do with what, kid?'' Smith asked.

''With what happened.'' He looked upset. The fight had
left his eyes. He would talk now. He was through with
being difficult. He looked at Kelso. ''Elaine and me, we
were just fooling around down there. You know? And we
heard somebody coming. So we hid behind a tree and
waited to see who it was. Like, if it was somebody we
might know. So we're behind this tree, and somebody
comes into the clearing. And it looks like they put something down on Mary's grave. On that big stone to one
side.''

''The one with the engraving on it?'' Kelso asked.

''No. The other one.''

''And then what?''

''So then they left.''

''Which way'd they go?'' Smith asked.

''The way they came. Not from the lot, but from the
other way.''

''Did you see what they left on the stone?'' Kelso asked.

"We went over and looked as soon as they'd left. You already know, don't you? That's what this is all about. Well, we didn't have anything to do with it, I swear. It wasn't us."

"Nobody said it was," Kelso said. "What was on the stone?"

The boy shrugged. "You already know."

"Pretend we don't," Smith snapped. "And tell us."

"It was a hand." The boy took a deep breath and let it out. "You know, a human hand. Like it'd been cut off of an arm. Elaine screamed, and we got out of there."

"Is that what you were doing tonight?" Kelso asked. "Looking to see if it was still there?"

"Yeah. Well, I saw the news on TV, I knew it'd been found, but I was looking at where it'd been. You know—just curious."

"Okay," Kelso said. "What did the person look like?"

"Well, it was raining on and off," the boy said. "I didn't see him all that good. But I know he was tall. Tall and thin. And he had on glasses, because I remember seeing his flashlight reflecting in his lenses."

"How tall was he?"

"I'm not sure. I'm six feet; I'd say he was about my height. Maybe an inch or two taller."

"How was he dressed?"

"It was pretty dark, except for his flashlight. Dark pants, dark raincoat. That's all I can remember."

"Okay. Anything else? Hair? Eyes? Face?"

"I don't think so. Oh, yeah. He was bald. You know, with a fringe." He drew a finger around the side of his head from ear to ear. "Bald on top."

Smith said, "You sure about that, kid?"

"Yeah, I'm sure."

"How many times did Elaine scream?" Kelso asked.

"I didn't count."

"Twice," Elaine said from the car. "I screamed twice."

"And then you left?"

"In a hurry."

"Were there cars up here in the lot besides your own?"

"Yeah," the guy said. "Choir practice was letting out. I recognized Elaine's mother, but she didn't see us."

"Lucky for you," Smith said sarcastically, and the kid glared.

So much for witnesses, Kelso thought disgustedly. No one in the choir knew anybody with a red sports car, but one woman's daughter was dating a guy who drove one. Maybe she didn't know who her daughter dated. Probably she didn't care.

"Okay, Bill," Kelso said. "That's all we need. You can go now."

Bill stood there with his jaw muscles working, ready to get into his car but not quite doing it yet. He seemed to want something else. Finally he looked almost sideways at Kelso and asked in a low voice, "Were you and your partner down there just now? I mean, for a long time?"

"It was dark," Kelso said. "We couldn't see anything."

"But we heard a lot," Smith said, and chuckled.

The boy's face went red. He jerked open the driver's door and got in, slamming it shut. The engine caught and revved, the car turned sharply, tires squealing, and accelerated down the driveway. Just before it turned into Amsterdam Avenue, Kelso caught a glimpse of the girl's face peering out from her passenger window, then the Trans Am roared away into the night.

"Kids." Smith put away his handcuffs. "You suppose her mother and father know she's running around at this hour with some bastard who takes her to the woods and feels her up and wants her to lie down?"

"They probably don't care."

"Yeah." He stepped over to his car. "Well, I'm going home and get some sleep now."

"Same here." Kelso opened the door of his VW. "That bald guy they saw, that's got to be the same guy Rosemary saw on Monday with the murdered girl and the same guy she saw hit me over the head last night."

"It would seem so."

"I still can't figure out why he wanted her hand found, but not her body."

"Because he's nuts," Smith said. "See you tomorrow."

"There's got to be more of a reason than that. And by the way, if the bald guy wore glasses, that more or less eliminates Ullman."

"No, it doesn't. Ullman could own a pair of specs."

"We'll have to find out," Kelso said.

"You got any other theories about the case as we stand here freezing our asses in the wee hours of the morning?" Smith asked.

"No," Kelso said, and got into the VW Beetle. "See you at work."

"Okay."

They drove away from the place. Kelso proceeded south to the opposite end of the city, and it was past twelve-thirty when he pulled up in the parking space in front of his apartment door. Inside, he fed his cat, drank some milk, and ate a stale yeast donut, then trudged upstairs to bed.

Tossing restlessly, he tried to recall what it was that had bothered him about Susan's aunt's séance. Somehow it seemed to fit in with Rosemary McAllister's similarity to Charlotte, the schizophrenic girl at the house. His mind filled with images of girls without hands and a bald monster that moved through the dark night woods in search of women to maim. He slept, and the images became nightmares from which he did not awaken until dawn.

Chapter Nineteen

Picture of a Ghost

The next day was Thursday, October 30. Kelso awoke early with a bad taste in his mouth, grimacing at the bright sunlight streaming in through his bedroom windows. Immediately the problem was back in his mind: something about a séance. But he could get no further with it than that. The cat was on his bed, pressing its body against his hip. When he rolled over to get up, it glared, then began to lick itself.

He showered, shaved, dressed in corduroys, a blue Oxford shirt, wool sweater, and crepe-soled shoes. He had a cup of instant coffee, fed the cat, stuck his pipe between his teeth, put on his jacket, and went out.

The sunlight wasn't going to last long; already, large grayish clouds were blowing in from the northwest and the forecast was for an increasing chance of rain with temperatures mostly in the low fifties. Something about a séance. He frowned, cranked up the yellow Bug, and drove off toward town.

For once he was more interested in getting to work than in eating, so he headed directly to the Municipal Building. He had the feeling that something would happen and he'd miss it, or that something was about to happen.

The duty room was the same as usual: Broom sat at his desk, wiping his red nose with a tissue, while Smith sat idly flipping the pages of a magazine. Kelso couldn't make out the title, but on the cover could be seen a photo of a nude girl with long hair, smiling at the camera. Kelso went to his desk, removed his jacket, and sat down.

"Sleep well?" Smith asked without looking up.

"More or less."

"Huh." Whether a reference to Kelso's statement or to something in the sex magazine wasn't clear.

"I hate this cold," Broom said, blowing his nose.

"Then why in hell did you come in?" Smith eyed Broom briefly. "Why come in here and infect the rest of us? You should've stayed home."

"Possibly."

"Try doubling your antihistamine," Kelso said, and left the room. He went down the hall to Identification and asked to see their current mug books. In reality there were too many books for him to examine in a short period of time, but he'd already gone through a number of them recently. The clerk, a young uniformed policewoman, handed him five of the latest. He thanked her, wondered if her slow smile meant anything, and carried the books back to the duty room. He stacked them on his desk, sat down, and began going through them one by one.

"What are you looking for?" Smith asked, tossing his magazine into a drawer.

"A six-foot bald man in glasses."

"Can't tell how tall they are from the pictures, can you?"

Broom chuckled and sneezed.

"All the statistics are with the photos," Kelso said. Smith knew, of course; he was just being funny.

"Meyer says to tell you nobody in the neighborhood could identify the girl's picture," Broom said, blowing his nose. "Except one old man, a retired physics professor, who recalled having seen a girl of that description walking late at night. He often strolls at nine-thirty or so in the evenings, and says he thinks he's passed her a few times."

Kelso looked up. "Was she ever with a bald man?"

"No. Alone."

"When was the last time?"

"About a week ago. He thinks it was on a Wednesday night."

"That would be the twentieth," Smith said, looking at his calendar.

"The twentieth." Kelso opened his notebook. "Dr.

Paul's estimate would place the amputation on the next day. No, wait a minute. You're looking at the wrong calendar, Smith. Wednesday was the twenty-second. The hand could have been amputated on either Tuesday or Wednesday.''

"I thought we had secretaries to change the calendars,'' Smith said irritably, ripping a page off and crumpling it into a ball.

"Also,'' Broom said, "the red car is a deadend. No one in that neighborhood has seen a red sports car recently.''

"We found the car.'' Kelso told him about the young couple. "Now we're looking for a bald man with glasses.''

"Has anything come of the dental records?'' Smith asked.

"No.'' Broom shook his head and sniffed loudly. "Her impressions and X-rays were sent to all the area dentists, but so far that's a deadend, too.''

"She was a real person,'' Smith said. "Somebody had to know her.''

An hour passed. Kelso found seventeen tall bald men with glasses, but none were good prospects. They were doing time in various institutions, or they were on probation, or they'd been arrested recently and were awaiting trial. He made a note to check out five of them who might have been free to cut the girl's hand off the week before and then murder her a few days later, but he had no great hopes of turning up anything.

"Hell with it,'' he muttered, closed the last book, and carried them back down the hall to Identification. The female clerk smiled at him again. "Doing anything for lunch today?'' he asked experimentally.

"Eating with my boyfriend,'' she replied, the smile fading instantly.

"Have fun,'' he told her. So much for smiles.

Back in the duty room he said, "So what's on the agenda today? Where's Meyer, anyway?''

"He called,'' Broom said, "and won't be in till this afternoon. Leill's got him doing something or other.'' He sniffed loudly.

"Huh. Hey, Smith, have you ever been to a séance?"

"Sure."

"What was it like?"

"I don't know. Not much happened. I sat around a table with four other people and after about an hour we all got bored and left."

"Want to get some breakfast?"

"Sure."

Kelso put on his jacket again. As he and Smith moved to the door he glanced back at Broom, who again was blowing his nose. "Hey, Broom, want to come with us?"

"I think I may go home."

"You should," Kelso told him. "Frankly, you look like hell."

"Frankly, I feel like hell." He sneezed.

"Bless you."

Smith drove, as usual, and on the way he asked. "What are we doing today?"

"I think there's a bald guy with glasses in that house," Kelso said. "I want to find out."

"Sounds great, Kelso. How do you plan to do it? Go up to the door and ask to see a bald guy with glasses?"

"We're a little testy today, aren't we?"

Smith swerved to avoid a city bus that had decided to occupy two lanes at once, sounded his horn, and shook a raised fist at the driver. "No, we are not testy this morning. *I* am testy this morning. I had a lousy night. My stomach was upset and kept me awake, and when I did sleep I had these terrible dreams about somebody trying to cut off my hands."

"I'm surprised," Kelso said mildly.

"What?"

"I didn't know vegetarians ever had upset stomachs or sleepless nights."

"Fuck you, Kelso."

"What about that séance you were telling me about? Do you remember if there was a medium?"

"A medium? No, not a real one. Just me and four other people."

"Were you trying to contact any particular person's spirit?"

"I don't remember. What difference does it make?"

"I'm not sure."

They pulled into the parking lot of a Pancake House and went in. Over pancakes and links, Kelso brooded about the séance and the bald man, while Smith ate cold cereal with raisin toast. He brought out the photo of the dead girl and examined it while he drank his second cup of coffee and puffed at his pipe, which, for once, stayed lit.

"Dark hair and dark eyes," he said. "Thin pale face. Small features."

"So what," Smith said, still in a foul mood. His ice-blue eyes had been tracking the younger waitresses around the restaurant.

"I wonder where the descriptions of Mary come from."

"Mary?"

"Yeah. You know—Mary's ghost. I mean, what is it? Some kind of rumor thing? Why does everybody have the same idea of the way she looked? A girl who was buried at the turn of the century, eighty years ago, and everybody gives the same description of her. That's sort of strange, don't you think?"

"I suppose."

A thin redheaded waitress with heavy eyeliner came over with their check and a coffee pot. "Everything all right?"

"Just fine," Kelso said. "Say, have you ever heard of Mary's grave?"

She nodded. "Sure. I've been there, lots of times."

"Really?"

"Sure. With my boyfriend." She refilled their cups.

"Have you ever seen Mary's ghost?"

"Me?" She gave a quiet laugh. "No, not me. But a friend of mine did once. You guys going down there? It really is sorta spooky, you know?"

"Did your friend say what Mary looked like?" Kelso asked.

"Well, I don't know. Hmm, let's see. I don't know if it was her or somebody else, okay? But somebody told me she's supposed to look, you know, not too tall, dark hair, dark eyes, maybe a sort of thin face. But it's just stuff I've heard. Well, you guys have a nice day.''

Kelso couldn't resist. ''Just a minute.'' He held out the dead girl's picture. ''Did she look anything like this, do you think?''

The waitress blinked a couple of times, then she frowned. ''That's not very funny,'' she said. ''Not very funny at all.'' She hurried off.

He looked at Smith. ''See what I mean?''

Smith shrugged, lighting a Kent. ''I'm not impressed. So what? So five people think they know what Mary looked like, and they tell a bunch of other people, and it spreads. What's so great about that?''

''I don't know. But I've got a feeling it's important. Damn, I wish I could figure out what's bothering me about that séance.''

They left and drove out Amsterdam Avenue, parked at the curb, and got out.

''Wait a minute,'' Kelso said, ''I'm tired of going through the woods. Let's go see what the front of the house looks like.''

''You mean you want to walk right up in their front yard?'' Smith asked.

''Sure. Why not?''

Smith shrugged and got back in the car. ''Nothing, I guess.'' Kelso got in and they drove around the corner onto Wilhelm Drive and parked a few feet from the driveway. A heavy chain was fastened across the drive between two stone pillars. The sky had become completely overcast; a cold wind moved leaves along the street and brought more fluttering down from the trees.

''Looks like the trick-or-treaters are going to freeze their butts tomorrow night,'' Smith said.

''Looks like it. Do you do anything for Halloween?''

Smith grimaced. ''If you mean, do I sit around with bags of candy and wait for creepy little kids to show up at my door, no, I do not. I hate 'em. I try to be away if I can. Don't tell me *you* do it.''

''Well, Susan and her aunt enjoy it, so usually I spend

the evening with them. They like to see the kids in their costumes and all. We pop some corn and—''

''I don't want to hear about it,'' Smith snapped, and strode quickly toward the yard.

A long paved walk bisected the immense front lawn, which sloped uphill toward the house. Tall trees, stone benches, and numerous marble statues made it like a park. In the cold flat light of the overcast morning it looked eerie. Leaves rustled everywhere.

Before them the house loomed, an imposing three-story Tudor with leaded-glass windows. Kelso had the uneasy feeling that they were trespassing, and had to remind himself that they were here on official business.

''I think we're being watched,'' Smith said, slowing his pace slightly.

''Why, do you see something?'' Kelso scanned the front of the house for movement. The door was closed, the windows were blank. Nothing.

''It's just a feeling I've got. A bad feeling.''

''It's your imagination,'' Kelso said. But he wasn't so sure.

At the front door Kelso found a button and pressed it. They could hear no sound from inside, but a few seconds later—so quickly that he wondered if in fact they *had* been observed—the huge wooden door opened slowly inward. It didn't squeak on its hinges but it should have. He recognized the thin dark-haired woman scowling out at them; Winthrop's sister, the woman who'd tried to keep them from entering the day before. She looked like the classic spinster, or the classic misconception of one—gaunt, angry, rigidly straight in a severe black dress which hid everything but her head, hands, and shoes.

''Yes?'' she said harshly. ''What is it this time?''

''Good morning,'' Kelso said politely. ''Sergeant Kelso and Detective Smith. I wonder if we could see Dr. Winthrop again for a few minutes.''

She stared him down like a cat. ''Why?'' The word came out hard and demanding.

He kept his voice pleasant with an effort. He thought she was an old bat, and it would've been nice to tell her so, but instead he said: "We're still investigating the murder of a girl near here, ma'am." He started to add something else, but didn't. That was all she needed to know.

He thought she was going to protest again, but then something flickered in her yellowish eyes and she stepped back, pulled the heavy door the rest of the way open and stood to one side with a pained expression on her skull-like face.

"Very well. Come in and I'll get him."

"Thanks," Smith said, overly cheerful. "We sure appreciate it." If she recognized his irony, she didn't acknowledge it.

"Wait here," she told him icily, closed the door, glared once as if wondering whether to trust them with the hall carpet, then stalked away. The carpet was a thick Oriental thing which they couldn't have stolen without a crew of experts.

"Charming lady," Smith said. "Almost asked her out."

"Good thing you didn't. She might've accepted."

"Reminds me of somebody in one of those Charles Addams cartoons."

"I think she *is* somebody in one of those Charles Addams cartoons," Kelso replied.

Smith smiled faintly. His mood seemed to have lightened. After a time, a door opened and closed somewhere down in the shadows at the far end of the hall and presently the bulky well-dressed form of Dr. Winthrop approached, looking distinguished in a dark blue three-piece suit, his gut bulging out royally, a silk tie knotted neatly at his starched white collar.

"Well, well, my detective friends again. Welcome, welcome. Would you gentlemen care for some coffee?"

"No thanks," Kelso said. "We won't take up much of your time today, Doctor."

"Come along, it's drafty in the hall." He seemed more stilted than before. "Let's adjourn to the drawing room, shall we? There's a cozy fire in there. This way, please."

They followed him down the hall and were ushered through a door on the right, into the same room they'd been in before, though yesterday he'd called it the living room. Maybe it depended on the time of day, Kelso speculated, and sank into a large overstuffed chair. Smith did likewise. The doctor remained standing with his back to the fire, hands behind him, small dark eyes watching them carefully. The room seemed as drab and lifeless as ever. The cigarettes were still in the small china cup on the table in the middle of the room.

"Now then, gentlemen. Did you wish refreshment?"

"No, thanks," Kelso said. "All we really need is for you to take a look at a picture. If you don't mind."

"A picture. A photograph, I assume you mean. Most assuredly. Anyone I know?" He smiled, but somehow it didn't seem genuine. Kelso stood, got out the picture, and took it over to the doctor. Winthrop held it. There wasn't the slightest change in his expression. He gazed at it for a while, then raised his eyes.

"Yes?" he asked blandly.

"Do you recognize her?"

"It's no one I know."

"Not one of your patients or anything?"

"Definitely not. Although, if you'll permit me an observation, Sergeant Kelso, it does bear a certain similarity, in fact a remarkable similarity, to descriptions of Mary's ghost." He smiled.

"Mary's ghost," Smith said. He went over to the center table, peered at the china cup, and pulled out one of the cigarettes. He rolled it in his fingers, sniffed at it, and lit it.

"Help yourself," Winthrop said dryly.

"You think it looks like Mary's ghost?" Smith asked.

"I think it looks like *descriptions* of the ghost." Winthrop was a very careful man.

"Have you ever seen Mary's ghost?" Kelso asked.

"There's a ghost in this house, as I've told you." Winthrop shrugged his heavy shoulders. "I've seen it several times. But I've never had the good fortune to see the spirit of Mary Carter." He paused, then added softly, "As I believe I have also told you."

"We'd like Margaret to look at the photograph," Kelso said.

"Of course. Anything to help the police."

As you have often told us, Kelso thought.

"Anything for the cause, eh?" Winthrop went to the door, opened it, and called out into the hall, "Margaret, would you come in here for a moment?" Leaving the hall door open, he returned to the fireplace and stood with his back to the fire, rubbing his hands briskly together as if they were cold. It did seem fairly drafty in the room. Probably hard to heat a place this large, Kelso imagined.

Presently Margaret entered. It struck Kelso that she must have been hovering around out there fairly near the door to have heard her brother. Winthrop hadn't called *that* loudly. Now she stood just inside the room, her narrow face cold and hostile, as if she were being asked to shed her clothes in public.

"Our friends here," Winthrop said, with a sweep of his arm, "have something they'd like you to look at."

Margaret turned her face toward her brother and for a few seconds their eyes locked in combat. Kelso had the distinct impression of a fierce struggle; then Margaret seemed to wilt a little, shrugged, and said sullenly, "Oh, all right. What is it?"

"Just a photo, ma'am." Kelso took it over to her. "Would you take a look and tell us if it's anybody you've seen before?"

She stood with both hands at her sides and glared. Kelso almost stepped back; a kind of malevolence seemed to emanate from her yellowish-brown eyes, he could feel it pressing against him, as if suddenly he had come upon something tangibly evil. Now he could appreciate the tremendous force of will that must have been exerted by Winthrop in staring her down. But he stood his ground, stubbornly and defiantly. A girl's hand had been cut off and she'd been shot; Kelso wasn't going to allow the investigation to be obstructed by a particularly evil woman with a particularly malignant personality.

Finally she must have decided that it was useless, or that she didn't want to spend the rest of the morning defying him, or that she was in effect defying Winthrop. For whatever reason, she reached out suddenly with one clawlike hand—she had very long sharp nails—and snatched the picture from Kelso's fingers. Her face had gone pink. She held the thing to her eyes, glared briefly, then shoved it back at him. He took it, avoiding her nails.

"Anybody you know?" Smith asked cheerfully.

Her face twitched but she ignored him, keeping her scowl fastened on Kelso. In a sharp, biting voice she said, "I've never seen her before in my life. Does that satisfy you? May I go now?"

There was nothing more to be gotten from Margaret. Kelso shrugged.

"Yes, that's all."

She jerked her head around to shoot a last narrow-eyed glance at her brother, then turned and moved quickly out of the room. The door banged shut.

Winthrop laughed suddenly, so that his belly shook. When he'd quit, he smiled and said, "Well, gentlemen, I'm afraid we haven't been able to help you very much. May I offer you that coffee now? Or a brandy? Or is it time for you to go back out into the cold and pursue your inquiries elsewhere?"

Yes, thought Kelso, that's what he'd like. He'd like us to pursue our inquiries elsewhere.

"Excuse me," he said, "but I wonder if we could have Charlotte take a look at it, and maybe the—"

"Absolutely not." Dr. Winthrop's smile disappeared and his face went tight and hard. His eyes narrowed to slits. "Out of the question. I'm sorry. She's decompensated, been having psychotic symptoms today."

"If she could just look at it—"

"I told you, it's out of the question. Do you really want an insane woman to look at a photograph?"

"Isn't she on medication?" Smith asked.

"Of course."

"What's she doing right now? Is she here? We can get a warrant."

"Of all the . . . a warrant is—"

"I'm not kidding around," Smith said, as if he meant it. And maybe he did. "This is a homicide investigation, not some game. We didn't come here to look for ghosts,

Doctor. We've got a dead girl on our hands, and somebody in this house might have seen her. Is Charlotte on medication right now? Is she stable? I want to see her. Or we'll come back with a warrant.''

Winthrop's thick hands came around from behind his bulk and became fists. The muscles at his jaws moved, as if he were chewing something. He said hotly, "Charlotte believes literally in Mary's ghost. This picture you have greatly resembles descriptions of such a ghost. Do you understand? Are you too dense to understand? If Charlotte sees this, she will think it is a picture of the ghost, and she's likely to become hysterical.''

"Isn't she tranquilized?''

"She's medicated. It's not the same thing at all.''

"Go get her,'' Smith said.

Another battle of wills. But this time the doctor was up against, not his sister, but the power of the police and the authority of the state. He seemed to know that. Even so, Kelso was mildly surprised when Winthrop's anger faded to sullenness and he said sourly, "Oh very well, if you must have your way. But I hope you will understand that any setback in her condition is entirely your fault, and I'll take it up with your superiors if necessary.''

"We understand,'' Smith replied, his eyes like ice.

"I will go and get her. If she's awake and cognizant, you may see her. Otherwise, I'll ask you to come back another time.'' He crossed to the door and went out. The door slammed.

Kelso's pipe had gone out. He prowled around the room until he found the ashtray, knocked out the ashes, then shoved the pipe into a pocket.

"You think he's really worried about her health?'' he asked.

"Smokescreen,'' Smith said. "He's covering up something.''

"He's her analyst. Maybe she's really overtly psychotic today.''

"Very conveniently timed.''

The door opened and Winthrop came in with the girl. At once something about her appearance and demeanor struck Kelso. It was almost like *déjà vu*, and not just because they'd been here and seen her once before. He frowned. Once again he realized what a striking resemblance Charlotte bore to Rosemary McAllister. And then, like a second bolt of lightning just after a first: both resembled the murdered girl.

Winthrop acted formal and impatient. "Shall we get it over with, gentlemen? As her psychiatrist, I must insist that she stay here only a moment or two. Charlotte, these gentlemen would like to show you a photograph."

She stood uncertainly near the door, small pale hands clasped before her like a serving girl, enhancing her resemblance to Rosemary. Her dark eyes were downcast, her face was narrow and pale, her expression was dull and almost lifeless. As if she were on some sort of drug. Her antipsychotic medication?

"All right," she whispered.

The feeling of *déjà vu* continued. The same scene had been played out before, but the other time it had been in Father Ullman's office, and Rosemary McAllister had been the dull lifeless girl wringing her hands and afraid to raise her glance to anyone's eyes.

Kelso, beginning to wonder if he was making a mistake but determined now to see it through, stepped up to the girl and offered her the snapshot of the murder victim's face. He spoke as gently as possible.

"Miss, would you just look at this and tell me if you know her?"

Without unclasping her hands, Charlotte brought her eyes up. For a count of three there was no reaction, and Kelso speculated that whatever drug coursed through the girl's veins had shut off any possibility of a response. Then her eyes widened abruptly and she sucked in her breath.

"It's her!" Charlotte stepped back, her face contorting in fear. "It's her!"

"Gentlemen—" Winthrop boomed.

Quickly, Kelso asked, "Who is it, Charlotte?"

"It's her!" The girl screamed. "It's Mary!" Then she was simply screaming, eyes bulging, mouth wide, screaming over and over. The sounds shot through Kelso's nervous system like electric shocks as Margaret rushed into the room.

Dr. Winthrop had reached the girl's side. "Hold her!" he snapped, and from somewhere in the vast bulk of his clothing he produced a syringe and a small vial. He stabbed the needle into the top of the vial, pulled out the plunger to suck clear liquid into the syringe, jerked it free of the vial, and jammed the needle into Charlotte's upper arm.

The girl jerked convulsively, still screaming. Margaret's face was screwed up into rage. Winthrop looked pale and angry. He pressed the plunger home and withdrew the needle. A droplet of blood formed at the point of injection and glistened like a tiny ruby in the light from the chandelier. Charlotte took a breath, seemed about to scream again; then her eyes fluttered and a dazed look came into them as she sagged into Margaret's arms.

"Take her to bed, please," Winthrop said.

Margaret walked the girl out of the room, practically carrying her. The door closed. The doctor glared. Kelso could see little beads of sweat on the man's broad forehead.

"Well, I hope you gentlemen are satisfied."

"I'm sorry," Kelso said. "But we had to show her the photo." He hesitated, then added, "Could we see Harold for a minute?"

"Harold is off today. I'm going to have to ask you to leave now."

"We want to see Harold," Smith said.

"I told you. He's off."

"Where is he?" Kelso asked.

Winthrop drew himself up. He seemed about to explode. His voice came out low and hard. "He's in Chicago. He won't be back until tomorrow."

"Okay." Kelso felt deflated by Charlotte's reaction, or he might have pressed harder. He turned and went with Smith out into the hall. There was no sign of Margaret and the girl.

Winthrop opened the massive front door. "I'll thank

you not to disturb us again unless you have urgent business,'' he said. "Or a warrant."

"I'm sorry," Kelso said again. They went outside and stood on the porch. The door closed. A sharp cold wind whisked leaves past their feet with a rattling sound. The morning was so gray and bleak that it resembled late November rather than the end of October. The black naked trees clawed skyward like charred fingers.

"Well, that's that," Smith said.

"No, it's not. Not till Harold gets back and I get a look at him."

"What makes you think—" Smith began, then shrugged and muttered something beneath his breath.

"What?"

"Forget it."

They went down the long walk, through the yard with its statues and benches, to Wilhelm Drive, the girl's screams echoing in Kelso's ears like the wails of the damned.

Chapter Twenty

The People in the House

The dispatcher radioed them and relayed a message from Detective Sergeant Meyer: meeting at the duty room, 1 P.M. Kelso sat in the LTD's passenger seat and chewed thoughtfully at the stem of his pipe, not even filling it, while Smith drove them downtown again through cold impersonal streets.

"The dead girl looks a little like Rosemary," Kelso said.

"Hmmm," Smith replied. "I think you mentioned that once."

"The dead girl also looks a little like Charlotte."

"One young girl with dark hair and dark eyes looks about like another," Smith said. "Especially if they both happen to have pale skin and a narrow face. And if you don't know them personally."

"That's not really true, you know."

"What isn't?"

Kelso sucked at his pipe, then replied, "Dark hair and eyes don't make two girls resemble each other, not close up. Not necessarily."

"So," Smith said, sounding a little impatient, "they resemble each other. What's the point?"

"I was just thinking. Did I tell you about Susan's aunt and her séance?"

"You mean they had one recently?"

"No. It was something she did when she was young, right after one of her uncles died."

Smith turned a corner and had to stop while a guy in a

three-piece suit crossed in front of them against the DON'T WALK light. He made the LTD leap forward at the first possible instant, missing the guy by inches, and muttered something about pedestrians. "So what?" he asked.

"She and her sisters decided to try and call his spirit back. They needed a medium, so Eleanor put on her uncle's old hat and his watch chain and smudged her upper lip to look like his mustache."

"What's the point?"

"If she looked like her uncle, maybe he'd speak to them through her."

Silence again. A misting rain began gradually blurring the view through the windshield and making the streets glisten. They pulled into the parking lot and got out.

"Let's go get some coffee," Smith said. "Damn, it feels like winter out here. Isn't this supposed to be fall?"

Kelso glanced at his watch. "It's eleven o'clock already. We may as well eat lunch."

"Okay."

They walked four blocks to a cafeteria and went through the line. It wasn't yet crowded, so they had their choice of places to sit and took a large booth in the front, where they could watch the street through tall windows. Muzak flooded into the room, which was decorated in Early American and included a real fireplace with a fire, huge chandeliers, and imitation antique furnishings. All the tablecloths and napkins were dark red.

"You always have vegetable plates," Kelso said.

"And you always have meat, potatoes, and dessert."

"We're creatures of habit, I guess."

"I guess."

"You sound really down."

Smith shrugged. "It's this case. It's depressing. We aren't going to get anything out of the people in that house, and frankly I'm beginning to doubt they have anything to do with the murder or the hand. I think we're spinning our wheels and not even looking in the right direction."

"What's the right direction?" Kelso took a bite of meatloaf.

"Damned if I know. That priest, maybe. He's tall and

bald. No one ever suspects a priest. He could get away
with murder, literally, if he wanted to.''

"I can't imagine a priest being able to do something
like that,'' Kelso said. "Not a real priest. They go through
too much training, and have too many chances to opt out
before being ordained. I'd think a man who made it all the
way through and got his own church would be too indoc-
trinated. It'd be impossible for him to shed enough of his
faith to commit a sin as terrible as murder.''

"Well, maybe so, but priests have crises of faith all the
time, don't they?''

"On TV,'' Kelso said. "And in movies. But I've never
known a real priest who had a murder crises.''

Smith chewed and swallowed green beans. "What's this
stuff you keep bringing up about the dead girl looking like
Rosemary and Charlotte?''

"I haven't reasoned it out completely. I'm just turning
it over in my mind. All I can say is, I think it's important.
And the séance . . .'' He shrugged. There was no use
going into it till he could be more specific.

He swallowed mashed potatoes and looked out the window. The mist had become rain, slanting and needlelike,
reminding him of Dr. Winthrop's syringe. He heard Charlotte's screams again. People hurried along the sidewalk,
hunched over and bent against the rain or huddled beneath
umbrellas. In the street the cars had their windshield wipers going now and their tires were leaving tracks on the
wet pavement.

"I think I'll try calling Marie tonight,'' Smith said.
"Maybe she'll change her mind and go out with me.''

"Marie?''

"The waitress I was telling you about. Like a young
Sophia Loren. So far she only smiles and says no.''

"It's always worth another shot. You know, Smith, I
was thinking . . . what if something weird really is going
on in that house?''

"The house again? I thought we'd exhausted that.''

"We never exhausted it. For one thing, there's still Harold, the cook, and I still want to see if he's bald and wears
glasses. For another, I think Winthrop was scared to death

that Charlotte would tell us something. The more I think about it, the more I'm convinced he gave her that shot more to keep her from blurting something out than to sedate her. He looked really worried.''

"She's his patient.''

"I know. But something's going on. And this thing about Harold. Very convenient. We want to see Harold and he's off today. He's in Chicago. How do we know Harold's off? It's a big house.''

"So what are you going to do, Kelso? Get a warrant to search for Harold? I suppose it would authorize us to search the premises at such and such an address for one tall thin baldheaded man with glasses.''

"I don't think we've got enough for a warrant yet,'' Kelso replied, ignoring Smith's sarcasm, "And I'm pretty sure Winthrop won't let us in again without one. But if we went over there tonight, after dark, we might be able to get close enough to see in through the windows. If Harold's really there, maybe we could catch a glimpse of him.''

Smith chuckled. "And what would that prove?''

"It would prove that Harold's tall, thin, and bald, or he's not. Also it would tell us whether Winthrop lied.''

"Sounds crazy to me, Kelso. And if they caught us sneaking around on their property, they'd raise hell. Can you imagine what Leill would do?''

"Probably take my gun and badge and show me the door.''

"You said it.''

They finished lunch and walked back to the Municipal Building in the rain. In the third-floor duty room Broom sat eating a cheeseburger and fries and sipping a large chocolate shake, a box of Kleenex at his elbow. Meyer had returned early and was pacing the room, a chicken sandwich in one hand and a mug of coffee in the other. He scowled up as Smith and Kelso entered.

"Well, well. The wandering minstrels return. You guys got anything to report?''

"Nothing important,'' Smith said, and Kelso shrugged.

"Nothing important. Well . . .'' Meyer put his sandwich down on his desk and picked up a sheet of paper. "I've got a few things here."

Broom sneezed and blew his nose noisily, muttering. Smith sat down and put his feet up on his desk. Kelso leaned against a filing cabinet and began tamping tobacco into his pipe.

"I talked to Dr. Paul this morning," Meyer said. "The rest of the autopsy results are in. They found a lot of Pentothal in her system, and a lot of morphine. Paul says the morphine was probably used after the amputation. Death from a gunshot wound to the head is confirmed. Thirty-two caliber slug, lodged in the brain. Death is estimated between 6 P.M. and midnight on Monday, the twenty-seventh. The amputation most likely took place about six days before that. Make it sometime during the day of Tuesday the twenty-first, but that's not firm." Meyer paused, took a deep breath, let it out.

"Sounds like somebody went to a lot of trouble over the amputation," Smith said. "Pentothal and morphine. Maybe they hadn't decided to kill her when they cut off her hand."

"You think they wanted her without the hand, for some reason?" Kelso asked.

Smith shrugged. "I don't know. Six days. All I'm saying is, why should they make such a neat job of the amputation, only to put a bullet in her brain a few days later?"

"If the amputation was done that well," Broom said, sniffling, "couldn't that mean she might've been to a doctor? And there might be a medical report?"

"We could take her picture to every doctor and clinic in the area and ask if they remember doing an amputation on a broad like that," Meyer said, rather sarcastically. "But for my money it was her killer, not some doctor."

"It could've been a doctor," Smith said stubbornly.

Meyer glared at him. "Well of course it *could* have been."

Smith shrugged.

"The amputation wasn't exactly a professional job," Meyer said, "if you remember what Dr. Paul said."

No one said anything. Then Meyer glared at the sheet

of paper again and said, "According to Paul, the operation was probably done by somebody other than a professional. He suggests a medical intern without much experience or competence, for example."

"So where does that get us?" Smith asked brightly.

"If you'll shut up, I'll tell you."

"Tell us," Smith said.

"I checked the background on this shrink, Winthrop," Meyer said. "And here's what I came up with. He'd got an M.D. with a residency in psychiatry, just like he says, and he's been to some kind of psychoanalytical thing, some institute. Like a lot of these guys, he only sees a few long-term rich patients on a regular basis. He's never practiced medicine except for psychiatry."

"So he's not a surgeon," Smith concluded.

Meyer glared. "Perhaps you didn't hear what I said. He's a psychoanalyst."

"But has he ever *been* a surgeon?" Kelso asked politely.

"No. You're trying to connect his medical background to the girl's murder and her amputation. Forget about it. He's never practiced anything but psychiatry. He's never held a scalpel in his hand. Now where was I? Oh yeah. His sister, Margaret Winthrop. She's never been married and she's lived with him in that house for years. She doesn't work and never goes out, as far as anyone knows. But I found out she was a nurse, a long time ago, and worked in a hospital briefly. Seems they canned her when she made a mistake with some medicine and a guy almost died."

"Was she by any chance a surgical nurse?" Broom asked.

"No. She worked in the emergency room for a while, but not in surgery."

"Too bad," Broom said, and sneezed. "She was my favorite for the killer." He blew his nose.

"Then there's Charlotte," Meyer said, looking at his notes again. "She apparently is Margaret's illegitimate daughter by some guy twenty-odd years back down the line. If anybody knows who the father was, nobody's talking. Nobody I've questioned, anyway.''

"I don't suppose Charlotte's ever been a nurse or a doctor or anything like that?'' Smith asked.

"Charlotte's never been anything but a schizophrenic,'' Meyer said.

Kelso's pipe went out. "What about Harold?''

Meyer looked surly. "There's no evidence of any cook named Harold.''

"What do you mean?''

"I mean, Kelso, exactly what I just said. No evidence. The information I was able to get is that three people live in that house. Winthrop, Margaret, and Charlotte. Broom and I asked around the neighborhood, and nobody ever heard of a cook named Harold.''

"That doesn't mean a thing,'' Smith said. "Why would the neighbors know? I don't suppose Winthrop invites them for dinner a lot.''

Rain blew against the windows. Kelso got his pipe going again and puffed at it. It went out. He tossed it into an ashtray and looked up.

"Smith and I thought we might go up to the house tonight, to see if we can spot anybody through the windows. Our witnesses saw a tall bald man with glasses put the girl's hand on Mary's grave and head into the woods toward the house. I'd like to see if we can catch a glimpse of a man like that.''

Meyer glared. "So?''

"So I was just wondering if you and Broom would like to come along for the ride. Four sets of eyes are better than two.''

"Broom's at death's door with whatever the hell he's got,'' Meyer said. "Besides, do you have any idea what Leill would do if we got caught prowling around in the dark outside that guy's house?''

Kelso shrugged and began cleaning his pipe. Smith played with a paper clip. Broom swallowed the last bite of his cheeseburger, drained the chocolate shake, burped, and patted at his lips with a napkin. Rain beat at the windowpanes.

Meyer sighed heavily. "Ah, what the hell. I guess we may as well see if there's anything to it and eliminate it as a possibility."

Kelso smiled, and suddenly he began to remember something about the séance. Simultaneously, he began to realize the significance of the dead girl's resemblance to both Rosemary McAllister and Charlotte. It was one of those moments of inspiration. He stared at his pipe, not seeing it. At the séance, Eleanor had worn her dead uncle's hat—

"Meet you guys here tonight, or at the house?" Meyer asked, killing Kelso's train of thought. The idea about the séance vanished again.

"May as well meet at the house," Smith said. "St. Luke's parking lot at nine o'clock?"

Meyer nodded. "Okay. One thing, though. If anything happens, I'm running like hell and I wasn't there, I didn't know you guys were going to be there, and it's your asses, not mine." He picked up his sandwich. "See you later."

Kelso spent the rest of the afternoon catching up on his paperwork, and the idea about the séance again remained as elusive as a ghost.

Chapter Twenty-One

The House

The rain had stopped but the sky remained overcast. A clear night might have been better because it would have made the darkness more complete; but the clouds were dark and seemed to reflect very little light. Every now and then lightning flickered on the horizon, followed after a few seconds by a dull rumble. The temperature seemed, if anything, to be rising. It was almost balmy.

At five minutes till nine Smith lit a cigarette and leaned back in the driver's seat of the dark blue unmarked LTD with his window rolled down, while Kelso, in the passenger seat, used his thumb to press tobacco into the bowl of his pipe but didn't light it. They were the first to arrive and there were no other cars in the church parking lot. Evidently the continuing news stories about the girl's hand and her body were enough to keep away the usual neckers for the time being.

A short while later Smith said, "Where is everybody? It's four minutes till nine."

"They'll be here."

"Meyer probably chickened out at the last minute. All he's worried about is his butt, you heard him say so himself. And Broom's probably in the hospital with pneumonia by now, the way he's been going."

"Here they come," Kelso said. "Probably."

A car swung into the driveway from Amsterdam Avenue, its headlight beams raking the area as it came up and into the lot. It was a dark blue Toyota—Broom's car.

"All these damned foreign cars," Smith muttered. "You and your VW, Broom's Toyota, girl I had a date with last week's driving a Renault now. Doesn't anybody believe in buying American anymore?''

"People are looking for quality and economy," Kelso replied mildly.

"That's not very patriotic."

"A lot of the American cars fall apart fast."

"Well, you should be willing to make a few sacrifices for the good of the country once in a while," Smith said. He stabbed out his cigarette in the ashtray and opened his door. "That's them. Come on."

The Toyota stopped a few feet away and its lights blinked out. Kelso climbed out and walked over, the wind whipping the tails of his raincoat around the legs of his corduroys. He gripped his umbrella in one hand, just in case. Meyer and Broom got out of the Toyota and faced Smith and Kelso. The new floodlight bathed the area in a yellowish glare that cast sharp black shadows from their bodies, making Kelso feel very conspicuous.

"Well," Meyer said, "let's get at it."

"I was thinking," Kelso said. "Are we going down through the woods to the grave and then up to the rear of the house, or what?"

"I thought that's what we'd do," Meyer said.

"If we approach it from the rear, there's nothing but a big open yard between the woods and the house. Anybody happening to look out the window could spot us easily in the yard."

"So what are you suggesting, Kelso?"

"I think the front's better. Let's go down to the street and around to the front. The yard's got all kinds of big trees and things for cover."

"Kelso's right," Broom said, sniffling loudly. "I've seen that house in the daytime. They've got statues in the yard, plus the trees. Be harder to see us coming up that way."

Meyer sighed. "It doesn't matter to me. I don't like this whole thing. Well, let's get it over with. Remember what I said, if anything happens it's every man for himself. I didn't drive, I don't have a car here, I was never here."

"Just like Watergate," Smith said with a slight edge to his voice.

There was a silence. Lightning jumped over the far tree-tops and the thunder was louder when it came. Then Meyer said, "Broom and I'll go on ahead. You two wait here a couple of minutes, then follow us. We'll meet you in the yard. And for Godsake don't let anybody see you."

"I brought along my handy-dandy invisible gun," Smith said. "If anybody tries to look my way, I'll just zap myself and disappear."

Kelso chuckled. Broom sneezed and blew his nose.

"I hope you don't intend to do that up close to the house," Meyer muttered.

"I'll try not to," Broom said, and the two of them turned and walked down the driveway to the street and passed from view. Kelso was still chuckling.

"What's so funny?" Smith demanded.

"Handy-dandy invisible gun. That's pretty good."

"Meyer has no sense of humor."

The wind sighed in the trees and a few leaves skittered along the asphalt with a dry rattle. The breeze smelled sweet and moist, like winter in Florida, except that it was filled with the lush decaying aroma of dying leaves. Some-one nearby had been burning them, probably illegally, and the smell was everywhere.

"You know this is crazy, don't you?" Smith said. "Sneaking up on this place in the dark like a bunch of kids. Did it ever occur to you that those people in there are basically nuts, and they might have guns? I wouldn't be surprised if they started shooting at us."

"I guess we'll just have to be careful then," Kelso said. "It's time."

"This is crazy," Smith repeated, and led the way down to the street.

Two cars went past as they went around the corner onto Wilhelm Drive. A dog barked. There were more trees for a while, then the trees ended. The yard was three feet or so higher than the sidewalk and separated from it by a brick wall. They reached the two stone pillars with the heavy chain that blocked the drive and stood for a moment, watching. The nearest light was a streetlamp back at the intersection of Wilhelm and Amsterdam. Here, it was relatively dark. Nothing moved. All was quiet.

"Okay," Kelso whispered, "let's go." He stepped over the chain, which was about hip-high, and Smith followed. They moved into the yard. Their feet seemed to make a lot of noise on the dead leaves. Far up the sloping ground they could just make out the dark shape of the house through the trees; a few of its windows were lighted. They came to the sidewalk in the middle of the yard and two people stepped out from behind trees.

"About time," Meyer muttered. "I thought you'd gotten lost."

"How do you want to do this?" Kelso asked.

"It's your show, Kelso. You call it."

"Okay. Let's just make our way forward. Try to move from tree to tree, a short distance at a time. Two of us on either side of the walk. When we get close to the house, we'll try to get a look into some of those windows."

"This is really crazy," Smith said.

"Well, are you ready?" Kelso asked.

"Wait," Broom said. He blew his nose several times. "Okay."

"Maybe you should stay here and wait for us," Smith told him.

Broom shook his head. "I'll be fine now."

"This is nuts."

"Let's go," Kelso said, and moved away to his right toward a tall tree with a thick trunk. Smith moved with him, toward another tree. To their left, Broom and Meyer faded into the darkness.

Thunder rumbled. Leaves rustled continuously all around them. In the shadows of the trees the yard was darker than the street, but Kelso knew that anyone looking out could spot them, so it was essential to stay with the shadows. Their footsteps were loud.

Looking to his left, he thought he caught a glimpse of someone darting between two trees, but then there was only dimness and shadow; maybe they weren't so visible after all. He headed for the next tree, hoping the intolerable loudness of his shoes in the leaves wouldn't penetrate the house's walls.

A statue loomed in the darkness like a ghost, its empty eyes seeming to watch him as he approached it. All was eerie and dreamlike. He passed a stone bench, its seat soggy with leaves. Something rustled to his right, probably Smith. He thought of a spy movie he'd once seen, and cringed at the thought of floodlights crashing suddenly into life, pinning them like bugs caught in a flashlight's beam. Directly behind the house a thin yellow bolt of lightning seemed to dance on the roof and was followed a few seconds later by a crackle that fell into an angry rumble. The wind gusted. He hurried forward, watching the house.

Now only a few trees remained between him and the lighted windows. There were no outside lights. He could count the trees—three of them, like a follow-the-dots map—standing between him and a large leaded-glass window directly ahead, casting a pale glow onto the lawn. He moved forward.

Two more trees. Then one. He was fifty feet from the window, standing behind the last tree. Cautiously, he peered around its trunk, smelling wet bark, and looked directly into an empty room. Disappointed, he listened. Where was Smith? Nothing happened. Far away, a dog barked several times. He thought dogs sounded different at night; darkness made everything hollow. Other windows spilled light onto the ground. He'd have to reach one of them.

He jumped as a twig snapped to his right and someone hissed, "Kelso!"

"Smith?"

"Over here."

Several feet away someone stood behind another tree. Smith's blond hair was pale and white in the gloom. Kelso trotted over quickly. The trunk was just wide enough to hide them both.

"Kelso," Smith whispered, "they're in there."

"Through that window?"

"Yes. Take a look. But be careful, one of 'em's facing us."

Kelso moved his face around the trunk until one eye saw the lighted window. Again he looked directly into a room, but in this one two people sat at a table. Winthrop was recognizable even from the rear because of his enormous bulk and huge round head. The person facing him was Margaret. Between them on the table a black candle burned. On one wall was a door.

The door opened and Charlotte entered, wearing a white robe or gown—almost like a hospital gown, he thought. Her face was very pale, her expression dull and lifeless. She sat down at the table. Margaret's lips moved.

Winthrop got up, momentarily blocking the view, and reached out to one wall. The light went out, leaving only the flickering candle. Winthrop sat down again. The flame cast a weird glow onto the faces of Margaret and the girl.

Kelso moved back behind the trees and whispered, "They're having a séance."

"Really? How do you know?"

"I just know. I'd give anything to get inside."

"What the hell would you do inside?"

"I don't know. I'm not sure."

"There's nothing illegal about a séance," Smith whispered.

"I want another look." Kelso leaned around the tree again, not as carefully as before. After all, they were paying no attention to anything but themselves. But he could see nothing. It took him a moment to realize that the candle must have gone out, or been doused. The window was black. He turned back to Smith and was about to say something when the scream came.

It came high and piercing, cutting through the stillness like the shriek of automobile brakes on the verge of a fatal collision. It penetrated Kelso's brain and made him suck in his breath, and his flesh crawled.

It came again.

"Jesus Christ," Smith said out loud.

"Come on," Kelso told him, and broke into a run for the front door. He reached it just as Meyer and Broom emerged, running, from the trees. Smith pounded up behind him. He pressed the bell button over and over again while Smith beat at the heavy door with his umbrella's wooden handle.

"Open up!" Smith yelled. "Police! Open up!"

The door was pulled inward suddenly. Dr. Winthrop glared out, his dark brows knitted, his eyes narrowed. He glanced from one to the other of them, four men in raincoats, and shook his large head.

"What in the name of all creation is going on out here? What do you *want?*" He made no move to step back.

"Meyer," the little detective-sergeant said, holding up his I.D. "We were on the way to see you, and all of a sudden we heard this screaming."

"Screaming?"

"Don't play dumb with *me,*" Meyer snapped. "You may be a big-shot psychiatrist, but you're dealing with the police now, and this is a homicide investigation. And if you think that's funny, I'll haul your butt downtown and put you in a cell and you can call your lawyer. Do we come in or not?"

There was a moment of indecision, then the hard look faded from the fat man's face and he smiled vaguely.

"Gentlemen, gentlemen, no need for harsh words. I always cooperate with the police. Even at this hour of the evening. If your investigation brings you here so urgently, then by all means come in. Come in." He stepped back and raised one big hand in a wide gesture for them to enter, beaming, totally in control.

Meyer grunted and stalked past him into the hallway; the others followed. Not many lights were on, it seemed drab and cold and gloomy. They looked around, uncertain what they were looking for or what they expected to see.

"Where's that broad?" Meyer asked. "That young broad. Your niece."

"Charlotte?" the doctor asked blandly.

"Yeah. Charlotte. Where is she?"

"In bed, I believe."

"Who was that screaming just now?"

"Ah, you heard the screams." Winthrop nodded. "Of course, that explains all this. You're disturbed about the screams. What an amazing coincidence, that you and your men should have arrived on my doorstep precisely at the instant when the poor girl awoke from some terrible nightmare.''

''Where is she?'' Smith asked, his tone as icy as his eyes.

''Why, upstairs in her bed, as I've already told you. Gentlemen, nothing is without explanation. May I offer you some refreshment? A brandy?''

''Save it, Doctor,'' Meyer snapped. ''We want to see the girl, and we're not leaving till we do.''

Winthrop smiled less cheerfully. ''You have a warrant, of course?''

''We don't need a warrant,'' Meyer told him. ''We heard evidence of violence in here, that gives us probable cause to check it out. You show her to us, or we'll go through this place like a wrecking crew.''

This wasn't technically true, but Winthrop seemed to buy it. At least, he pretended to buy it. He nodded, shrugged, and said pleasantly, ''Well, well, by all means, you shall see the girl. She was sleeping, of course, and it's late, and probably she is being attended to by my sister, who is a trained nurse, but by all means you shall see her. This way, please, gentlemen.'' He turned, enormous in a dark blue suit, and led the way down the shadowy hall.

They followed him to a staircase and up to the second floor. It reminded Kelso of an expensive hotel—all thick carpeting, patterned wallpaper, very hushed, subdued lighting. They passed a series of closed doors; he wondered what lay behind them. At one door Winthrop paused, knocked softly with his knuckles, and called, ''Margaret? Is she decent? There are some gentlemen here who wish to see her.''

''Come in,'' a harsh voice replied.

Winthrop opened the door and led them inside. It was a large bedroom, the only light a small low-watt lamp on a side table. In the bed a pale dark-haired girl lay under blankets up to her chin. Her eyes were closed. Margaret, scowling fiercely, sat on the edge of the bed holding one hand on the girl's forehead as if to comfort her.

"What's wrong with her?" Meyer asked. "Why was she screaming?"

"There is nothing wrong with her," Winthrop said. "She has nightmares. Many emotionally unstable people do. She's resting now, as you can see for yourselves. And now I suggest that we leave and allow her to sleep."

Charlotte's eyes opened. She glanced around dully, as if half asleep, then closed her eyes again. Margaret stared at the girl and did not look up.

Kelso stepped forward suddenly, grabbed the edge of the bedcovers, and jerked them back, baring the girl's right side. He scowled.

"What is the meaning of this?" Winthrop thundered.

Charlotte was not missing her right hand.

The trip was a waste. He knew they'd find nothing now, if ever there had been anything to find in the first place. Kelso shrugged, dropped the covers, and went out into the hall. Smith, Broom, and Meyer followed. The doctor came out and shut the door.

"We've got a few questions," Meyer began, but Winthrop cut him off.

"That's it. That's the end of my patience. I'm sorry, but that really is absolutely it. Now, you've barged into my home without any kind of warrant or other legal cause, and violated the privacy of my sister and my niece as well as myself. I've tolerated it, in the spirit of cooperation, but I will tolerate it no further. You may be the police, but I am a citizen with constitutional rights and protections. You will now leave, and if you desire to return for any reason it will be with an official document signed by a judge of this state. This way, gentlemen." He pointed down the hall toward the stairs.

Kelso thought Meyer was about to argue, but the small detective must have come to the same conclusion as Kelso—that they'd seen all they were going to see, anything else was pointless, now they were merely wasting their time. Meyer shrugged his narrow shoulders and went down the hall. The others followed.

"Good night, gentlemen," Winthrop told them at the front door, but his dark eyes were like steel.

"Sorry for the trouble," Kelso said.

The door closed, and they heard it lock. Broom sneezed and began blowing his nose. Smith lit a cigarette and strode off by himself, down the walk that split the yard.

Meyer said, "Well, that was a big fat nothing."

"Something was wrong with that girl," Kelso said. "I sure wish I knew what." He felt afraid, and wondered if the others did, too. It seemed darker and colder than before.

"I'm cold and tired and pissed off," Meyer said. "Let's go home."

They walked along the sidewalk to the street, past trees and benches and ghostly statues, their shoes scattering leaves and echoing on the pavement. Thunder boomed very close by and the wind gusted suddenly. It started to rain.

Chapter Twenty-Two

Clues

Tired and depressed, Kelso went home. Smith dropped him off and said good night. Inside the apartment, the telephone rang while he was feeding the cat. It was Susan, wanting to know if he could come over and watch TV.

"Eleanor's gone to spend the night with a friend," Susan said. "We'll have the whole place to ourselves."

Kelso thought about it. He had a headache and he was worried about the situation at the house. He wanted to try to fit together the pieces of the puzzle, especially since he thought he had most of them by now and it should only be a matter of placing them next to each other in the proper way. And he had a feeling that there was an urgency about it, that he had only a limited time in which to act before something else happened, something as terrible as the dead girl and her severed hand.

He thought about Susan Overstreet alone in her aunt's house, with a warm fire and something good to eat, and no one to bother them.

"I can't make it tonight," he said. "It's the case. I'm really beat, I've got a headache, I think I'm just going to go to bed early."

"Would you like me to come over there? I could fix your supper and rub your back." Her voice lowered. "I could tell you a bedtime story."

"I appreciate the thought," he told her, "but I'd be terrible company. Another night, okay?"

"You're taking a chance. There might not be another night."

"Very funny."

"Good night, George." She hung up.

He went to the kitchen and made himself a bologna sandwich with lots of mustard on it, opened a beer, and sat in the living room, with the cat watching for any clue that it might get a bite. He switched on the TV, found a movie, muted the sound, and ate and sipped while the screen flickered. His mind began to work.

There were three girls, all somewhat alike physically. Dark hair, dark eyes, pale narrow faces, around twenty years old. All very similar to the general description of Mary's ghost. One was a retarded girl named Rosemary McAllister, who worked at the Episcopal church where the priest was tall and bald. The second was a schizophrenic who lived in the house near the grave, the daughter of an ex-nurse, the niece of a psychiatrist. The third girl was unknown, unidentified, except that her hand had been cut off and left on Mary's grave and she'd been murdered and buried near the grave.

He handed a piece of bologna to the cat—who snapped it up greedily—and thought some more.

On the night the hand was found, a young couple had seen a tall bald man in glasses leave the hand on the gravestone. The bald man had headed into the woods toward the house where Winthrop lived. Later that night, Rosemary McAllister had watched a bald man hit Kelso over the head in the clearing, and when Kelso had come to, both the girl and the bald man had gone.

In the house with Winthrop and the others there was supposedly a cook named Harold, who might be tall and bald with glasses. Was Winthrop protecting him? Was he, for example, Margaret's illegitimate son, also psychotic, and given to chopping off the hands of young girls? Would Winthrop protect such a person?

Apparently Dr. Winthrop believed in ghosts and had recently tried to conduct a séance with Margaret and Charlotte and a black candle. Then Charlotte had screamed—had she seen something? Maybe she'd seen the ghost Winthrop kept insisting lived in his house. Or maybe it had been the ghost of Mary Carter.

And what had happened after that, when they'd found

her moments later in her bed, apparently drugged or heavily sedated, watched over by Margaret?

Then there was the teasing, tickling, slithering problem of Eleanor's séance. Eleanor as a child, up in the attic with her sisters, wearing her dead uncle's hat and watch chain and a simulation of his mustache, calling to his spirit.

Three girls, he thought, suddenly too tired to figure out anything. Three girls looking like Mary's ghost. One dismembered and dead, one retarded, one intermittently schizophrenic. The dead girl's hand on Mary's grave like some weird offering. Little Eleanor in a dead man's hat.

Kelso finished the sandwich. The movie was relatively incomprehensible without the sound, but seemed to involve a young woman with two lovers. Every few moments she was seminude. Probably erotic under the proper conditions, which these weren't. He gave the cat another small bit of meat he'd saved. If he'd allowed Susan to come over tonight, they might have been watching this movie together on the sofa with the lamp turned low, and it might have been very erotic indeed, probably even without the movie. But Susan was at home, the movie was as interesting as an Army training film, and he was tired. He turned off the set and finished his beer.

Somehow, he thought, climbing the stairs, there had to be a connection between the three girls. Charlotte, Rosemary, and the victim. Maybe there was a connection between the girls and Aunt Eleanor's séance. Father Ullman might be connected.

But his brain was a muddle of ghosts, tombstones, Episcopal priests, psychiatrists, nurses, retardation, psychosis, bald men in glasses, black candles, screams.

He undressed and got into bed. Turned out the light. Felt vaguely uneasy. Maybe it was the beer. Or the sandwich. Or his headache. He got up, took two aspirin, and got back into bed, leaving the bathroom light on under the pretext that if he felt sick he could get to the toilet faster. The real reason was that tonight, despite his thirty-six years, his maturity, and his steel nerve, he was afraid to sleep in the dark.

When the cat jumped onto the bed he started violently,

then felt sheepish. The animal turned three times, hunkered close to his legs, and began its nightly bath. The sound of its steady licking calmed him, finally, and he relaxed, wondering, just before he fell into sleep, about the connection between Eleanor's uncle's hat and Mary's ghost and the dead girl's hand.

When he opened his eyes again, it was six fifty-five in the morning, and he had the answer.

Chapter Twenty-Three

Rosemary Is Missing

Under the comfortably hot cascading water of his shower he thought about the answer. Was he certain? No, but it sounded reasonable. Had he dreamed it? Not really. Maybe Freud was right, maybe some part of his mind worked independently of his normal awareness, and during the night it had continued to attack the problem and had, somehow or other, arrived at a plausible solution.

Because that's all he had, really. A plausible solution, something which fit the facts. He had no real proof. He got out and dried off, shaved, dressed, and hurried downstairs. His telephone was ringing. It was seven-twenty, Halloween.

"Hello?" He crooked the receiver between neck and shoulder to reach for the jar of coffee.

"Sergeant Kelso?" It was Father Ullman's voice, sounding tense.

"Yes?"

"Sergeant, something's happened to Rosemary, and I'm not sure what to do. I think I need your help."

Kelso frowned. "Rosemary? What's the problem?"

"She was supposed to come to the church last night and do some filing, but she never showed up. I telephoned her mother. According to Mrs. McAllister, the girl left the house just before seven-thirty last night and never came back."

"Did Mrs. McAllister report it to the police?"

"She doesn't seem concerned. I just spoke to her again five minutes ago. She says Rosemary does this from time to time, because she's slow. That's her term for it—slow."

That bitch, Kelso thought. He said, "I see."

"She says the girl often goes out, forgets where she was supposed to be going, and winds up at some friend's house. She expects Rosemary to come back today or to contact her. But she's always come to my office when she said she would. I believe something's happened to her, Sergeant."

"You haven't reported this officially yet?"

"Not yet. I wanted to get your reaction first."

"Under the circumstances," Kelso said, trying not to sound as grim as he felt, "I think you were wise to call. You never can tell. I'll see that a bulletin's put out, and we'll start looking for her right away. Are you at the church?"

"No, at home."

"Okay, give me your number there. I'll call you if we turn up anything."

"Thanks, Sergeant." The priest gave him a number.

"Don't worry," Kelso said. "We'll find her. It's probably nothing."

"I hope so."

He hung up. The cat wanted breakfast. He fed it, thinking about what a bitch Barbara McAllister was. He made a cup of coffee and thought about Rosemary. There'd been no need to alarm the priest at this point, but he had a gut feeling that something had happened to the girl. He diluted the coffee with cold water, gulped it down, and left.

In the duty room Smith was already at his desk, feet up, munching a carrot stick. Kelso walked in and shook his head.

"Another carrot? You're going to turn into a rabbit."

Smith gazed at him, blue eyes calm, and chewed without replying.

"Something's happened to Rosemary," Kelso said.

"What?"

"Rosemary McAllister's missing." He related his phone conversation with Ullman as Smith nodded thoughtfully and finished the carrot.

"Doesn't surprise me," Smith said.

"Really? Why?"

"Because nothing surprises me." He wiped his lips with a napkin.

"I think we should get over to the grave and check around in the woods for her."

This made Smith look up with a slightly different expression. He took his feet off the desk and sat up straight. "Oh. I thought you meant she was—you know—missing. I didn't know you were associating it with the case."

"I think it *is* the case," Kelso said, wanting him to hurry. "Come on, I don't think we've got a lot of time."

"Meyer called," Smith said. "He wants us to wait for him, so he can brief us before we start the day. He's due here about eight-thirty."

"I don't have time to wait for him." Kelso took his .38 out, checked it, and put it back in the holster at his hip. "I've got to look for her right now. She could be in trouble. I'll go by myself if you want to stay here and wait for Meyer. Tell him—"

"Okay, okay." Smith got up, opened a drawer, took out his revolver and checked it, shoved it into his shoulder holster. He put on his jacket. He was wearing a brown suit with a yellow shirt and a silk tie with a paisley print. "Okay," he said. "Let's go."

Smith drove. Inside the LTD he said, "Are you sitting on something?"

"Not really. All I know is what I told you. Just what the priest told me."

"Sounds like Rosemary ought to dump her old lady and move in with the priest," Smith observed dryly.

"Parents are more sacred than priests in this society," Kelso said.

"Uh huh."

They pulled into the church lot and parked at the end near the path, then got out and stood for several minutes glancing around. In the bright sun everything seemed different. It was clear and cool, the wind had a hard biting edge. Yellow leaves rattled across the asphalt. Theirs was the only car in the lot.

"What now?" Smith lit a Kent. He had on aviator-style

sunglasses tinted dark brown. Kelso thought he looked like a German spy in a cold-war movie.

"Let's take a look down at the grave," he said.

They negotiated the path. This time it was easy to see the sharp branches in time to avoid being whipped across the face, and to step over the raised roots or vines. It was like moving through a forest in the middle of nowhere, for a few minutes nothing could be seen but the plants and trees, and it was easy to imagine that there was no church, no house or grave, no city, nothing but woods and underbrush for miles. Then they made the sharp turn to the right and came out into the clearing.

No one was there.

The large stone with the engraving still occupied the center, and the monument base still rested on the ground at one side. This morning there was nothing on it but leaves. No severed hands. The wind made the leaves hiss.

"Today's Halloween," Smith said pleasantly. "There's supposed to be a heavy frost tonight in low-lying areas. Those little bastards in their plastic masks are going to freeze their asses off trying to rob everybody of cookies and candy tonight."

"Halloween used to be my favorite holiday," Kelso said. "Next to Christmas."

"Really?"

"I looked forward to it for weeks. When I put on a sheet and a mask and went outside after supper, walking up and down the sidewalks with a paper bag, I thought there really were witches and goblins out there, and I didn't just hear dogs barking and kids laughing, I heard ghosts and devils."

"And it scared you?"

"Not at all. It thrilled me. I loved it. But it's not the same now. I don't think today's kids are thrilled by it, I think they regard it as just another handout, another freebie. The magic's gone. You know, I can still smell the masks we used to buy. They were sort of stiff and had a special peculiar smell inside. That was before the age of plastics."

"Everything's plastic now," Smith said. "But society

keeps getting better. That special smell in your mask was probably a toxic chemical.''

"Probably."

Kelso went around the clearing, poking at leaves here and there with his toe, finding nothing.

"I don't know what to do," he said. "What do you think happened to her?" Although, he thought suddenly, he might know.

"Maybe she took a bus somewhere," Smith said, lighting a cigarette and walking over to sit on the edge of the monument base. "I knew an old lady once who did that. Took bus rides all over the country. Nutty as a fruitcake. She'd buy a one-way ticket to Phoenix or Boston or Seattle and not even tell anybody. When she got there, she'd check into a hotel and wander around town until her money ran out. Then the cops would pick her up, find out who she was, and contact her relatives. They'd wire her some money and she'd get on a plane and fly home, or they'd come and get her."

"Did she do that very often?"

"No. The fifth time, some guy hit her over the head with a bottle to grab her purse. Killed her."

Kelso shook his head. "You're smoking on Mary's grave again."

"I know."

"Tell me something, Smith, and no bullshit this time. That other time, you threw your cigarette away, right? It wasn't knocked out of your hand."

"I'd never lie to you, Kelso. It was a ghost."

The wind made an unpleasant rattling noise in the trees. Smith finished his cigarette and ground it out with his shoe.

Kelso sighed. "Rosemary looks like Mary's ghost," he said. "At least, she looks like Mary Carter."

"Yeah. I believe you've mentioned that."

"Charlotte looks like her, too. So does the dead girl."

"Yep."

"I think I've figured out something about Susan's aunt and her séance."

"What'd you figure out, Kelso?"

"Last night, when Winthrop was in that room with Margaret and Charlotte, suppose they were trying to communicate with Mary's ghost. Suppose he wanted a medium—you know, somebody for Mary to speak through."

"Yeah?"

"Maybe he'd want somebody who looked like Mary, just the way Eleanor tried to look like her dead Uncle Mortimer."

"So he used Charlotte?"

Kelso nodded. "Yes. But before he used Charlotte, suppose he used somebody else. Somebody who looked like Mary Carter except for one thing. Smith, suppose Mary Carter had lost one of her hands. Her right hand. And Winthrop knew it."

Smith stood up. His eyes narrowed. "Jesus, Kelso, are you trying to say he chopped off that girl's hand so she'd look like Mary Carter?"

"Why not? Suppose you were going to hold a séance and you were a fanatic about trying to communicate with the dead, the spirit world, whatever. And suppose you used to be a surgeon."

"Winthrop didn't used to be a surgeon."

"I'm talking about Harold the cook. Only I don't think he's a cook, I think he's probably an ex-surgeon, maybe a doctor who got his license pulled for malpractice or performing illegal abortions, that kind of thing. I think he and Winthrop and Margaret are all into the supernatural. So, they get this girl, this Mary Carter look-alike, and they have a séance, but nothing happens. So this bald ex-doctor decides they've got to get rid of the girl's hand, to make her more like the real Mary, so Mary's spirit will come and speak to them through her."

"I suppose it's possible," Smith said in a flat voice.

"I think it happened."

Smith got up and paced around, kicking at leaves. "I don't know, Kelso. It makes sense in a way, but it's too . . ."

"Evil?"

"No," Smith said. "Not evil. Just sick."

"Well, they're all supposed to be crazy in that house," Kelso said.

"So what do we do now? Is this just speculation? Have you got any proof?"

"Not yet." Kelso went over toward the path to the house. "Listen, I think there's a chance Rosemary's in there with them right now."

"I hope to God she's not."

"So do I. But I think she probably is. I'm going up there and take a look."

"You're crazy. In broad daylight? After what happened last night?"

"I just want to watch the house for a while and see if anybody comes or goes." He checked his watch. It was eight twenty-five. "It's still early in the morning. After last night, they won't expect us again for a while. They should be off their guard. Maybe Harold will show up."

"Yeah, and maybe he'll come up behind you and whack you over your head. A little harder than last time."

"Why don't you go back to town and check in with Meyer. Tell him I'm keeping the place under surveillance. Get some other people looking for Rosemary, just in case, and check with her mother again, and that priest. And come back for me in a couple of hours."

Smith shook his head. "I don't like this, Kelso. Leave you to mess around with those people, with no backup or anything?"

"I'd rather do it this way." Kelso tried to think of a plausible reason for Smith to leave. He didn't want him to know what he was about to do.

"Kelso—"

"Look, there's a chance the girl's not here at all. I need you to coordinate the effort to find her, if she's somewhere else. And besides, if anybody looks out the windows of the house in this sunlight, two of us will be easier to spot than one. Just go on, and come back about ten-thirty, okay?"

Smith started to say something else, then shrugged. "Have it your own way. I'll come back in two hours. Rear of the house?"

"Check the rear first. If I'm not there, I'll probably be in front."

"I hope you know what you're doing, Kelso."

"I know what I'm doing," he said. Just go, he thought. "See you."

"Yeah." Smith turned and started up the path toward the parking lot. He disappeared, and after a few minutes the crunch of his footsteps faded. Seconds ticked off. Kelso heard a car door slam. An engine started up. When the sound of the engine had blended with the faint hum of traffic on Amsterdam Avenue he took a deep breath and headed up the path through the woods, through the maze of black and yellow—Halloween, he thought—to the house.

Chapter Twenty-Four

Inside the House

At the edge of the woods he stopped, peering out from behind a tree at the bright expanse of yard separating him from the rear of the house. The building loomed somehow unpleasantly, even in the morning's light. The sun, on the far side of the house, cast a black shadow onto the grass. There was no one in sight.

Kelso was struck again at how foreign it looked, like a French château or something in an Impressionist painting. He had the sudden feeling that the structure existed in a kind of warp in space and time, that the events which occurred within its walls weren't subject to the ordinary laws of men and science. It made him shiver and recall those eager frightening Halloween nights with the sounds of unearthly things all around him in the cold darkness, and the smell of his mask.

For a moment he stepped back into the woods, acutely aware of the continuing passage of time. What he hadn't told Smith was that he hoped to get inside the house. Somehow. He was convinced of a high probability that Rosemary was in there, and that she was with Harold, who wasn't a cook but rather an unstable and possibly perverted ex-surgeon with a lust for the grave and the supernatural. The only questions were whether Rosemary was still whole and alive and how to get inside.

He considered and rejected the direct approach. If he presented himself at the front door, Dr. Winthrop might or might not let him in, but either way, Kelso would catch no one in the act of doing anything. He needed evidence, and it wasn't going to be handed to him on a platter.

187

The other way meant breaking and entering. Leill could have his badge. He might even be prosecuted. They wouldn't send him to jail, he had a clean record, but it would mean the end of his career. He weighed that against leaving Rosemary at the mercy of someone who might have her under the knife already, and moved.

He began skirting the edge of the woods, moving from tree to tree the way he'd done last night, only now he was doing it in broad daylight. All anyone had to do was to look out of a rear window at exactly the time he was between trees and he'd be spotted—a somewhat bulky figure in corduroy jeans and running shoes, a padded nylon jacket—ducking rather ludicrously through the dead leaves and underbrush. He'd be seen. And then what?

But he made it to the far end of the house without incident and started along the side. Of course, there was no way of knowing what was happening inside the house. Possibly he'd already been observed, and even now the enormous bulk of Dr. Winthrop and the tall thin figure of the bald man would be following his every move. They'd bide their time, plot, wait for the exact right moment to sneak up, grab him, and kill him.

Something make a noise behind him and he whirled, but it was only a squirrel. He turned back to the side of the house.

The woods were much closer to the building here than in back, only a matter of ten feet or so. And now he noticed a small metal door that seemed to be set down below the ground's surface, probably opening onto a lower floor or a basement. Next to the door was a small window, through which Kelso could see a figure passing back and forth, as if pacing. He risked peering around a tree, completely exposing himself for several seconds to get a good look.

He stared.

The person moving past the window was clearly visible. It was a man, rather thin, wearing glasses. He was bald, except for a fringe around the sides.

Kelso stepped back behind the tree and took several deep breaths. So there really was a tall bald man with glasses, and he was inside the house. Was he Harold the cook? Or a demented surgeon who had practiced but not perfected the procedure for an amputation?

This had to be the man Rosemary had seen coming up behind Kelso and hitting him over the head three nights ago, as he'd watched her turn from the grave to regard him with that vaguely mocking smile. This had to be the man she'd described as coming into the clearing earlier that week, in the company of someone who looked like Mary Carter. And this had to be the guy the young couple had observed leaving the severed hand on Mary's grave.

He had a killer here, someone who performed amputations casually in order to produce a medium for a séance. And someone who murdered just as casually. No time to mess with a warrant. By the time he got to the parking lot and a telephone, tried to call Meyer or Leill, tried to convince some judge, with Rosemary in there, and this monster with his knives and scalpels . . .

Kelso decided. There was no other way.

He peered out again. The bald man was no longer visible in the window. He stepped out of the woods and sprinted across the grass to the metal door, pressed his body against the rough stone next to it, and felt cold through his clothing. He reached out and tried the handle. Locked. Damn, he thought. Why couldn't I have had a break?

No breaks. Life doesn't give you breaks. He tried again. Locked securely. But it looked like a flimsy lock, a simple keyhole affair, probably not a dead bolt. For some reason people liked to make their front and back doors secure, but ignored basement doors. So much the better for burglars. He took out his wallet and found a credit card, a MasterCard. After receiving a nasty letter about exceeding his credit limit, he'd stopped using the thing. Now maybe it would prove useful for something, at least.

Not expecting much, he shoved it between the door and the jamb and brought it down until he felt resistance. He pressed hard, and used his other hand to turn the handle.

Unbelievably, it turned and the door opened. He experienced a mixture of surprise and terror and peered inside.

He saw an empty hall. Four steps led down to it.

Without hesitation, he went in and closed the door behind him.

Chapter Twenty-Five

Kelso in Trouble

The hall was long and narrow. He stood with his back against the door, holding it closed but not latched, in case someone appeared and he wanted to back out fast. There was a faint familiar smell in the hall, reminding him of flowers but not smelling at all like flowers. Then he realized what it was, and why.

It was a medicinal smell, almost the odor that slightly irritates your nose when you walk into a hospital ward, a combination of disinfectants, medicines, rubbing alcohol, unpronounceable chemicals in tinkly glass vials ready to be sucked into disposable syringes and stabbed into various hips and arms. White sheets. Rubber mattress covers—or did they use plastic in this modern era? Nurses in starched uniforms, stethoscopes flopping from pockets or draped around necks. Doctors huddling in hallways to speak meaningless babble in subdued voices, telling the fate of their patients like soothsayers: recovery or doom.

Kelso had been inside hospitals twice in his life as a patient, and often as a policeman. Neither as patient nor as policeman had it been pleasant. Bad things went on in hospitals, no matter how hard they tried to keep it hidden and covered over and dressed up with lounges and coffee shops and professional smiles. He remembered getting lost once. He'd wandered up this hall and down that one, looking for X-Ray, hopelessly disoriented in the maze of color-coded stripes that were supposed to guide him on his way. Finally, he'd turned a corner and there, directly ahead, was Operating Room B—Cardiac Surgery. He'd stood riv-ited, fascinated, alone in the tiled hall that smelled of its bottles and syringes, staring intensely at the opening which had no door but was hung with a pale green curtain suspended from a plastic rod. Inside that room existed all the life and death and thrill and horror and art and science and flesh and blood of humanity, the struggle for survival. That room was a little antechamber which might or might not lead to the other side. You went in, and you came back to this world or you went on to the next. Depending.

The same sense of terror, of finality, of a crossroads, flooded him now, standing with his back against the metal door, gazing the length of this hospital-smelling hall. Because it wasn't right. It was all wrong.

This hall didn't belong in a house. Not in a *home*. The floor was green tiles, not a carpet or hardwood boards. The walls were white tiles, not wallpaper or pine paneling or plaster. The ceiling was white acoustical tile; lights set into the surface behind rectangular glass covers provided a harsh white illumination. And he could smell the alcohol, the medicine, the antiseptic.

Get a grip, he thought, and let the door ease shut behind him. There was something final about the little click it made, as if he'd just been locked inside a cell. The way a prisoner feels, he thought, and shuddered.

Cautiously, thankful for his rubber soles, he went down the four steps and started along the corridor, almost tiptoeing on the green tiles, sniffing at the chemical smells. It was hushed. The house sprawled hugely above him but made no sound.

At intervals along either side were doors with frosted-glass windows, impossible to see through. Rather than try their handles, he continued on his way, uncertain where he was going, not sure what he would find, wondering where the bald man had gone and where Rosemary was. Down at the far end the corridor seemed to turn; it must lead somewhere.

Several feet ahead on his right a door opened. Kelso froze, then stepped sideways to his right and pressed his body against the wall as best he could. The bald man emerged into the glare, dressed in brown trousers, brown shoes, a white shirt. He looked gaunt and skeletal, somewhere in his forties probably, with a high forehead and reddish brown horn-rimmed glasses. It was the man Kelso had seen pacing in front of the window.

The bald man entered the hall with a young dark-haired girl whom Kelso immediately recognized as Rosemary. As they moved away, the girl stumbled and seemed to lean against the bald man for support, and he had to put an arm around her narrow shoulders to hold her up. Kelso noted that she still had both hands.

A second door opened just as the couple reached it, and the hugely obese figure of Dr. Winthrop appeared. He took Rosemary's other arm.

Kelso felt nervous, even with his revolver at his hip. The three people moving away from him in the medicine-reeking hall weren't especially horrifying in and of themselves; it was what they represented that was horrifying.

He came to his senses. He must have been right. They had cut off the dead girl's hand to make themselves a medium for Mary's ghost. For some reason they'd decided to kill her, and now they were going to try it with Rosemary. He wondered if it would be possible to follow them, to wait until the last instant, so he could catch them in the act. On the other hand, if he tried to wait they might see him, or they might succeed in butchering her.

Kelso took a quick step forward, his right hand going to his .38. As he touched the grip someone yelled behind him, "Stop!" A harsh, rasping female voice. Gritty and furious.

He spun and there was Margaret, her lips pulled back from her long teeth in a snarl of hatred. She lunged forward. As he drew his revolver her shoe came up and struck his groin. The pain was instant and overwhelming.

For a moment he was helpless and she came at him, kicking and clawing—he remembered those long fingernails—and making a low animal sound deep in her throat. He aimed his revolver and stepped back, fighting nausea. She kicked again, but missed. He had no wish to shoot an unarmed woman, but he might be forced to. The pain ebbed slightly. He sucked in air and raised the gun.

A powerful hand gripped his right arm just above the

elbow and jerked backward, twisting hard. The weapon fell from his hand and clattered onto the tiles. Someone grabbed his left arm. He caught a glimpse of a syringe in pale thick fingers, and thought of hospitals and doctors and the operating room he'd found that day by mistake. Cardiac Surgery, the crossroads in and out.

He felt the painful stab of a needle being rammed into his left arm and opened his mouth to say "Wait." But the word never came out. Margaret had stopped kicking and stood quietly a few feet away, glaring at him. She blurred as the hall darkened and his ears filled with a buzzing noise like the drone of bees, louder and louder, as he fell. . . .

Chapter Twenty-Six

Mary Carter

Smith sat at his desk in the duty room, puffing at a Kent and skipping irritably through the pages of a report on a robbery he was supposed to be following up at the same time that he was helping Kelso investigate the murder of the girl with the missing hand. In addition to the murder and the robbery, which involved a Days Inn Motel out on the north edge of the city close to the interstate, he was also involved with: the rape of a high-school girl at a party attended by several of her current and former boyfriends; the murder of a vagrant discovered stuffed inside a garbage dumpster behind a downtown restaurant a few evenings ago (a busboy had failed to show up for work since then and was being sought); and a series of apartment break-ins involving the unusual element of a burglar who confronted young female tenants at gunpoint, forced them to disrobe, then snapped their pictures and fled (a previous tenant with a record of trading in pornography was being sought).

Detective-Sergeant Meyer entered the room at two minutes after 9 A.M., lit a cigarette, glared at Smith, and said, "What have you got?"

Smith had no idea what the little cop was talking about.

"I don't know what I've got," he replied testily, "unless you make it more specific. I'm working on more than one case, you know."

"I'm talking about the thing with Mary's grave. What the hell else would I be talking about? We do have priorities around here, you know. Where's Broom? And Kelso?"

Smith held back the most appropriate reply. He'd never liked the short little creep, and it had nothing to do with race. Smith had once dated a Jewish girl and would've married her except that at the last minute she'd backed out and gone off to New York to become the assistant editor of some glamour magazine. It was Meyer's personality, nothing else, that grated on Smith. Sometime he'd have to ask Kelso how he put up with it.

"Broom's in the crapper," he said, trying to be obnoxious. "Kelso's at that house with the psycho broad and the other loonies, keeping an eye on it."

"What for?"

"Rosemary McAllister's missing. Kelso thinks she might be in the house, and he thinks the bald man's in there too. I guess he thinks the bald man's getting ready to chop Rosemary up into little pieces to leave on the grave, for the kids to play with, I suppose." He sneaked a sideways glance to see if his macabre descriptions were having any effect, but Meyer puffed at his cigarette and seemed oblivious.

"I don't like my detectives going off by themselves," Meyer said. "It's not standard operating procedure. He knows it, too. He only does it to annoy me. Since when is Rosemary McAllister missing?"

"Since last night, when she left for St. Luke's and never got there. Never got back home, either. Didn't you see the bulletin I put out on it? Her mother's not worried, the priest is. The priest called Kelso this morning about it."

"Anybody talk to Mrs. McAllister this morning? I can't keep up with every single bulletin every minute of the day."

"Obviously," Smith said. "The priest talked to that woman this morning, and I spoke to her myself about ten minutes ago. Rosemary's still missing, but her mother's still not worried. Retards will be retards, that seems to be her philosophy."

"Good for her," Meyer replied sarcastically. "I've been doing some research on that priest. Ullman. He's as clean as a whistle. I don't see how we can include him as a suspect at this point."

Broom came out of the men's room blowing his nose, though not as loudly as before. He looked a little better.

"Speaking of research," he said, going over to his desk and plopping down heavily, "I've got some interesting information about Mary Carter if anyone would like to hear it."

"I've got until ten-thirty," Smith told him. "Then I've got to meet Kelso." He was well aware of how long-winded Broom could be at times.

"This is short," Broom said. "I went to the public library last night. Did you know they keep a lot of material that the general public doesn't have access to? It's true. Pornography, for one thing. Smith, that ought to interest you. Just go in and show them your badge, say you're working on a case, and ask to see it."

"Huh," Smith said noncommittally.

"Anyway, they have some historical records of no interest to most people. Stuff on some of the older families from around here, people who've lived here for generations and built museums or donated land or whatever. So I found some material on Mary Carter."

"What kind of material?" Meyer asked gruffly, glaring up from his desk.

"I made some notes. They wouldn't let me check it out." Broom opened a notebook and looked at it. "Mary Carter came up here from Atlanta in May, 1916, and stayed in that house, which was called Hawthorne House at the time because that's who lived there. A family called the Hawthornes. No relation to the writer, as far as the librarian knows."

"What writer?" Smith asked, refusing to admit that he knew anything that could be considered literary.

Broom ignored the question and continued. "Anyway, Mary was eighteen. Uh, I'll skip the less pertinent parts."

"Nice of you," Meyer grumbled.

"Thank you," Broom said politely. Broom never appeared to get irony.

"Tell us the pertinent parts," Smith said, lighting a cigarette.

"Well, there was an accident with her hand. She hurt it

somehow, the records aren't clear, something involving a machine. There were a lot of problems with gangrene back in those days. It could kill you, so the librarian said. In early July they took her to a doctor who amputated her hand."

Smith looked up. "You're kidding."

"Yes, the whole thing is merely a joke," Broom said. Then: "No, I'm not kidding. Mary Carter's hand was amputated in July 1916."

"That's a hell of a coincidence," Smith said.

Broom scrutinized his notes and sneezed lightly. Blew his nose. Sniffed.

Smith began to think. A dead girl with her hand cut off. Mary Carter with her hand cut off. He didn't like coincidences. What was it Kelso had been talking about earlier— a Mary Carter look-alike, using her for a séance? He admitted to himself that he hadn't given it much credence, but now, with this new evidence of Broom's, maybe there was something to it after all.

"What happened to her?" he asked, beginning to feel vaguely worried.

"It says in one of the diaries I found that she died almost right after the amputation," Broom said. "Within a couple of weeks."

"Because of the amputation?" Meyer asked, sounding incredulous.

"No. She contracted pneumonia."

"Too much of a coincidence," Smith muttered. "Kelso has this theory that—" He stopped. Meyer was glaring at him. He knew what Meyer thought about Kelso's theories.

"What did you say, Karl?" Broom asked, closing his notebook.

"Nothing. Is that it? That's all you found?"

"No, there's something else," Broom replied. He shoved a large bound volume to the center of his desk. It looked old and dusty. "I found this, and they let me take it out. An old family album. You know—a picture album."

Smith started. "You're kidding."

"I'm not kidding. There are pictures of various family

members, and one is of three people on a bench under a tree.'' He opened the book and began flipping pages of thick paper. ''They didn't want me to take the album, but I told them it was police business. Ah, here it is. Look at this.''

Meyer and Smith went over to Broom's desk to see.

The photograph showed three people sitting close together on a stone bench, with the house visible in the background. The sun was on their faces and they were squinting. The one on the left was a large heavyset woman in a long dress with old-fashioned shoes. In the middle was a man in a dark suit, high collar and tie, a large mustache. On the right was a young girl, moderately attractive, thick dark hair, dark eyes, pale narrow face, wearing a long white dress. On her lips was a faintly mocking smile. At the bottom of the picture someone had written three names:

Henry and Bessie Hawthorne, with Mary Carter.

''This is incredible,'' Meyer said.

Broom nodded, looking proud of himself. ''I know.''

''Look at her hands,'' Smith said in a tense voice.

The girl had some sort of shawl in her lap. Her left hand lay on top, but the shawl obscured her right hand.

''If this was taken after the amputation,'' Broom observed, ''the shawl might've been used to hide it, so she wouldn't feel uncomfortable about having her picture made.''

''She looks like Rosemary McAllister and Charlotte and the dead broad,'' Smith said, looking at his watch. He didn't like any of this, the implications of it, the possibilities. It fit too well with Kelso's theory. The amputations, in both cases the right hand, the idea of using a medium physically similar to Mary Carter—there was something sort of sick and dangerous about it all. And Kelso was lurking around outside that damned house.

He ground out his cigarette, went to his desk, and reached into a drawer for his revolver.

''I'm going over to that house,'' he said. ''Anybody want to come along?''

''What for?'' Meyer asked.

"I've got a bad feeling about this. He might need some help."

"I've got an appointment to meet a robbery witness in fifteen minutes," Broom said. "Maybe I can get somebody else to do it."

"Is that the Connors robbery?" Meyer asked. Broom nodded. "Forget it. This case has priority." He scowled at Smith. "We'll both go."

"Okay," Smith said, putting on his coat. "Let's go."

"That damn Kelso," Meyer muttered as they headed for the elevators. "Always getting into some kind of trouble. One of these days his luck's going to run out."

Outside it was still bright and sunny, but cold, and the temperature seemed to be falling. It was 9:15 A.M. Halloween.

Chapter Twenty-Seven

The Monster

Kelso opened his eyes and shut them again quickly. It was dark. There was a dull throbbing in his head, and his stomach felt queasy, as if the slightest movement would result in vomiting. Buzzing still filled his ears, making him wonder for a moment whether he was actually awake. But when he opened his eyes again he knew that this was real, he wasn't dreaming, he was awake. The memory of the events in the tiled hall returned.

He wriggled the fingers of both hands—for an instant he'd had the absurd fear that one or both his hands were missing. He pressed them against each other, relishing the feeling of fingers and thumbs in contact. At least that part of the nightmare hadn't come true. Not for him, anyway. But as for Rosemary . . .

His watch read nine forty-seven. Frowning, he realized he'd been out for at least an hour since the struggle in the corridor. He recalled Rosemary reeling between the huge shape of Winthrop and the gaunt figure of the bald man. Which of them was the monster? He closed his eyes and saw her arm dangling, her hand gone. But it hadn't happened yet. He opened his eyes wide to make the image go away.

It was difficult to sit up. Dizziness almost made him pass out again, almost made him throw up, but somehow he remained sitting and swallowed several times, fighting back the vile taste rising up from his throat. His head pounded. They'd stabbed him with a needle, doubtless a sedative of some kind, something vicious and painful. He stood up and looked around.

The room was small, almost a closet. The tiny frosted-glass window in its upper half let in enough light for him to see the cot he'd been on, a low ceiling, a tiled floor, tiled walls. His stomach flip-flopped. Gritting his teeth, he fought his way to the door, through nausea and the buzzing dizziness, and tried the handle. It turned.

He felt at his hip, but the holster was empty. Naturally, they'd taken his gun. So now he'd have to be even more careful—He laughed to himself, a bitter laugh. Careful. The way he'd let them jump him, the way he'd allowed an unarmed woman to kick him into submission? He opened the door.

His only advantage was that they might have miscalculated the dosage in the rush of the struggle. If they thought he was still asleep, he might have a chance to find Rosemary before they could do anything to her. But he would have to hurry.

He peered up and down the hall, not wanting to fail before he could begin, but the hall was clear in both directions. It was the same tiled and medicine-smelling hall, with its harsh ceiling lights. Like a hospital. Where was the operating room, and the monster in it?

Warily, he went down the hall, checking doors, wishing he'd done it differently, wishing he'd kept his gun. He must still be under the influence of the drug they'd used. His thoughts came clearly now, but then in a jumble, and he walked straight and steadily, but then his knees were weak and the tiles seemed to blur, like a television show where they kept losing the transmission. He remembered the first and only time he'd been really drunk, in college, late at night, trying to negotiate his way from his room in the dormitory down to the men's room. The hall had stretched longer and longer before his eyes, and he'd had to reach out with both hands and feel his way along the walls. He gripped the knob of a door to his left and turned. The door opened.

No light slanted out into the corridor from the room. No one called out or tried to emerge. He opened the door wide and looked inside. By the glare from the hall he saw a wooden table, a chair, and a straw broom leaning against the wall in a corner. Belongs to the resident witch, he thought, and closed the door.

Once, the nausea returned without warning and he grabbed his stomach, almost choked, bent over double, felt that it was all coming up. Then miraculously it subsided, the pain eased, he was left with a terrible burning vomit-tasting grittiness in the back of his throat. His head pounded harder again, his knees didn't want to bend, his vision kept coming and going. At times the smell of medicines seemed to come from inside his head; at other times it was clearly an aspect of the tiled corridor.

Again the buzzing and throbbing eased slightly. As quickly as he could, he checked other doors, feeling that his time was severely limited: not only might he pass out again at any moment, but also Rosemary must have very little time left to her, a few minutes, possibly a matter of seconds.

A door opened into a large office. Another revealed a bedroom with a small bed, chairs, and a table. A third showed him another hallway at right angles to this one, dark and musty; he decided to bypass it until there was nothing left to check. The buzzing intensified in his ears so that he could no longer hear the faint squeak of his rubber shoes on the waxed tiles—frightening him, since now someone could walk up behind him without his even hearing it.

Maybe his movements were causing the drug to circulate, some part of it that had gotten stuck in his legs now surging into his brain to put him to sleep for another long time. He remembered to check his watch. Its numerals were blurred, but it seemed to read nine forty-seven. With a sinking feeling he realized that it had read the same thing when he'd awakened. It must have gotten broken during the struggle, possibly when he'd fallen to the floor after the injection. Now there was no way to tell how long it was taking. Hurry, he thought, and moved forward once more.

It was the end of the hall, but there was a final door. His legs throbbed and supported him unsteadily as he made his way toward it. If it proved locked or opened onto an empty room, he'd work his way back to the other hall. He began to think that he'd failed, he wouldn't be in time, Rosemary would be discovered in a crate in a shallow grave, minus her right hand. Because of me, he thought, and reached for the doorknob.

It turned. The door opened inward an inch or two. Kelso breathed out a long shuddering sigh that made his nose and throat burn; he tasted the stuff from his stomach and the medicines and drugs.

A light burned inside the room.

His pulse banged in his ears and his heart beat in his chest like a kettledrum roll. Somehow he was able to ease his head forward to the opening and look through, into the room.

Dr. Winthrop stood over a raised wheeled examining table. His profile was to the door. He wore a white surgical gown, cap, and mask. One upraised latex-gloved hand held something with a sharp glistening blade.

On the other side of the table stood Margaret, also in white gown, mask, and gloves, fiddling with a syringe, glaring at it with her yellowish eyes, pulling liquid into it from a vial.

On the raised table between them lay a girl on her back, her face pale beneath the white glare of an operating-theater light. Leather straps secured her at her waist. Her arms were bare. She still had both hands.

Kelso could see her face, her dark hair spread back from her head, her eyes closed. Apparently she was not conscious. She lay there, vulnerable, exposed to scalpel and needle, while Margaret played with her syringe and the obese doctor gripped his knife.

Kelso started forward, but something hit him hard on the left shoulder. He rolled with the force of the blow and spun around. Facing him was the tall bald man with glasses, his sunken eyes strangely empty behind the lenses, pointing a revolver.

It reminded Kelso of one of his nightmares. He made a quick estimate of the distances and the general situation. There were possibilities, he thought. For example, he might lunge forward and grab the bald man's gun away from him before he could fire. Or something unexpected, a charge in the direction of the operating table, catch the doctor off guard, get that scalpel and use it as a weapon. But the nightmare was real. None of the possibilities seemed workable.

"Put your hands up, bastard," the bald man said. He had a hoarse voice, as if his throat were sore. He gestured angrily with the gun.

Slowly, Kelso raised his hands, hating himself for having fallen into another trap. The bald man moved forward, forcing Kelso back into the room and to one side; then he leaned against the doorjamb, pointing the revolver at Kelso's chest, and sneered.

"Got you now, bastard," he said.

"Well, well, Sergeant Kelso." Dr. Winthrop's eyes smiled. "It seems that Harold is correct, and we have you at a disadvantage. It really is too bad you couldn't have minded your own business."

"This *is* my business," Kelso said.

"I'll splatter your guts all over the wall," Harold said, and cocked back the hammer.

The only thing left now was to stall. Ignoring Harold, he looked at Winthrop.

"Okay, so it's over. Do you mind telling me what I missed?" His voice sounded funny to him, over the buzz in his head, and it hurt to talk.

"Since you're headed for a box in the ground, Sergeant, I don't mind at all," the doctor said amiably. He was holding the scalpel up in the air again, standing with his back to the girl on the table. On the other side, Margaret glared.

"Did you kill that girl we found?" Kelso asked.

Winthrop's eyes smiled. His words came slightly muffled through the surgical mask. "That girl is Harold's wife. Or was. Her name was Carolyn. They came here about a year ago, from Florida, looking for work. Harold actually is a rather accomplished cook, and his wife served as a maid. In a house this large some help is needed. His wife served in other capacities as well. It was part of the . . . um . . . bargain."

Kelso glanced at Harold. The bald man's expression remained the same—surly, mean, sneering. The revolver remained steady. There had to be a chance to get out of this. He'd have to watch for it and be ready when it came. He looked at Winthrop again.

"Why'd you kill his wife?"

"Margaret and I have devoted much of our lives, Sergeant Kelso, to the quest of knowledge of the Other Side. You see, I am convinced that it is entirely possible. We have taken up where others left off. The great Harry Houdini, for example, probably communicated with the dead, and Sir Arthur Conan Doyle believed in it and tried. My own mother was a psychic and often received vibrations of things to come."

"Why don't we just get on with it," Margaret said suddenly. "He doesn't need to know all this."

"My dear sister, poor Kelso has managed to get this far in some way or another, quite possibly because of your attitude, which no doubt made him suspicious enough to persist. And since I intend to have him disposed of shortly, it's only fair that I satisfy his curiosity in the few moments that remain to him."

"When it's time," Harold said, hefting the revolver, "I want to do it."

Winthrop ignored that. "As I was saying, Margaret and I are convinced that communication with the departed is possible. According to my mother, there have been séances in which a medium succeeded in making contact with a spirit whom she greatly resembled physically. So we decided to use someone who resembled Mary Carter."

"Why Mary?" Kelso asked. The buzzing in his ears was louder again. He swallowed, trying to stay alert.

"Two reasons. One, her spirit was observed numerous times near here, which meant she was attempting to make contact with our world. Two, we already had a ready-made medium—Harold's wife Carolyn, who greatly resembled Mary."

"How'd you know that?"

"I discovered a photograph of Mary Carter in an old album at the public library, along with some diaries and other materials. It seems that the Hawthorne branch of my family is of historical significance to the community.''

''But why'd you kill her?''

''Let's just do the bastard now,'' Harold said.

''Not yet, Harold. We didn't really intend to kill her, Sergeant, not at first. You see, I discovered in these historical documents that Mary Carter stayed at this house for a time in the summer of . . . um . . . it was 1916, I believe. She suffered an unfortunate accident which severely damaged her right hand, and shortly afterward it became necessary for it to be amputated. So, in order to create a medium as physically close to Mary as possible, we amputated Carolyn's hand.''

Kelso heard his voice come out angrily. ''You're a doctor?''

''I began an internship in surgery,'' Winthrop said, ''but I had . . . umm . . . a falling out, shall we say, with my instructors, and went instead into psychiatry.''

''He means he washed out,'' Harold said, and grinned.

''Shut up, Harold,'' Winthrop snapped, then became amiable again. ''They failed me for spite, Sergeant, after I complained of their incompetence. Well, it doesn't matter. I gained a little experience, enough for this simple procedure.''

Kelso felt cold. Harold aimed the gun. The light glinted from Winthrop's scalpel. On the table the sheet-covered form of Rosemary lay waiting, while Margaret glared and fingered her syringes like a witch playing with magic potions. Kelso was aware of his hands in the air on either side of his head, helpless. He forced himself to speak.

''So what happened? Why was she killed?''

''Unfortunately,'' Winthrop replied, ''Carolyn proved uncooperative after the operation. At times she verged on the hysterical. She and her husband were not exactly of the best stock, as you may have noticed.''

Harold glared and opened his mouth to say something, but shut it again at a look from the psychiatrist. Winthrop continued.

''She began to complain. Although she had agreed to the surgery, she began to deny it. She had to be watched constantly, lest she attempt to leave the house on her own. Finally she signed her own death warrant by threatening to notify the police. We could afford to take no more chances.'' He shrugged. ''On Monday of this week, I injected her with a large dose of barbiturate—it was Pentothal, I believe—rendering her unconscious. I did this for humanitarian reasons.''

''Had you been giving her morphine?'' Kelso asked.

''Of course. From the time of the surgery. Then, she was sacrificed.''

''In other words, you killed her.''

''Yes.''

''How?''

Winthrop hesitated, then shrugged. ''With a bullet in the back of her head. From that thirty-two caliber revolver which Harold is about to use to send you to the Other Side.''

''What'd you do next?''

''Next, Harold and I took her down to Mary's grave in a box, in the early morning hours of Tuesday. About 2 A.M., I'd estimate. We buried her where you found her, under the stone in the center of the clearing. Incidentally, Sergeant, how did you know to look for her there?''

''It was a lucky guess.''

''Ah.'' The big man nodded. ''Well, I suppose the police are entitled to a bit of luck on occasion. Proved rather unlucky for you, though, didn't it?''

Harold laughed briefly. His eyes were bright with hatred.

''Well, then,'' Winthrop said, ''now we had two different spirits for our experiments. I was certain we could communicate with one of them.''

''What about the hand? Why'd you leave it on the gravestone?''

''Oh, that.'' Winthrop's eyes smiled over the top of his mask. ''An offering, you see. We felt, at least I myself felt, that it might entice Mary's spirit up to the house, indicate to her that we understood something about her.'' He glanced at the bald man. ''Actually, Harold was supposed to take it down there after midnight, then retrieve it before sunrise, but as usual he failed to get it right and took it down about 9 P.M. on Tuesday. That, of course, is why it was discovered.''

"So you didn't want it discovered."

"Absolutely not. Except by Mary Carter."

"Then why didn't he take it with him when he found me down there with Rosemary and hit me over the head?"

"Time to shut the bastard up for good now, ain't it, Doc?" Harold said, rasping.

"Not yet, Harold. I will tell you when it is time. Well, Sergeant, I'll admit to one mistake, and that was in allowing myself to place too much confidence in Harold. It turns out that he's a fool. From what he later told me, he happened into the clearing shortly after ten that night, and found you holding Rosemary at gunpoint, for some reason.''

"I thought she was trying to take the hand," Kelso said.

"Ah." Winthrop nodded. "Well, I'd already become interested in Rosemary as a possible medium, and Harold had spoken to her a few times in the woods, where she tended to wander on her way to and from the . . . um . . . church. Evidently Harold thought you were about to arrest the girl, so he struck you over the head with a rock and allowed her to get away. Then he forgot all about the hand, or he meant to return for it later—with Harold it's difficult to tell—and he simply left." Winthrop shrugged. "He is a particularly stupid individual, but he's a good cook and I find him useful for less savory work. After all, he usually does what I tell him."

"Look, Doc—"

"I told you to shut up."

The revolver wavered. But there was one more question to be asked.

"What about Charlotte?" Kelso felt slightly better, but he was sweating. His hands felt numb from being held up. When the question was answered, he would have to think of a way out. Harold was stupid; maybe that would help.

"Charlotte," said the doctor, "was to have been the next medium, and we even tried a session with her, but she really is psychotic, and I decided we'd only be wasting our time. True, she bears a strong resemblence to Mary Carter, but she was unstable. The use of drugs to control psychotic symptoms is still something of an art. No, Rosemary here is a much better candidate—quiet, shy, thoughtful. Possibly even psychic. Retarded people are often aware of the other world, much more than the rest of us. Perhaps it's because they don't have as much to think about and they can devote their thoughts to the spirit world.'' He glanced over one massive shoulder at the girl on the table. ''She has other charms, too, which I have not overlooked.''

Kelso thought about lunging for him, but Harold's gun was steady and Winthrop looked back, his eyes dark and intense above the surgical mask.

''It was indeed fortuitous that she happened to wander up to my house last night,'' Winthrop said. ''Saved us the trouble of . . . um . . . inviting her.'' He chuckled. ''We asked her in for some tea, and gave her a sedative. She fasted during the night, a requirement for surgery, and we were almost ready to proceed when you blundered into our hallway. Well, I believe all your questions have been answered, Sergeant.''

Harold held the gun out, aiming now at Kelso's head.

''Listen—''

''Don't protest, Sergeant. It really is over. You must accept it. In case you're interested, I will tell you that Rosemary will undergo the same amputation of her right hand that Carolyn did. As did, indeed, Mary Carter. I am going to be a famous man someday, Sergeant. Pity you won't be around to congratulate me, but perhaps I will contact your spirit.'' He looked at the bald man. ''Use the den, Harold, it's sound-proofed. And don't waste a lot of ammunition. One in his head should suffice.''

Harold leered. ''Come on, bastard. It's just you and me, now.'' He stood away from the jamb and stepped backward into the hall, keeping the .32 level with Kelso's chest, and motioned with his free hand. ''Come on, bastard.''

There was one chance. Gritting his teeth, Kelso staggered forward as if the drug were still affecting him. Then he threw his left hand out and knocked the revolver sideways. The bald man hadn't expected this from a drugged cop; mild surprise registered in his staring eyes.

The gun went off, deafening in the stillness. Kelso slammed his right fist forward, into the man's jaw. Harold's head whipped back. The sound of his teeth snapping together echoed in the hall. He sagged. Kelso grabbed the gun before it could fall, and whirled to face the operating table.

Winthrop's eyes were black and hard. For one instant everything seemed frozen in time, as if Kelso had suddenly snapped a picture of the scene. He saw the doctor, his enormous bulk draped in the white gown and gloves and mask, the sharp blade glinting in the operating light. The witchlike Margaret, glaring vicious hatred at him, trying to murder him with her eyes. Rosemary lying motionless on the table.

"Kelso," said the doctor, his voice tight, "you're a dead man."

Margaret's hand came up, ending the snapshot. Everything was in motion again. Without warning, before Kelso could comprehend, Margaret tossed a syringe. He thought of darts. The thing flew over the table at him and he felt the needle penetrate his left hand, which he'd held up as a reflex. It hung there like a plastic insect that had just bitten him and was still hanging on, sucking his blood. This only happenes in nightmares, he thought, and tried to pull the trigger of the revolver, but found that his finger refused the command. The room spun.

She threw a second syringe. He tried to dodge and fell into its path; it stuck in his arm.

The terrible buzzing came again, the darkness, the falling. He tried to shout the word *monster*, but it came out as a thin scream. The tiles hit him in the face and it was night.

Chapter Twenty-Eight

Smith

Smith stood in the woods outside the house, glaring at its walls. Rain was coming down hard and they hadn't brought umbrellas up from their cars. Behind him, Broom and Meyer shuffled through the leaves and undergrowth and Meyer muttered, "He's not here, Smith. The son of a bitch."

"Let's go see what's along the side," Smith said.

"Why not?" Meyer glared. "We're only soaked and cold and catching pneumonia. Broom will probably die from all this."

"Probably," Smith said, and Broom sneezed.

They trudged to the far end of the house and through the woods that lined the side, only about ten feet from the wall. Smith was worried. He knew Kelso. He'd known the idiot might try to get inside. If they couldn't find him soon, the only thing left would be knocking at the front door and demanding to know where he was. He glared at the house and saw a door.

"That little metal door looks like it might open into a basement or something," he said.

Meyer said, "So what?"

"So maybe Kelso tried to get inside the house."

"If he did, then he's a dumb-ass."

At that moment they heard a loud noise.

"What the hell—" Meyer began.

"Gunshot," Smith said. He pictured Kelso lying on the floor, bleeding from a large hole in his head. "Come on, Meyer." He charged out of the woods for the side door, Meyer and Broom at his heels. He grabbed the handle.

"It's open." They followed him through and down four steps into a hallway.

He was convinced that Kelso was in here. In a place like this, he thought, they wouldn't have left a side door unlocked. Somehow Kelso must have gotten in and left it unlocked. They've shot the little idiot, he thought, and ran forward at full speed, drawing his revolver.

At the far end of the hall, which for some reason was tiled and smelled of medicine or antiseptic, a bald man with glasses lay on the floor, either dazed or unconscious. Smith reached the man and saw an open door. He halted— so suddenly that Meyer and Broom almost collided with him—and stared.

A young woman, whom Smith recognized immediately as Rosemary McAllister, lay strapped to an operating table. On the near side of the table stood Dr. Winthrop, clad in gown and gloves and holding a scalpel. On the far side stood his sister Margaret, also gowned, holding a syringe poised as if to throw it like a dart. Just inside the doorway lay Kelso, one syringe sticking up from his arm like an angry mosquito, a second sticking into the palm of his left hand. His eyes were closed and he wasn't moving.

It took Smith only three seconds to react.

He held his revolver forward, aimed directly at the fat psychiatrist, and said loudly, "Drop the knife, Winthrop, or you're dead, and I'm not kidding."

Winthrop's eyes blazed for an instant, then he dropped the knife. It bounced once on the tiles.

Margaret drew back her arm as if to throw.

Meyer was aiming his .38. "You've got two seconds to get both hands over your head with your fingers spread apart," he said, "or, lady, I swear I'll blow your fucking head right off."

Margaret glared. Her hands came up over her head and stayed there. The syringe fell to the tiles. The venom in her yellow eyes faded, giving way to a dull sullenness.

In the doorway, Kelso stirred briefly. On the operating table the girl had started to moan.

Chapter Twenty-Nine

Mary's Grave

When Kelso opened his eyes he was lying on his back on a large comfortable sofa. Looking around, he recognized the living room in which he and Smith had twice interviewed Dr. Winthrop. Uniformed cops were everywhere. Detective-Sergeant Meyer was there, and Smith. Even Broom. He closed his eyes, opened them again. Even . . . over by the door to the hall, the tall jut-jawed steel-eyed figure of Lieutenant Leill. Everyone has come to my party, he thought.

"Kelso? Are you all right?"

Dr. Paul was bending over him, peering down with intelligent brown eyes.

"I'm okay," Kelso said. His tongue felt thick.

"I gave you something to counter the stuff they pumped you up with," Dr. Paul said. "You received enough Pentothal to undergo minor surgery."

"I don't want to hear about surgery," Kelso said.

"Drink this."

After a while he felt well enough to sit up, and Smith came over to sit next to him.

"What a dumb bastard," Smith told him. "You almost got yourself killed. Why didn't you wait?"

"If I'd waited, that girl might've . . ."

"Yeah." Smith nodded. "I know. Hey, you want anything? Coffee?"

"Just some water."

Smith went to get it. Everyone in the room seemed to be talking at once. Kelso's head felt enlarged. He had the shakes. When Smith returned with a glass of water he sat up straighter, sipped a little of it, and asked, "So what happened?"

"Just after that bitch used you for a pin cushion with her syringes, we came down the hall. Me and Meyer and Broom. We arrested her and that fat shrink, and they're in a little room down the hall with Harold, spilling their guts. Especially Harold. He's almost hysterical. Personally, I think he's nuts."

"They all are," Kelso said. "Is Rosemary all right?"

"Yeah, for the most part. Dr. Paul's taking care of her. They had her pretty well doped up, but she's coming out of it. If you hadn't gotten there when you did, she'd probably be minus a hand now."

"They, uh, Margaret, shot me full of something once before. When I first got inside. I guess she miscalculated the effect of the drug."

"Well, Margaret's not a great nurse, and she's as crazy as the rest of 'em. Winthrop fathered her daughter, by the way, they've admitted to that."

"I'm not surprised."

Meyer came over to the sofa and scowled down at Kelso.

"Well, well. Quite the hero, huh? Saved the world and all."

"Whatever." Kelso shrugged. "But thanks for saving *me.*"

For one of the few times that Kelso could remember, Meyer smiled. It lasted approximately three seconds, then the famous scowl returned and he said gruffly, "I'd have done it for anybody."

Lieutenant Leill came over and Kelso attempted to stand, but the lieutenant shook his head. "Stay there, Kelso. I just wanted to congratulate you. Good job, saving that girl."

"Yes, sir."

"Dr. Paul tells me she'll be okay. You okay, Kelso?"

"Yes, sir."

"Good. Take the afternoon off."

"Thank you, sir."

"No problem." Leill nodded sternly, this favor having been bestowed, and wandered off to talk to the coroner.

"I almost forgot," Smith said. "When you feel like it, Susan wants you to call."

"Okay."

But he sat there for a while. It all seemed unreal. The congregation in the living room might have been a cocktail party. An image of the white tiled room came back, the snapshot he'd taken in his mind's eye of Winthrop in gown, gloves, and mask, Margaret with her syringes, Rosemary strapped to the table—he had to shake his head to make it go away. Even then, it kept coming back.

At two-thirty that afternoon Kelso stood in the clearing with Smith, Meyer, Broom, Dr. Paul from the coroner's office, Father Ullman from St. Luke's, and five cops in blue overalls. A cold wind blew the leaves and once in a while a drop of rain landed on Kelso's face. The monument base had been moved to one side and the men in overalls had used shovels. Six feet down into the packed earth had lain the coffin, very old. It had been hoisted up, and now two policemen were using crowbars to pry loose the lid.

There was some question as to whether Mary Carter was really buried here. Lieutenant Leill had begun asking if the people in the house might not have murdered some other girl and put her body down in the clearing under Mary's gravestone. Now that question would be answered.

"It's off," one of the officers said. They pulled the coffin lid away.

Kelso and the others shuffled forward to see.

Dr. Paul bent over it. "Consistent with the skeleton of an adolescent female." He peered. "Hmm. Right hand missing."

Dr. Paul poked and prodded. Photographs were taken. An official from some department of city government and one from the state witnessed the event and signed various documents. An attorney for the church signed something.

"I think we can say that this is in fact the mortal remains of Mary Carter," Dr. Paul said.

More signatures were applied to official documents.

Then they stood awkwardly, looking at the thing. At last

Meyer said, "Father Ullman, you want to say a few words?"

"When she is reinterred," the priest replied.

Meyer nodded. "There's no reason to wait."

The overalled men sighed, closed the lid, secured it with nails, and lowered the coffin into the ground. Again they waited. Father Ullman brought out a small black book with gilt edges and opened it. The day was blustery, overcast, and threatened rain. A few more drops fell and around them the woods sighed loudly. Everyone stood silently, awkwardly, around the grave, while the priest read from his book.

" 'In the midst of life we are in death,' " he said, and paused. He turned a page, as if changing his mind, then started again.

" 'Unto Almighty God we commend the soul of our sister departed, Mary Carter, and we commit her body to the ground; earth to earth, ashes to ashes, dust to dust; in sure and certain hope of the Resurrection unto eternal life, through our Lord Jesus Christ; at whose coming in glorious majesty to judge the world, the earth and the sea shall give up their dead; and the corruptible bodies of those who sleep in Him shall be changed, and made like unto His own glorious body; according to the mighty working whereby He is able to subdue all things unto Himself.' " He closed the book and for a moment there was nothing but the wind in the trees. Then: "The Lord be with you," he said.

"And with thy spirit," Broom replied.

"Lord, have mercy upon us," the priest said.

"Christ, have mercy upon us."

"Lord, have mercy upon us," Ullman said, then said the Lord's Prayer in words that were almost inaudible over the rising wind.

"Amen," Broom said.

The men in overalls began filling up the grave. The others turned and shuffled out of the clearing, up the crooked path to the parking lot, not speaking. In the lot, Kelso caught up with Broom.

"I didn't know you were an Episcopalian, Broom."

"Yes." He smiled peacefully at Kelso.

Smith came up. "You okay, Kelso?"

"I think so." Actually, it had been something of an ordeal, but he'd wanted to be there when they opened the casket. "I still feel weird."

"You want to go get a drink or something? A bite to eat?"

"I promised Susan . . ."

"Yeah. Okay. Well, see you Monday."

Kelso nodded and went to his VW. He drove to Susan's house, got out, and stood for a minute in the driveway with the wind blowing leaves all around him and a huge flock of migrating birds filling the gray sky like a thousand witches.

The front door opened. Susan came out onto the porch and looked at him. He went up the curving walk, stepped up to her, and put his arms around her. After a while, they went inside.